inside
the
mind of
gideon
rayburn

inside
the
mind of
gideon
rayburn

Sarah Miller

 ST. MARTIN'S GRIFFIN NEW YORK

ALLOYENTERTAINMENT

Produced by Alloy Entertainment
151 West 26th Street, New York, NY 10001

www.stmartins.com

Book design by Irene Vallye

Library of Congress Cataloging-in-Publication Data

Miller, Sarah, 1969–
    Inside the mind of Gideon Rayburn / Sarah Miller.
       p. cm.
    ISBN-13: 978-0-312-33376-8
    ISBN-10: 0-312-33376-5
    1. Teenage boys—Fiction.   2. Adolescent psychology—Fiction.
  3. Students—Social life and customs—Fiction. 4. Boarding schools—Fiction.
  5. New England—Fiction. I. Title.

PS3613.I55294 I57 2006
823'.92—dc22

2006298664

First St. Martin's Griffin Edition: June 2007

10 9 8 7 6 5 4 3 2 1

for eric

acknowledgments

First and foremost I am grateful to everyone at Alloy Entertainment and St. Martin's Press for the opportunity to write this book, and I single out the following individuals: Josh Bank, Bob Levy, Les Morgenstein, Sally Richardson, and Jennifer Weis.

Thanks also to Peter Lopez.

Clearly, I am most indebted to Jennifer Rudolph Walsh at William Morris.

Thanks to Joy Gorman, my manager and beloved friend, who makes sure I don't do anything too stupid, and to Tom McGrath, my *Men's Health* editor, who makes sure I don't starve to death.

Thanks to Mike Abssy and my parents.

The following is a list of people who either read this book in various incarnations or provided general goodwill and support: Nancy Bell, Phil D'Amecourt, Colin Dickerman, Jennifer Doyle, Melissa Kantor, Liz Kinder, Martha Lucy, Heather Lukes, Jennifer Lyne, the real Molly McGarry, Michael James Reed, Anna Reich, Bill Stavru, Kim Stenton, Nancy Updike, and Valerie Van Galder.

Last I thank Ben Schrank. Many people helped with this book, but Ben was the one constant. There are a lot of things I could say about him, all nice, but I'll just say the only one that matters: I could not have written this book without him.

inside
the
mind of
gideon
rayburn

who
am i?

Like most girls, I want a lot. Fame and fortune. Equal rights. Shoes no one else has. But I'd trade all that in for the Perfect Guy. (Don't tell me there's something wrong with that. I don't know of a single person who doesn't spend most of her time thinking about love.) Anyway, ever since I could think, I have been imagining and reimagining the exact sort of boy I want to love and who would love me back. Basically, I imagine someone who has all the good attributes of the male species and whose bad ones wouldn't ruin my life.

I never thought it would be a guy like Gideon Rayburn. He's not gorgeous, not overwhelmingly brilliant, not all that great at sports. Jesus. Why am I bothering to explain to you why he isn't stereotypically crushworthy? Trust me, you'll see for yourself soon enough.

The point is, he's so not the kind of guy I ever thought I would fall for. But then again, how would I have guessed that I'd be seeing what goes on inside his head? That my eyes and thoughts would go with him everywhere? When you know someone like Gideon this well, it's kind of impossible not to fall in love with him. And when I say I know him well, understand: As I tell you his story, as it happens, I not only know what he's doing, I know what he wishes he were doing, what he thinks he should be doing, and what he would wish he were doing if he were just a slightly better person. (Don't get me wrong. Gideon's amazing. But he's a boy. He's fifteen. And he's a typical American kid from the suburbs. My point: He's got a lot working for and against him.)

By the way, Gideon has no idea I'm inside his head. Guys are cute, but they're not very observant.

My feelings, though perhaps passionate for someone of my age and experience, are pretty normal. But my situation—that is unique, and that's what puts me in a position to tell you everything. I mean it. Everything you've ever wondered about what guys think (and feared about what they want), I'm going to tell you. You are going to learn what boys say when girls are not in the room and how they feel when they're on top of one. I will, for now, leave out one very crucial thing: who I am. I'm in this story too, and not just inside Gid's head. But there are a lot of girls—and women—in this story. Which one am I?

where
am
i?

The first thoughts I hear that are not my own are disjointed, weird, and uncertain. That should have been my first clue that something was wrong. They are: Do I like this place or do I want to go home? I'm just a simple kid from the suburbs of Virginia. What do I know about how to act at a prep school? But I'm not a total idiot, right? Hmm. Or maybe I am. Oh, God. And these boxers . . . the seam is stretched so uncomfortably against the left side of my nut sack. What earthly reason is there for my not having thrown them out?

Like everyone else, I am used to hearing my own thoughts. These are not my thoughts. I would never refer to myself as simple. I am not from Virginia. I am not remotely an idiot, even at my most self-hating. Naturally, it is *nut sack* that throws me like an earthquake up against a very hard wall.

Thoughts keep coming: Don't be scared, everything's going to be fine. Yes, prep school's a little alien to you but it's not literally alien. I mean, it's not as if I have left this world. Some of the same rules must apply. And then: Don't let Dad know you're scared, because he'll just make it about him.

Then I start to see and hear things that I am not actually seeing or hearing. I mean, I am actually seeing and hearing them. But I am not in the place where these things are being seen and heard. I do not know how I got here. But I am in someone else's head.

The boy whose head I'm in is looking out the window of a car. He (we?) is in the passenger seat. He swings his head to the left. What I am seeing, through these eyes that are not mine, in this place where I am not, is a man I don't know, about fifty years old, and he's driving a late-model Ford Silverado. He fiddles with the radio and settles on an Eagles song, "Lyin' Eyes." (For those of you not familiar with their repertoire, this song's about a guilty but incorrigibly unfaithful woman.) The man nods through the chorus, a faraway look in his eyes, then starts to twist an unfashionable and graying mustache.

A new thought accompanies this not terribly pleasant image. It is: God, I hate this song, because this song reminds me of Mom. Except that it's so seventies and Mom is so nineties. I see a flash of hair with very obvious chunky highlights, a brightly colored yoga bag, a dark pedicure inside a pair of lime green slip-on wedge open-toed mules, and finally a matching New Beetle.

This, I take it, is his mom. Nice to meet you.

And suddenly . . . no thoughts. Just . . . buildings. The prep school. The source of anxiety, the major one at least.

I see brick dormitories around one end of an academic quad and in the middle of it, a statue of a man on a horse. On the other end is a very old building—a tiny-windowed wooden two-story colonial—and a considerably more imposing building with a clock tower. There are a few graceful stands of maple and ash trees, the tips of their branches just starting to redden and yellow. At the far end, past the quad, is a chapel, made of stone as well. Its stained-glass windows glow blue and violet through a web of foliage.

On a patch of grass in front of the clock tower building is a wooden sign reading: MIDVALE ACADEMY.

A question: Does Gideon know I'm here? I guess not, because then we would be having a conversation.

He/I/We won't stop looking at the chapel. Why? Is young Gid interested in stained-glass? No. I wonder if this chapel would be a good place to . . . The thought trips on itself. First it is, a good place to have sex. Then, holy fuck, which one?

I laugh out loud, forgetting that I am with friends, who look at me like I am crazy. I think about sex, but never like this, never with a twinge of ashamed panic, like, Oh God, I'm thinking about sex again.

Now this: That chapel would be a good place to hook up with a girl if I were the kind of guy who could get girls to hook up with me. Do I like this place or do I want to go home? The grass here is so green. I feel like it's laughing at me.

The boy who owns this mind is very vulnerable. And rather sweet. He has been on the road since dawn. He is hungry and craving root beer. He's holding in his hands a glossy black-and-red folder that reads MIDVALE ACADEMY: NEW STUDENT INFORMATION. He opens the folder, and the first sheet of paper is addressed to Gideon Rayburn, 989 Christmas Park Circle, Fairfax, Virginia.

The Silverado has stopped in front of a brick Georgian-style dorm called Proctor. This person, this Gideon Rayburn, knows he's going to have to get out of the car eventually, but he's not ready. A glance inside the windows of this building, his new home, is not at all heartening. On the first floor, a kid with floppy blonde hair hangs a Bruce Lee poster above his bed, then goes to the closet and lovingly hangs up a white gi with a brown karate belt. On the second floor, a lumbering sort in a baseball hat and overalls conducts a symphony (Schubert) with a plastic spoon.

Gid's reaction to them is both surprising and cute. He thinks, Fuck these guys. Okay, he knows he's partly jealous, but he's also heard how everyone at Midvale is good at something, and confronted with it for the first time, he kind of wants to puke. Why, he wonders, does everyone have to be talented?

I am sympathetic to what Gid sees as an insidious moment in history, one where everyone has to be a star. Appealingly, he seems to lack this drive. He doesn't lack ambition altogether, but even though we've just "met," I can safely say he seems most invested in being a well-liked person. It's just a hunch. A warm hunch.

Gid enjoys a righteous moment of feeling just regular, decent. He looks in the mirror and for the first time, I can see his face. This feels extremely weird because up to now, when I looked in a mirror, I saw me. Instead I see a boy who does a handsome job of regular. I like the squareness of his mouth, and the way his nut brown eyes and wavy hair match. His hair isn't creepy, run-your-hand-over-it wavy, it's loose, cute, beachy wavy. A little too long. Anyway, looking in the mirror, what Gid sees is a guy who—despite his anxieties about this place—really, really doesn't want to go home. And the reason is sitting right next to him.

Jim Rayburn. Gid's mind isn't quite sure where to start on this, and neither am I, but here goes. Jim Rayburn, born 1959, Newport News, Virginia (Pisces, Dog). He is a contractor. He was dumped about two years ago by Gid's mother. (Capricorn, Pig . . . What a terrible match. That is my thought, not Gid's. Boys don't know anything about astrology, although, Gid's dad being a perfect example, they really should.) Wendy Rayburn—a carefree spirit in her lime green mules if there ever was one—fell in love with Gid's middle-school science teacher, Mr. Soames. Gid thought Mr. Soames was gay. He now has proof (some of it, unfortunately, audible) that this is not true.

Gid's dad spends a lot of time tugging his mustache, smoking Carlton 100s, and looking at Gid with a forlorn expression that says, *Don't make the same mistakes I've made.* Jim is a weird combination of emotionally clueless and needy. He never asks Gid a single question about anything—school, girls, visits to his mother—but he's real big on things like hugs and punching Gid on the arm, lots of forced bonhomie.

They say a boy needs his father. And I would never say that Jim Rayburn is a terrible person. But it's probably good that Gid's getting away, for both of us. Because Gid needs to figure out who he is. And if I'm going to be spending a lot of my time inside Gideon Rayburn's head for a reason that I do not yet understand, there are a lot better things to think about than why Gid and his dad don't have a perfect relationship. For example: I understand that Gid is unclear about when and if he will be having sex in the chapel, but how, exactly, can he be unclear on whether or not he's a virgin?

tiny
dancer

The last twelve hours of Gid's life are about as clear as the last twelve hours of my own. That is, they are very clear—almost as if I had lived them myself. I am glad I didn't, though, since he spent most of them trapped in the car with his dad.

Let's go back five hours. We are in the grass-blown, wild-flowered but not especially fascinating landscape of central Connecticut, and Gid is in the midst of a Things You Love exercise that he got from his mother's *Journal of the Zen Hut*. The exercise suggests that in times of negativity, you should think of, as the title not so subtly suggests, things you love. He intones: "Cookies. Street hockey. Kissing. My down comforter that smells like bleach. Kissing again."

Really? Interesting how he hasn't mentioned sex yet. Told you sometimes boys feel like girls.

"How are you feeling about your new school situation?" Jim Rayburn blurts out, ruining what was for everyone a nice moment. To Jim, everything is a fill-in-the-blank situation. When they're out of milk, it's a milk situation. When Gid's mother dumped him, he had a messed-up lady situation. Which, from a seminal image conjured in Gid's brain, has become a no-lady situation punctuated by Saturday nights with other romantically bereaved, similarly pathetic work buddies. They hang out in the basement den, listening to Neil Diamond and, as the hours tick by and the Carlton 100s pile up in the amber glass ashtrays, Merle Haggard.

"I'm not worried about school at all," Gid lies. "I think Midvale is going to be a very good place for me."

This seems to shut his dad up for a while. Gid takes advantage of the silence to employ another device he read about in *Journal of the Zen Hut:* relaxing the mind by listing and categorizing everything he sees. He observes cows in the field. A Buick LeSabre with a crushed back end, held together with a red bungee cord. A yellow house. A tree stump, recently cut. The splinters in the stump make him think of a girl's fingernails, and this makes Gid think of having his pants unzipped.

A jagged tree stump can make a guy think of having his pants unzipped? That's incredibly dirty! However, I am beginning to see that there are benefits to being in this boy's head. I will never again have to wonder how and why guys think and feel all that weird shit. I'm now *inside* the madness.

Midvale Academy draws closer and closer. They are twenty miles away, then ten, then, much too quickly, one. Gid starts to panic and can't keep from turning over and over one unacceptable possibility: If my fear is really this palpable, isn't there a good chance no one is going to like me? What if not one of these twelve hundred students from forty-two states and eighteen foreign countries wants to be my friend? His exhalations take on a tone of desperation. His father tugs on his mustache and says, "Hey, Gid, someone got your balls in a vise?"

"Dad, could you please just give me a minute?" Gid says.

His dad shrugs, as if to say, "Hey, when have I ever let you down?"

Gid knows that he cannot arrive at school with this much raw terror in his heart. Once again—I'm sensing that this flaky mysticism is the one thing Gid and his mom have in common—Gid turns to the venerable *Journal of the Zen Hut* for comfort. Many times, *Journal of the Zen Hut* had counseled that when feeling inadequate, you should merely focus on yourself, all aspects of yourself, good and bad, and concentrate on being open to those things existing all together at once. *You will see,* he remembered reading, *that when you accept yourself totally, when you lay yourself bare and accept yourself as you are, people are open to receive you, absolutely as you are.*

Gid closes his eyes and concentrates, starting to get a mental picture of his whole self, good and bad. The bad comes first. I think that's natural. He thinks about how he can be lazy. That he had cheated on his PSAT—just one question that he went back to after consulting a pocket dictionary—*nadir:* the lowest possible point—in the bathroom during the break. That he didn't know whether he was actually smart, even though people said he was. That he wasn't all that nice to his father, considering Jim wasn't such a terrible guy. Those were the not-so-painful things. Then he concentrates on the bad thing, the worst thing. That sometimes he just loathes himself, absolutely. That at times he suspects he is a total fraud.

In spite of all this, Gid commands himself, I am totally likable and lovable. I am great at math. I have good hair and I don't have those weird fat thighs some guys have. I am energy made by the universe [it is a good thing those *Journal of the Zen Hut*s are not going to be in his line of vision for a few months, isn't it?] and therefore perfect as I am.

Gid really manages to work himself into some kind of trance. I can feel how airy his brain gets at that moment, how his fears are melting away and he's kind of floating on a soft, light cloud of possibility.

His dad pulls onto the campus, and the clock begins to sound out the hour—three o'clock—in a stern, low, judgmental C. It is at this moment that Gid looks out onto the quad and beholds the spectacle that simultaneously represents all of his deepest wishes and doubts: the exquisite vast sea of girls occupying the quad of Midvale Academy.

They are beautiful. They are like sirens on rocks, except they are on the grass, fully clothed, with expensive handbags. They are everywhere. They sun their smooth, golden legs. They saunter in front of the car carrying toaster ovens and computer monitors and wicker baskets full of Pratesi sheets, patting each other's silky, shiny heads with their childlike and exuberant postsummer greetings. They are tall and short, brunette and blonde, mostly white but a few of them black or brown or Asian. They are all ridiculously pretty. There were pretty girls at his school in Fairfax, but they were so hard. They applied eyeliner in the library. They extinguished Parliament Lights in each other's Diet Cokes. These girls, uniformly slim and bursting with health, appear to have spent the day running up and down green hills. They have now returned to civilization for the sole purpose of fortifying themselves with strawberries and soy milk.

He looks and looks again, seeking out bulges, bad bone structure.

Forget it, Gid, you're not even going to find a bad haircut.

A trio of girls separate themselves from the herd and begin walking toward the car. Gideon stares first at the one in the middle, a medium-size girl, with longer brown hair and a heart-shaped, angular face. She has a red streak in her hair, unnaturally red, like cloth, with some of it spilling down her shoulders. To her left is a tall girl in blue shorts that hang low on her hips and with blonde hair cut sharp at her chin. She's sort of basic looking and preppy. And to her right is a small girl with giant eyes framed with eyeliner and dark blonde hair pulled back into a messy bun. Gid thinks, These girls are pretty, but he can't even really concentrate on them, because this prettiness on display has such a dizzying, hall-of-mirrors effect.

And that's when the Silverado horn—a custom horn, which plays Elton John's "Tiny Dancer"—blares out, loud and strong. Gideon squeezes his eyes shut, and he involuntarily clutches his heart, bracing himself for a crash. But when he opens his eyes, everything is fine. Except that off to the left of the car, the three girls stare back at him, shocked and wide-eyed.

Gid would have preferred a crash. "Dad, what are you doing? You scared the shit out of me! You scared the shit out of them!"

But Jim Rayburn is busy rolling down his window. "Hello there, ladies," he calls out, slowing down. He whispers to Gid, "Might as well meet these cuties, huh?"

This is not happening, Gid thinks. My father is not really this much of a loser.

The girls cast nervous glances at one another and start to whisper. Gid considers giving the girls a friendly smile, to let them know they aren't in any danger, but then, remembering that they probably hadn't yet gotten a good look at him, tries to press himself back as deeply as he can into the seat. "Dad," he groans, "I think these girls are a little freaked out. So can we—"

But his father ignores him. "Ladies! Hello! I'm Jim Rayburn, and this is my son, Gideon."

Now the girls come forward. They all have on little half-smiles—the polite, patient smiles teenagers summon up to mask their hostility for annoying adults. The tall blonde advances with the most brazenness toward the car, her smile very open, unguarded. But the other two hang back.

Jim Rayburn actually winks. "I don't suppose you could tell us where Midvale Academy is?"

I can't even get my mind around how someone might find humor in that, and I guess I am glad not to be that stupid, though I'd like to laugh right now because I am uncomfortable as hell. The dark-haired girl with the red streak and the ballet girl whisper to each other. The blonde girl narrows her eyes and tries to smile, but Gid can tell she's confused. He knows that dumb jokes make her feel guilty, ashamed, and paralyzed with feelings of inaction.

Well, that's how Gid feels. He's projecting. But it's an accurate projection. Very. Gid closes his eyes and imagines slitting his wrists, dark blood soaking into his father's custom oatmeal square-weave carpet.

Finally, Jim breaks into a loud, overcompensatory laugh. "Okay, okay," he says. "Can't pull the wool over your eyes. Okay, okay. Now, suppose I was going to relate this story about three lovely girls who made me feel a whole lot better about leaving my only son behind at this fine institution. If I was to tell that story to someone, what names might I call you by?"

Now his father is channeling Mark Twain.

"I'm Marcy Proctor," says the friendlier blonde one. "Great-great-granddaughter of Charles Peck Proctor, class of 1865, the guy who built Proctor."

Gid neglects to mention that's his dorm. I think that's cute.

"Midvale Academy royalty," Jim says, his blatant admiration laying bare his lowly social status for all the world to see. "Verrry nice!"

"Oh, and this is my friend and former roommate, Molly Mc-Garry." Marcy gestures to her companion.

Molly McGarry performs a slightly sarcastic curtsy. "Of the Buffalo McGarrys," she says. "And if you're going to put me in a story, please say, 'Once upon a time, there was a haughty and beautiful princess named Molly.' The haughty part is incredibly important." On this last part, she catches Gid's eye, raising one of her eyebrows.

Gid keeps his eyes on her face. He finds himself thinking the word *compelling,* then wonders what book he read that in because it's not a really automatic thing for a guy to call a girl. Then he looks away.

There is a horn blast behind them. Gid turns to see a white BMW (a big one) revving obnoxiously on their tail.

"Jeez, hold your horses," Jim Rayburn says. "Okay. Well, we've got to get a move on here, but that just leaves you." He points to the smallest girl, who shields her big eyes and looks ready to melt in the hot sun like a pat of butter. "My name is Edie," she says. "I hope you like it here."

Gid thinks, You and me both.

And then he/I/we are looking at the chapel. We are thinking about sex or almost-sex and there is the clock tower and here we are back at the Eagles song and thoughts of Mom. Now he is waiting to go into this dorm, looking at that hateful doofus conducting the Schubert symphony with the spoon.

I have no idea how I got into Gideon Rayburn's head. And now that I'm here, I don't really have any time to figure it out. It's taking everything I have to keep up, though Gid's thought process of "I'm okay, everything's fine, I'm not okay, everything's falling apart" is not so dissimilar to my own. If it weren't for the nut sack and the girl stuff and the consuming mortification at the thought of Jim Rayburn, whom I have the luxury of merely finding fucking odd, I'd say Gid and I are more alike than we are different.

cullen
and
nicholas

The dorms look grand from the outside. Inside they kind of give up. Gid likes the high windows and finds the fresh white paint cheery. But the carpet—lentil-soup brown, rough and short—and the hard fluorescent lights make him feel a little tricked. In a sense, he has been.

Places like Midvale are all about show. They're about what they're supposed to mean and say. What they actually mean and say, well, no one involved really cares all that much.

Gid joins a line forming in front of a table, above which there is a sign reading KEYS. Like everything else here, this sign bears the Midvale insignia—a statue of a man on a horse and a Latin inscription, which, roughly translated, means "Study forever."

Gideon is less than thrilled to see the kid from the white seven-series a few places ahead of him in line. The guy turns around twice to glare at him from under a lock of black hair. He is Asian but not all Asian. He has a chiseled, sleek handsomeness of which he seems acutely aware. He signs for his key, and as he leaves the room he looks at Gid with something like disdain. Gid narrows his eyes, hoping that will make him look intimidating. The kid lets out a snorting laugh to let Gid know he doesn't find him a worthy adversary. Gid peeks around, seeking out a sympathetic face. At least no one else is laughing at him. But no one seems to see him either. His fellow Midvalians, Gid notices, are almost uniformly tall and well formed. The kind of guys who match the kind of girls he saw outside. It's his turn. He squares his shoulders and steps up for his key.

The man he faces is in his mid-forties, stout but muscular, dressed in khakis (he's sitting down but I happen to know they're [yuck] pleated) and a white shirt that's straining at the neck and shoulders. His head is bald and pink, like a ham.

Gideon and Ham Head stare at each other for a moment.

"Gideon Rayburn," Gid says.

"Gideon Rayburn," repeats Ham Head, his tone wary. "I'm Mr. Cavanaugh." His thick fingers tap through a series of small manila envelopes alphabetized in a set of old gray tin boxes. There are a lot of *Rs*. "You might hear some people calling me Captain, or Captain Cavanaugh"—he finds the envelope and peers at it critically, as though he doesn't trust his own vision—"because that's what I used to be."

"A captain in the army?" Gid asks.

Cavanaugh stiffens. "No," he says. "I was captain of a boat." He frowns again. Gid feels as if he said something wrong. I feel like, Well, whatever yesterday held for you, today you're hamlike and handing out keys at a prep school dorm.

"Room 302. Card for outside, key's for the room. Any chance you spoke to your roommates over the summer?"

Gid had not. He called both and e-mailed each of them twice, but they didn't call or write back. "No," he tells Mr. Cavanaugh. "We never connected."

"Cullen McKay and Nicholas Westerbeck," Mr. Cavanaugh says. "Tell them I've got my eye on all of you." He winks, the least friendly wink in the history of winks.

Gid takes the lentil-soup brown stairs two at a time, his heart light with anticipation. From the second landing, he can see his door, 302. It is slightly ajar.

I sense intrigue.

Gideon slowly guides it open with his foot. The room is large, with that fresh white paint and, Gid is pleased to see, polished hardwood floors and dormer windows. On one side, the ceiling slopes charmingly over three school-issue plain black iron single beds. Gid's room at home had *Battlestar Galactica* wallpaper and green-and-blue-flecked shag carpet. These hardwood floors make him feel clean and smart.

There's a black suitcase on one of the beds and a few more on the floor. And . . . someone is standing in the closet. No, there are two people. Are they making out?

Holy shit. They are. They are really making out too. Lots of hands in lots of places and lots of things undone.

"Excuse me!" Gid stands in the middle of the room, unsure of what he just saw. The girl had long dark hair, and her shirt was un-buttoned down to her navel, which was pierced. But the guy—so tall. Even in the half-light, Gid could see that he definitely had to shave daily. (Gid shaves about once a week, if that.) Wasn't he kind of manly to be a boy? I am only a boy, Gid thinks. My roommates should only be boys.

"Sorry," Gid stammers, "this is my room, and . . ."

The closet door opens and the guy steps out. He lunges for the door, which Gid has left wide open, his long legs carrying him across the room in about one and a half strides. God, he's big. He has strong cheekbones, green eyes, huge shoulders, and hips so slim they're almost not there. "You always gotta watch out for that," the guy says. "The fucking teachers around here are totally after us."

Gid takes a step back. The black-haired kid might have been technically more handsome than this guy, but this combination of aristocratic beauty, sexual maturity, easy confidence, and sheer physicality, well, it is really alarming. "Especially Mr. Cavanaugh—Captain Cavanaugh," the guy intones in a perfect imitation of the Ham Head's voice—angry, low, but with a certain pathetic tightness to it. "Ha! Captain Cockweed! He can blow me! You must be the new guy . . . Gilbert, is it?"

The girl goes to the mirror and starts to smooth her blouse and hair.

"Gideon," he says. Until this moment, Gid's been pretty oblivious of the fact that he has a body. Now, suddenly, in one sickening wave, he feels like a giant, disgusting amoeba.

"I'm Cullen McKay." He blinks, and then, as if noticing her for the first time, says to the girl, "Katie, you gotta get out of here." He taps Katie on the ass—if you ask me, Katie was put on this earth to be tapped on the ass—and to Gid's utter amazement, the girl blushes and smiles.

That's what I need to be like, Gideon thinks. I want to have girls so into me that when I tap them on the ass, they smile at me.

Oh see, now, that's kind of gross. But I get it. What teenage boy wouldn't want that? What teenage girl wouldn't want her version of that? I know I would.

"Anyway," Cullen continues, "Cockweed tried so hard to get me kicked out last year, but shit, he could never catch me!"

"Catch you?" Gideon says. "Catch you doing what?"

Katie laughs and, keeping her eyes on Cullen the whole time, struts out of the room. Her butt in red pants is like an upside-down box of Valentine candy.

"Does that girl go to school here?" Gideon asks.

Cullen laughs. "Her brother does. I know her from the Vineyard. She was dropping her brother off, and she just came over to say hi."

When girls say hi to me, Gideon thinks, they really just say hi.

The wall opposite the door has two large windows, one of

which leads to a fire escape. Gideon sees a green rim of the quad; a few branches touch the edge of the outer pane. The wall to his left, the plain wall, has two doors to reveal one large (the make-out place) and one small closet. The small one has a pull-up bar in the doorframe. The furniture is all standard campus issue, but there's a white iPod attached to a stereo and a pair of freestanding Bang & Olufsen speakers.

"Nicholas and I chose this room especially for ease of exit," Cullen says, gesturing at the fire escape. "That's White, the girl's dorm where our friends live," he says, pointing through a window on the side of the room, down to a modern brick building across another expanse of grass.

Ease of exit? Gid wonders. This means sneaking out, right? A nervous-making, exciting idea.

Right, Gideon. Prep school is the site of the cool euphemism. You'll get used to it.

Jim Rayburn walks in, swinging his truck key around his finger. I think it says something about fishing, but I can't read it. Jim Rayburn's face falls when he sees Cullen. Not in an "I can't believe my son's living with this obvious delinquent" kind of way, but in a "Why did this actually-not-so-obvious delinquent get a higher rung on the male food chain than I did?" way. Jim Rayburn is deeply insecure. Hence Gid's panic. Gid hopes (somewhere deep down) that he's getting away from Jim soon enough so as not to absorb this trait.

"A pleasure," Cullen says. The big hand grips Jim's with confidence and warmth. "Nicholas and I have been looking forward to meeting your son." Jim Rayburn widens his stance, his body opening up a little under Cullen's disarming friendliness.

The door squeaks and opens a crack. Gideon sees a sliver of a head with shiny straight black hair and one unnaturally blue eye. The door opens some more. A boy's face. The boy is not smiling. He's carrying a large jug of water. He uses a brown leather duffel to nudge the door open farther and walks into the room. He hoists the duffel up onto a low wooden dresser, then, still without a word, disappears into the hallway, returning with an identical duffel. He sets it down, then walks over to the middle bed and pulls it all the way across the room, setting it in a shadowed area where the roof slopes down. He stands back, stares at it for a second, then moves the bed about two inches to the left. He drinks deeply from the jug, then puts it under the bed.

"I'm Nicholas," he says to Gideon, still not smiling. "I assume you're Gid." He nods at Jim. "And I assume you're Gid's dad?"

"When you assume . . . ," says Jim, even though there's really no joke to be made here. Nicholas's smile is thin and tolerant as he shakes Jim's hand, then Gid's. Nicholas is smaller than Cullen, about three inches shorter and about two thirds as wide, but somehow he's more intimidating. He has fantastic posture.

Nicholas goes to the duffel and places his hands on top as if to steady himself. He unzips it and removes first a hammer, followed by a single nail, which he proceeds to pound into the wall with just a few short, sound whacks. Next he produces from the duffel a black wooden 8 × 10 framed black-and-white photograph of a young, pretty girl. As Nicholas arranges it on the wall, Gid leans in for a closer look. The girl has dark hair and bright, sparkling eyes.

"Wow," Gideon says. "Is that your girlfriend?"

Cullen throws his head back and howls. Nicholas says nothing and rummages in his duffel again. He removes a white sheet and, with a firm, almost angry shake, tosses it over the bed. "No," he says, without a trace of warmth in his voice. "It's my mother." He constructs two perfect sets of hospital corners. Then he sits down, unties and removes a pair of New Balance sneakers, and, as if in pain, eases himself onto his back.

"I apologize for not being more social," he says. "Being in a car with my stepmother emotionally exhausts me, and I have to rest."

Cullen is still giggling into his hand, and Nicholas throws him a disapproving look before he closes his eyes and pulls the sheet up under his chin. Within a few moments he's snoring.

Cullen reaches into his pocket and produces a tiny silver camera. "How about a picture of me and your son on our first day as friends?"

Jim loves this. He forgets himself for a minute, grateful that his son is in caring hands.

Or so it seems.

Mugging for the pose, Cullen throws a heavy arm around Gid's shoulder. "Hey," he whispers in Gid's ear, "say booze, bongs, and bitches."

Minutes later, when his father drives away, Gid watches from the window.

Cullen squats in front of the open CD changer. "Sad?" he asks. He puts on Cat Power. Which is really sad. Too sad. It's good, though, because Gid knows he's not *that* sad.

"No," says Gid. He doesn't know exactly how he feels. There's some guilt, but only because he's so relieved. He watches his father drive away partly because it seems like the right thing to do, but also because he wants to make sure he's really gone.

Cullen nods. "There comes a certain age in a boy's life . . ." And with this, he reaches under the bed and produces a contraption, like a plastic vase with tubes coming out of it, "where Dad steps out and the Vaportech steps in." Gideon is about to ask what the Vaportech is when Cullen reaches into his pocket and produces a very large and heavy-looking Ziploc bag full of pot.

Gid is speechless. I feel a strong responsibility toward him, and I will him, as hard as I can, to say something like, "You know, I thought I would have a little bit more time to figure out the extent to which I'm interested in misbehaving," or, "Let me figure out what the rules are before I start breaking them." But I'm clearly not reaching him, because he not only says nothing, he smiles, takes the Ziploc, and opens it.

"Smells like good stuff," he says, although this is the first time he's ever seen pot, let alone smelled it.

the
yellow
thong

Gideon spends the afternoon with his face wrapped around the Va-portech. Nicholas sleeps. Cullen talks, ceasing the relay of informa-tion only long enough to smoke more pot himself.

"So we get our pot delivered from Sanders, the maintenance man. He also put sealant around the doors for us over the summer, so Cockweed, who lives across the hall, can't smell it." Notice Cullen doesn't mention that he pays the maintenance man, dearly. Cullen is one of those rich people who seem to have forgotten about that little element of his transactions and sees the world as this place where people are, miraculously, just really into doing nice things for him.

Gideon tunes in and out. Mostly, he's picturing the girl Cullen was making out with earlier in the closet. If he were friends with Cullen, would girls like Katie like him? That makes sense. Or is he just high?

It makes some sense. But, yes, he is extremely high. "When I got my key from, uhh . . . Cockweed . . . he said to tell you guys he was keeping an eye on me," Gid says, and is pleased when Cullen throws his head back in a joyous whoop. "On all of us."

"He's so not going to win this year." Cullen buzzes with energy, walking around the room, picking up and putting down CD cases, running his hands through his hair, which, Gid notes, is blond and both angelically curly and thick enough to be virile. Gid finds himself going down a bad road, worrying that he is not as handsome as Cullen. And maybe he's not, but he's certainly handsome, if less brazenly so. And his eyes have a lot more kindness, a lot more soul than Cullen's. Maybe some girls are more into perfect abs than soul, but not me.

Cullen bounds over to the door and looks through the peephole into the hallway. "I'm the one who has my eye on him!" He beckons to Gid. "This is a great room on account of the fact that we have our own bathroom, and no other students live on this floor. But it's also a bad room because Captain Cockweed's apartment has an entrance up here. Look."

Indeed, there is the man himself, kneeling down, his head angled toward the ground so that Gid is looking right at his scalp. He holds what appears to be a soup can over a large metal box. "That's weird," Gid says. "He looks like he's using an electric can opener."

"Aha," says Cullen. "And he is. Those faculty apartments are free, because the teachers don't make any money. But they always have something major wrong with them. And the Cockweed-Cavanaughs have an electricity problem. We joke about it. Not a lot to talk about on campus, and I mean, look at that. It's pretty funny."

Gideon thinks, Electricity situation.

"So," Cullen continues, "you will often see them in the hallway using a blender or electric paper shredder or so on. Wait 'til you see Mrs. Cavanaugh out there with her vibrator!"

Gideon's eyes widen.

Cullen claps him on the shoulder. "Joking, my friend." Guys and vibrator jokes. A love that never ends. Cullen looks through the peephole again. "He's gone now. They have a son, Tim, who will be in juvie by the time we're in college. And sort of a cute daughter, Erin. I feel a little sorry for her."

"Really?" The mention of a girl makes Gid excited. "Have you fooled around with her?"

"She's six, dude. Maybe someday. Although she does have some rather attractive babysitters. This girl Fiona that I kind of would like to score with. I was gentleman enough to keep my hands off her last year since she was fourteen. . . . She takes care of Erin sometimes." Cullen gestures at the Vaportech, now loaded up and ready to go. He lights it.

Gid smokes. "You're a natural," Cullen says.

Gideon wonders, Is Cullen joking? Did you only call someone who really was not a natural a natural, because if they really were a natural, wouldn't they know it, and not have to hear it from you? To point out the naturalness of something, didn't that really call attention to its very unnaturalness? That word *natural* really undid him. He's got to remember: He's fucked up. Nothing matters.

"Hey," Gid says, taking a chance, "do you ever think that chicks babysit as a way of trying to say, 'Hey, guys, look, I'm good with kids'?"

Anyone can see this is an unbelievably brilliant insight. Just a second ago, when Cullen called Gid a natural, he was, in fact (I can't read Cullen's mind, of course, but I am almost certain), being a little patronizing. But now Cullen's face lights up. "Oh my God, I never thought of that. I was wondering why Fiona babysat, I mean. The chick's seriously loaded. Even for here. And that she babysits for Cockweed, in this dorm, of all places. Hmm. Now I'm sure she wanted me. Thanks, man."

Cullen stops pacing and squats on his heels, on the floor,

dangling his head in his hands. Gid imagines that Cullen might be quite at home in the jungle, a nice jungle, with pillows and refrigerators. Cullen springs up off the floor and hangs off the pull-up bar with one arm. "Did you see there are a lot of good-looking freshmen? A lot of foreign students, which seems great because they're often hot, but which is not so great, because they're all super well-behaved and generally have weird religious beliefs. Sometimes those beliefs keep them from having sex. Except for the ones who are maniacs, of course." Cullen switches to the other arm. "So, Gid, as far as girls go, do you have a type?"

"Well, I wouldn't mind finding myself a maniac," Gid says. No sooner is this out of his mouth than Gid realizes who he sounds like: Jim Rayburn.

Cullen doesn't go so far as to look annoyed with Gid. But for now, he's not asking any more questions. And he stops swinging around and sits back down on his heels.

Nicholas stirs, and Gid feels higher. That is to say, more fucked up. More paranoid. Nicholas turns over on his back and opens his eyes. He looks right at Gideon, then shuts his eyes again, as if Gid were a problem he wasn't quite ready to face. "I gotta go to the bathroom," Gid says.

The bathroom is cavernous. There are six toilet stalls and a hall of showers built, it seems, for an entire football team. There is woodwork in here. Wainscoting and stuff like that. Gid touches it, thinking, Fancy. One wall is taken up with three windows, all flung open to the sweet summer air. Down below, in the grass, a group of girls have made a circle. One of them lies down and settles her blonde head on her arm; another leans back and rests her dark head on this girl's ankles. Gid can't see their faces, but he can tell from the way they move, the seriousness with which they adjust their expanses of hair, that they are beautiful. He shuts the window, an attempt to temper the painful longing that has come over him.

He returns to the room to find Cullen tossing most of Gid's CDs—including, but not limited to, John Mayer, Norah Jones, Jack Johnson, and Maroon Five—into a Saks Fifth Avenue shopping bag.

"What's up?" Cullen says, as if nothing were happening. Then he grabs a black Magic Marker and across the bag scrawls *Lesbian Music*. Nicholas is awake, lying in bed, propped up on one elbow, reading *The New Yorker*. He scarcely glances at Gideon and seems similarly disinterested in Cullen's activities.

"My aunt's a lesbian," Gideon says stiffly, because this is all he can think of. His mother's sister, Clara. She's a nurse. *Quel* surprise.

"Whatever. So is everyone's," says Cullen. He crosses out *Lesbian* and in its place writes *Girl*. He grins at Gideon. "Now we can all relax and watch the LPGA Chick-fil-A Charity Championship in peace." He winks.

Nicholas snorts and turns a page of his magazine.

Cullen keeps thumbing through Gid's CDs. "Tori Amos? Weren't you afraid when you bought this that it would, like, turn into a little fairy and fly away?" He thumbs through a few more. "Dave Matthews," he says, holding it up. "That fat fuck."

"I think Dave Matthews is cool," Gideon says.

"Nope," Nicholas says, still not looking up. "Wrong."

Nothing is spared save some classic rock, some rap, and Stevie Nicks, which was his mother's and a total accident.

"I'm very into Stevie Nicks," Cullen says, and Gideon, formulating a speech about how it wasn't his, retreats to plain old general anxiety. "She was a fox, she had pipes, and she could fucking party. In my book, it doesn't get much cooler than that."

Gideon regards the shopping bag and asks, "Okay, so, do I just keep this music in a special place?"

Cullen bursts out laughing. "Not unless you consider my anus a special place."

Nicholas shakes his head but doesn't look up from his reading.

"Cullen wouldn't take the time to sort things into a Lesbian Music—"

"Girl Music," Cullen corrects him. "The point Nicholas is trying to make is that this isn't about organization. Did you see anyone make an appointment with Sheila from California Closets? I didn't. This shit is going where it *belongs*."

And he picks up the bag, walks onto the fire escape, and one by one frisbees the offending CDs out over the quad. They land in the grass, a few feet from the same girls Gid was looking at from the bathroom. One of them crawls over and picks up a CD, then another one, and looks up toward the dorm. She shrugs.

Within a minute, all the CDs have been cleared away.

"Wait," Gid pleads. "You can't do that." This seems abnormally cruel to him. Yet he senses that the right thing is to let it happen. That perhaps he will be better off without this music.

I think that's definitely true. Maroon Five, *ugh*.

Besides, no one appears to have heard Gid's pleas. Cullen slides the Vaportech over to Nicholas's bedside.

When Nicholas exhales, a giant smile spreads over his face. "I enjoy how much this place annoys me," he says. He goes to the bay window and surveys the campus. "All these spoiled, narcissistic rich people, of which I myself am one." So Nicholas, unlike Cullen, is totally aware of his richness; he's even self-deprecating about it. I guess that's a little less maddening than Cullen's cluelessness. But not much. "I just hope," Nicholas adds, looking a little somber, "that we can find a good way to make the time pass this year. It's our only hope."

He hoists his two matching leather duffels onto the bed and starts to unpack. His clothes are folded department-store neat and arranged by color.

I don't blame Gideon for having no idea what to do next. Is he supposed to get mad? Is he supposed to stand up for himself? He

goes to his bag and slowly unzips it, just to give himself something
to do. His stomach flutters and roils with a just-punched feeling.
He puts his hands around a stack of white T-shirts, feeling comfort
in their familiarity. One of them, he notes, is getting a little yellow.

He thinks, Yellow. Wait. The bag. Now I know what's in it.

Yellow? Wait? The bag? Now he knows what? Come on, Gid! I
guess I need to get better at piecing together fragmented thoughts,
but I'm not there yet.

Gideon reaches frantically into his suitcase, still thinking, un-
helpfully, Yellow, wait, the bag.

Slowly, I see it. It's strange how I can hear his thoughts, but it's
even stranger how his memories are starting to feel like my own.
There's a basketball hoop and a smell of blacktop, car wax and thin
milky coffee in a thermos. *The Washington Post* in its plastic wrapper
smacks against flagstone.

It's dawn in Fairfax, Virginia, and Gideon is saying good-bye to
a girl. The girl's name is Danielle. They stand underneath a basketball hoop in Gid's suburban cul-de-sac. She's handing him a little
paper bag, and Gideon puts it in his suitcase.

Here, back at Midvale, his hand sinks into the suitcase again.
Now he's panicking. He did put it in the suitcase, right? Yes, he remembers. So where, then, Gid thinks, his hand giving one more
frantic scoop inside the by now obviously very empty pocket of his
suitcase, is the fucking paper bag?

"Looking for this?" Cullen says. His hands are behind his back.
His left hand emerges, revealing the crumpled paper bag with just
the tiniest bit of yellow cloth peeking out of it. Cullen opens the
bag and holds up a pair of yellow thong underwear.

"How did you get that?" Gideon demands.

"Oh, you know, I was looking for some women's underwear,
and I thought to myself, Hey, before paying those expensive
department-store prices, why not rifle through the new kid's

luggage? Kidding. I saw a brown bag. Thought it might be something exciting I could eat or smoke or swallow. Turns out . . . well, this is pretty exciting in its own right, wouldn't you say?" He hands the underwear to Nicholas.

Nicholas's eyes turn bright. "Oh-ho," he says. "I need to hear the story behind these."

"Oh my God," Gid says, feeling panic and a sense of falling, of unreality, almost, more than anger. "You went through my bags. You guys are totally . . . you . . . you have no . . ."

It will take him months to put his finger on it. So let me complete what Gid can't.

Cullen and Nicholas don't care about much except their own amusement. They have no real sense of morality.

"These are my girlfriend's," Gid says, still bewildered to find his most private possession out in the open like this. "My girlfriend from home," he qualifies, not wanting word to get out that he's taken. Although he feels some blushing pride in being so. Sort of.

Nicholas mashes his lips together and makes a low, skeptical sound. "You brought these here as a memento?"

"That's right." Gid lifts his second, smaller suitcase onto the bed and starts to unpack. He makes a sudden decision, gathering his wits, swallowing his shock. He's going to act normal, because then they might just forget about this. "They're my girlfriend's, and I just have them to remember her by."

"I don't buy it," Nicholas replies.

Gid continues to unpack, monitoring his expression, keeping it still, without tells. Inside, he remembers. He remembers the way those underwear felt in his fingers, how the nylon threads stuck to his calluses.

As violated as he feels, he also wants to tell.

Then Cullen takes the underwear from Nicholas. He smells them. "Freshly laundered," he says.

Wow. That was . . . Cullen is some breed. There's a pause while Gid lets what his new roommate has done sink in.

Gideon doesn't like it that Cullen just smelled his girlfriend's underwear, but he admires it. These two boys are so comfortable in their own skins. Gid wants—hard to admit this to himself because he doesn't yet know what they want—to be around them, to be like them. Mostly it's because he thinks it would be a good way to get girls. But partly it's because these guys seem to have more fun being themselves than he does being himself.

"Uh, sorry I smelled your girlfriend's underwear," Cullen says. He doesn't sound all that sorry. He's just reacting to the length of the pause.

"Well," Gid says carefully, "I did spend the whole ride up here trying to forget her. Maybe letting some guy smell her underwear is a step in the right direction."

Wait. He wasn't trying to forget her. He was trying to forget feeling guilty about not remembering her.

Nicholas, still unpacking, is mostly faced the other way, but Gid can see the side of his mouth. He smiled. He smiled at one of Gid's jokes.

Gid, this is no small feat. You're my hero.

"I'll tell you," he says. Cullen's eyes light up with delight, and there is a hungry glint in Nicholas's "I'll tell you, but you have to promise—"

"Don't tell us not to laugh. You can't tell people not to laugh," Nicholas says. "I mean, you're our roommate, and we're going to try to like you, but if you end up embarrassing yourself, or being a complete asshole, we won't. We can't control how we're going to feel."

"I get it," Gid says, surprising himself. "You guys are auditioning me to be your friend."

And goddamn if those two masters of confidence aren't

speechless and awkward, just for a second. Gid hasn't beaten them at their own game, not by a long shot. But at least he's told them he knows what they're playing. The kid from Virginia is surprisingly smart. And the smarter they get, the cuter they get.

Because we're not like guys. The whole thong thing. Please. It's a pair of friggin' underwear. The most mundane thing in the world. But who am I to stop the magic? Who am I at all?

the
bet

They are nice enough to ease Gid's pain with some bourbon. "From the bar on my grandfather's boat," Cullen says.

"My grandfather has a boat," Gid says, enjoying the warm burn in his chest.

"Really?" Cullen says, pouring another small belt into Gid's mug. "My grandfather's is a forty-two-foot Chris-Craft. What's yours?"

Gid's grandfather keeps a twelve-foot Starcraft with a twenty-horsepower Mercury outboard in his garage in Manassas. He sometimes fishes for bass in the Potomac. "Let's just say it doesn't have a bar," Gid says. Cullen nods. Nicholas, Gid is pleased to see, smiles again. He's smoking pot, but not drinking. He only drinks when there's Guinness available, he says. A predictable eccentricity.

Gid's eagerness to be their friend is so understandable to me. Say what you want about these guys, they are charming mother-fuckers. Even though I've been making fun of them, I may already be friends with them, and if I'm not, if they wanted to be friends with me, I don't think I could say no. Gid loves the way the smoky liquor softens his pot buzz. The room is so warm and foggy now that it feels almost tropical.

Cullen removes the thong from his pocket and tosses it to Gid.

Gideon sits down on his own bed and draws his legs up, Indian style. He holds the underwear. "My girlfriend back in Fairfax was named Danielle Rogal," he says. "She lived down the street from me."

"God, this is great!" Cullen shouts.

Gideon shifts uncomfortably.

"I'm serious," Cullen says. "Don't leave anything out. What kind of body did she have?"

Gideon squeezes the underwear, thinking of Danielle's bare olive skin and sincere hazel eyes, which became more sincere, often disturbingly, the more naked she became. "Thin, maybe three inches shorter than me, normal, uh . . . chest," he says. "Dark hair. Anyway . . . uh . . ." Telling this story can't possibly enhance his reputation. But he's already started.

"I actually had no idea how long we'd been going out," Gid continues. "But when we were saying good-bye, she told me we had been going out for seven months, two weeks, and three days." This gets a snicker from the crowd, and from me too. Girls are supposed to be bad at math, but we're excellent at counting. "So, the night before I left . . . Well. I guess I should go back."

Cullen rubs his hands together with coarse greed. "Only if it involves anything remotely dirty!" Nicholas is flat on his back again. With every outburst from Cullen, his eyes dart to the side in annoyance.

"So once we'd been together for about two months, we basically started doing everything," says Gid. "But she always had her clothes on. Her pants had some weird thing about them . . . where I would have my hand in them, and they would kind of . . . expand?"

Nicholas and Cullen don't know, either.

Is he talking about *Lycra*? Oh my God. Guys are such retards!

"But she never took her clothes off, and then . . ."

Cullen leaps off the bed, screeching as if in pain. "For how long did she never take her clothes off?" he asks. He holds his head, bracing himself for the answer.

What, Gid wonders, has Cullen so confused and upset? "The whole time. The whole time we were . . . until the night before." Gid looks helplessly at Nicholas.

"No!!!" Cullen wails. "That's so horrible!"

"Cullen, just let him fucking finish," Nicholas says. "I think that what Gid's saying is that they did a lot of shit for a few months, but she always had her clothes on. I think it's sort of a boarding-school thing to just get totally naked and go for it."

Gid wants to know more about boarding school and nudity but doesn't know how to ask without sounding too eager.

"So the night before. We're in her basement."

"Don't leave out all the details," Nicholas advises. "I like a little atmosphere."

"Ass-mosphere!" says Cullen. "You like that?"

"The carpeting was green, shag. Her couch was like, tweed or something. And upstairs, I could hear her brother, Kevin, getting himself a bowl of ice cream. I knew something was different because her parents were out at a Kiwanis dance and her brother, he won't come downstairs because of his mold allergy . . ."

"Okay," Nicholas says. "Details can overwhelm."

Strangely, Gid is enjoying himself. Being the center of attention. "So sure enough, instead of just, like, unzipping her pants and, like, letting her bra just kind of hang off of her, she just jumps off and takes off all her clothes."

"Fucking finally!" Cullen shouts.

"Quiet!" Nicholas commands. His eyes take on that lightness, that sea-under-the-sun quality that indicates his rare excitement. "This is when it all happens."

This is indeed when it all happens. Gid takes what he hopes is a courage-stealing sip from his mug of bourbon. Stalling, he reads it. MIDVALE: CLASS OF '78 TWENTY-FIFTH REUNION. Cullen's dad went to school here too? Gid continues through a pang of outsiderness. "She's naked. Except for these." He holds up the underwear. "And she says, looking right at me, 'It's time.'"

Cullen jumps up and sits down, jumps up and sits down, delighted. Nicholas nods and smirks with real pleasure. Gid had been willing himself to say that Danielle said, "I want you to do it to me." But he chickened out. He's glad they're enjoying the story, but he can't help kicking himself, wishing he had the balls to embellish, make it even better.

"So was this the first you'd heard of it?" Cullen asks. "Were you like, 'What's it time for, cookies and ice cream?'"

"Oh no," Gid says. "I knew what she meant. She had said, 'I want my first time to be with you.' But I thought that was, you know, for some future date."

Nicholas and Cullen nod to each other. Gid senses vague, if not entirely genuine, approval. He also hopes this is over.

"How many girls have said that to you?" Nicholas asks Cullen.

"I don't know, eight? But each time I hear it, it's like the first time all over again."

"That's not true," Gid says, before he can control himself.

"Which part?" Cullen asks. He smiles. Gid watches him. His smile is innocent. This is a guy, Gid realizes, who could persuade a girl to part with just about anything.

Everything about Cullen suggests that Gid is one hundred percent right about this.

"They all say the same thing?" Gid asks.

"No," Cullen whispers. "Each one says the same thing very differently."

I would bet my place in Gideon's head that Cullen is lying.

"Did you two do it or not?" Nicholas asks. So it's not over.

Gid can't run away from the truly interesting, incriminating part of the story any longer. This is bad for him but good for the story. "We . . . started to, I mean, that was definitely the idea. I mean, I tried to get it off her, and then, you know, I couldn't, so we just kept doing it, but I kept fussing with the underwear, and . . ." He trails off. "I don't know how to say this."

"Let me help you," Nicholas says. "The underwear, and not what the underwear promised, ended up being the thing that ultimately drove you . . . um . . . over the edge. The underwear, and not the thing that the underwear promised, was the place where this particular spasm"—he lets the pure phonetics of the word sink in for a second, the soft S coming up against the harder M—"of passion found its final resting place."

"What*ever!*" Cullen says. "I come on girls' underwear all the time."

Gid winces.

"Dumbass," Nicholas says. "It's because he's a virgin."

"No way," says Cullen. "That sucks."

"I don't think I am technically a virgin," Gid protests.

Gid knows he told a good story. But good story or not, this virgin label, if at all possible, has to go.

He reaches for the bourbon, hoping to loosen the tightness growing in his rib cage.

"Not so fast," Nicholas says. "It's not Mountain Dew."

Cullen takes a few shirts to his bureau and drops them in a drawer. Everything he owns is old, cotton, and ripped in such a way so as to casually display his incredible physique. Gid decides that he likes Cullen, but that his particular brand of cockiness is going to become extremely annoying. "I don't think I am technically a virgin," he repeats.

"None of this matters," Nicholas says shortly. "What matters is what you, or rather we, do with these underwear. And I say, these underwear are a challenge."

Cullen agrees, "Yes! A challenge. Absolutely!"

Nicholas continues, "These underwear don't ask a question about the past. They ask a question about the future. Who cares whether you sort of got laid? When are you definitely going to get laid?" Nicholas paces the room, warming to his subject. He stops, facing Gideon with almost military precision. "I say the end of the year. June. It seems like a long time, but really, when you think about the fact that you have the rest of your life to have sex, it's not so bad."

"December!" Cullen shouts. "No, fuck that. He's going to get laid by Halloween." Cullen leaps onto the bed on his stomach again and humps it. "Workin' overtime!" he shouts.

Gideon wonders what this carnal outburst is regarding. I know it's really just that. A carnal outburst.

"I have to say I am impressed that the girl offered to have sex with you without your asking for it," Nicholas says. "Lack of desperation bodes well for your long-term success."

"Thanks," says Gideon, thinking, that's not the right thing to say to someone who thinks that even in an environment teeming with luscious girls, it's going to take you a whole ten months to get laid.

Now Nicholas does something really cold. He turns to Gideon and sizes him up. "The white Chuck Taylor low-tops are trying too hard to be old-school; the jeans are too neat. The shirt is the same color as the jeans, so you kind of look like a blueberry."

Cullen nods slowly, impressed. "Great call. But I still believe in October."

Okay, I feel bad that they said Gid looks like a blueberry. But I'm not going to say it's not true.

"You're just not doable yet," says Nicholas. "And that's not, like, me, that's just the truth of the universe filtering through me."

Oh God. Now, that is too mean. Girls have nothing on boys when it comes to outright cruelty. Behind-the-back stuff, we're better with that, sure. But saying it right to your face? Boys rule on that one.

"You've made your point; I've made mine. I say Gideon gets laid by the end of October," says Cullen.

"I say no way," Nicholas says. "But he definitely gets laid by June."

"I think you're making a mistake there," Cullen says. He backs up, and they regard Gid once again. "If he doesn't get laid by the end of October, I say there's no way he gets laid by June. I think you either have it or you don't."

"And I think that you definitely don't have it yet, but you could have it," Nicholas says. "So, to reiterate, you say by October or never. I say not by October, but definitely by June."

"I believe we have clearly defined our terms," Cullen says.

They shake hands.

"Wait a minute," Gid says. "You guys are making a bet about me?" He's still holding the underwear in his hand. God, that trip to the bathroom. That was his first mistake. The underwear would have been safe in his drawer, and they'd be talking about . . . Forget it, Gideon, the truth is, something equally awful probably would have happened. "I don't know. I mean, obviously, I'm going to try to have sex with girls, right. But I'd prefer to not have anything riding on it. I think it might . . . mess me up."

Cullen and Nicholas eye each other nervously. I can see that partly they don't want to hurt Gid's feelings. But also that they really want this bet. Bets are fun. Nicholas said he hoped they could find some way to entertain themselves this year, and this is it. "If you're going to be doing it anyway," Nicholas says, "what does it matter if we have an interest in it?" That was a pretty smart way of presenting it to Gid. Making him the star of the show.

"Last year, we bet our friend Liam Wu that he couldn't have sex with both Marcy Proctor and Erica Dewey, who were roommates, in the same week, in their room. We gave him a month to do it," Cullen said.

Marcy Proctor! That's the girl from this afternoon! She's pretty. And she was the only one who was vaguely nice to him during his father's asinine little episode. "Well, did he pull it off?" Gideon asks, hoping for a no. Poor sweet little Marcy Proctor.

"It took him three weeks," Nicholas says, smiling at the memory. "But he did them both . . . on the same day."

Gideon sits down on his bed. Liam Wu. "What does Liam Wu look like?"

Nicholas, as Gideon suspected he would, describes the Asian guy who honked at him this afternoon.

"He did that? You guys bet him that he couldn't do it, and he did, just for fun?"

Cullen looks at Nicholas, who shrugs. "Well," Cullen says, "we did give him Nicholas's mom's car. But look, what he was doing was really, really something to pull off. I mean, it was truly magical. Stunning entertainment. What you're going to do is what you're going to be doing anyway. Or trying to do."

"You gave him Nicholas's car?" Gideon and I are on the same page. Shocked about the car, also shocked that Liam Wu was so handsomely rewarded for pussy hounding.

"Yep," Cullen says. "He wouldn't do it otherwise."

"Well," Gideon says, "I won't do this. Not even for a car."

Though we are both wondering what kind of car it is.

Nicholas sidles up to Cullen and whispers to him. Cullen scowls, shakes his head, and whispers back. "Excuse us, won't you, for just a minute?" Cullen hides the bourbon under his bed. As he's doing so, his cell phone rings. "Answer that," he says to Gideon, then adds, "please." He and Nicholas leave.

Cullen has a silver flip phone. The caller ID says MADISON.

Before Gid can even say hello, a young female voice asks, "How's the new kid?"

God, this girl sounds pretty. Her voice is teasing, with a little layer of gravel in it. Gid bets she smokes, and even though he's watched a lot of filmstrips and ads that tell him to think otherwise, he finds this sexy. "I am the new kid," he says.

"Well, I guess he must not hate you, 'cause he let you answer his phone," the girl says.

"Yes," Gid says, "I guess."

"Are you guys going to come over tonight?" the girl asks. "Oh shit, I gotta go."

Cullen comes back into the room first. Nicholas follows. "That was someone called Madison," he tells Cullen. "She wants us to come over."

Cullen nods and starts to pack himself another bowl.

"We've decided that if you get laid by October, we're going to give you the car," Nicholas says. Cullen does a little dance, a side-step, snapping his fingers, swinging his arms in little loops.

"What car?" Gid says. "Is there another car?"

"The car is the car is the car," Cullen says, twirling around. "A 1991 seven-series BMW. Sunroof. Five-speed, of course."

Holy shit. The car that honked at him today.

"You can drive a standard?"

"Of course," Gideon says.

Thank God. That whole both-hands-on-the-steering-wheel thing is so Rust Belt.

"But you guys gave Liam the car, right?" Gid says. "You can't just take it away from him."

"Sure we can," Cullen says breezily. "By the way, this is a cool car, but it's also white. So it's not like, wow, totally bad ass. But you definitely should win it."

Gideon imagines a world where he has proved to his roommates he can get laid, actually gotten laid, and won the prior instrument of his humiliation. This is a world he wants to live in. It seems too good to be true. And of course, well, none of it has happened, but it could, right?

"You guys are going to give me the car? That's great," he says.

"Well, I wouldn't go out and buy your BMW racing jacket yet," Nicholas says darkly.

"Ha! Yeah!" Cullen says. "Better get some condoms first, and see if you use one of them."

Gid thinks about the girls on the quad. There were so many pretty ones. One of them is going to have to like him, right?

"I think this calls for a celebration," Cullen declares, pulling out the camera from this afternoon. Nicholas looks unenthusiastic but dutifully lines up for a pose, with Gideon in the middle.

Cullen holds out the camera with his impossibly long arm. Gid feels good here, flanked by his roommates. Then the flash goes off, and it occurs to him he's in the middle not as a gesture of support or affection, but because of symmetry. He's the shortest.

"Wait a minute," he says. "What do you guys get? Your bet is about me, but you're betting each other, right?"

Uneasy glances pass between Cullen and Nicholas.

"Uh," Nicholas stammers, "if I win, then I get the car back."

"Wait a minute," Gid says. "Doesn't your mother know the car's missing?"

I had the same question.

"She never leaves New York," Nicholas says. "She never leaves our neighborhood."

Gid looks at Cullen, who nods.

"Anyway," Nicholas says, "Liam knows that he might have to give it back. He just won't ever know why. It's our secret. He knows we're going to do something like this, but he just doesn't know what."

Gid likes the "our secret" part, but he's still not settled on this.

"Okay," he says. "So what does Cullen get if he wins?"

Cullen claps his hands together, his face brightens with eagerness. But Nicholas shoots him a stern look. He says one word: "No."

And that's the end of that conversation. Strangely, the refusal to divulge this last detail has made Gideon more, not less, interested in the bet.

more girls, more guys

Gid's so up and down; sometimes he likes himself, sometimes he doesn't. He's complicated. Most guys are so uncomplicated. They're either total nerds who look about ready to dive under the rug, or they're jock assholes who strut around like they own the world. Gid struggles with his ego. It makes me think that I could tell him anything.

I think I might have a little crush on him. But I get a lot of crushes.

On the short walk to dinner with Cullen and Nicholas, their fellow students spot them, admire, and clear to the side as they pass. Gid feels like he's riding the crest of a wave. Gideon sees beautiful girls—a swaying mane of chestnut hair here, a perfect jawline there, a set of luminous green eyes—and these girls are looking at *him*. It occurs to him that the attention is because of Cullen and Nicholas, but he pushes that out of his mind.

The bet scares him. But the bet is also fun, because Nicholas and Cullen made it up, and being around them, even on their terms, well, it's fairly enjoyable. Gid didn't ask to room with the coolest guys on campus, but since that's what happened, well, he'd be a fool to turn his back on the opportunity. Plus, he doesn't totally believe the bet's real.

"Start looking around. I know you can do October, buddy, but you're going to have to be proactive," Cullen says. He claps him on the back and strolls ahead. He sneaks up behind a girl with black hair, dressed in pink satin pants and a tight white tank top, and puts his hands over her eyes. The girl stops and runs her hands up his arms, then squeals, turns around, and hugs him. Cullen slips his hands inside the back of her pants, and she doesn't flinch.

That, Gideon, is a lot to live up to.

Gid turns to see if Nicholas is paying any attention to Cullen's antics, but he's clasped his hands behind his back, with a faraway look in his eyes. A blonde girl, medium height, athletic, and tan, falls into step beside him. "Hey," she says. She's wearing running shoes and blue-and-white-striped pants with a soccer ball stitched over the upper thigh.

"Hi," Nicholas says, not even looking at her.

So Cullen is the flirt. Nicholas is the strong silent type. I just need to find my thing, Gid thinks. How hard can that be?

It can be pretty hard, Gid. I mean, I'm falling for you, but I'm not sure I'm normal.

"I'm Erica," the blonde girl says, leaning across Nicholas. She's extremely healthy and Nordic-looking.

"Hi," Gid says. "I'm . . ."

"I know who you are," she says. "You're new. Madison talked to you on the phone. Madison's my best friend."

Gideon and I both think it's weird how girls are always identifying themselves as each other's best friends. Of course, I do it too. Hey! Maybe I just did.

Erica touches one of her blonde braids self-consciously and her blue eyes dart nervously in Nicholas's direction, but Nicholas appears to be daydreaming. She gives Gid a quick smile and takes off.

Even just running to catch up with her friends, she has a studied, symmetrical athleticism to her gait.

Erica. "She's one of the girls from Liam's bet?" Gid whispers to Nicholas.

"Yep," Nicholas says. "She sure is."

Just as they're about to go inside, Cullen doubles back and joins them. "Whew, Lucy is hot. I'm hooking up with her later. Oh, and by the way, that dorm—" Gid follows Cullen's finger to a building at the far end of the quad, not unlike their dorm, but older. "That's Emerson . . . that's the weirdo chick dorm. The Virgin Dorm. See how it's all pretty and pristine? Unlike where our friends live." He turns around, showing Gid the dorm he pointed out before.

"White," says Gid, to show that he has been listening.

"We call it White Wedding," Cullen says, punching Nicholas on the arm. Nicholas doesn't react and walks a few paces ahead.

"Don't worry about him," Cullen says. "He needs more alone time than a community like this affords."

The dining hall is one vast space with maybe eighty round tables and two doorways—one where students line up and the other where they emerge with their trays. Gideon was really hoping for something more grand, maybe with higher ceilings, or more dark wood. It's not much nicer than his high school cafeteria, and the smell and sound—cheap wheat bread and bananas, clinking silverware and ice thundering into squat glasses—is the same.

"So this girl that you're hooking up with that you were talking about, Lucy," Gid says to Cullen. "Have you hooked up with her before?"

"No," Cullen says. "She's new."

"So you never talked to her before?"

I can see where Gid's going with this, and he's not going to like where it leads.

"No, not before tonight. Wait . . . I'll catch up with you in a second." Cullen takes off.

So wait a minute. Gid would never dispute that Cullen's better with girls than he is, but according to the terms of the bet, Cullen believes he can get laid sixty times faster than Gideon, and Nicholas, even worse, thinks Cullen can get laid two hundred times faster!

Gideon finds Nicholas waiting in the food line with his tray and silverware. He tells Gideon exactly what I would tell him if I could. "I wouldn't think of it that way," he says, and, after accepting a scoop of rice, moves along.

Poor Gid looks miserably at a middle-aged cafeteria worker, with vapor covering her bifocals, poised to drop a greasy chicken breast onto his plate. He thinks she has some kind of weird skin disease. Gid, that's a hairnet. "How else should I think of it?" Gid says, out loud to no one in particular, nodding yes for the chicken, nodding again for rice.

Gideon finds Nicholas at the salad bar, where he is loading his plate with chickpeas and sunflower seeds. "Did you know," he asks, gesturing at the chicken on Gideon's plate, "that when an animal is slaughtered, it feels fear, and we're essentially eating that fear?"

I've heard this before and think that is total crap. But Gid thinks about the bet and how he never even asked out a girl in his whole life. Not even Danielle, who just wrote "I like u" to him on a Post-it note, then went to second base with him that very day. He throws the chicken away and decides not to eat chicken until the day he gets laid.

Gideon fills a beige plastic bowl with lettuce. "Put some beans in," Nicholas says. "You need some protein."

Now Nicholas is examining a bunch of bananas in a stainless-steel bowl, with oranges and some Red Delicious apples. "Don't eat those," he warns. "Nonorganic bananas are the worst." He takes an apple and smells it. "Pesticides," he says, putting it down. He takes an orange. "Look," he says. "It's all going to be okay."

Nicholas cocks his head and Gid follows him, wondering,

exactly, as I am, What is so okay about this? Nothing could be further from okay.

They pass a table of plain brown-haired girls who look like they're actually in prep school to study, a table of foreign students arguing and holding straws in their hands like cigarettes, a table of pretty, thin girls who eat slowly and deliberately to make their tiny amounts of food last. Again, Gideon can feel people looking at him. He has never, ever felt so visible.

To his right, about five tables over, he sees the girls from earlier in the day. Molly and Edie. The blonde, Marcy, isn't with them. He guesses that Molly and Edie are those sort of pretty but not spectacular girls who prefer each other's company to all others.

Twenty paces ahead, under a round window looking out on White, is Cullen. In front of him is an ugly heap of casserole and he holds a large spoon in his hand like a child. And next to him is Liam Wu. Across from them is a chubby redheaded guy with a gap between his two front teeth.

Gid and Nicholas settle across from Cullen and Liam, next to the redhead, who, making room, gives Gid a heavy-lidded nod and a wave. Liam Wu's perfect head moves, almost imperceptibly, in greeting. If he remembers Gid, he's not saying so. "I'm Devon," says the redheaded kid. He's wearing a Brian Jonestown Massacre T-shirt and smells like Fab detergent and pot.

Cullen picks up one of the four glasses of chocolate milk that he's got lined up on his tray. He presses a finger to his lips. Gid understands he's reminding him they're not telling Liam or Devon about the bet. This is a relief. Gideon tries to eat—the other boys aren't talking at all, just grimly bolting their food—but he can't keep his eyes off all these pretty girls. One with miraculously soft brown eyes, her pale hair piled on top of her head, stands ten feet away, looking for a table. Another, red-haired, in a purple halter top showing off freckled cleavage, stands up from her seat and waves to someone at the salad bar.

As gut-wrenching as it was for him to look at these girls this afternoon from the car, now it is much, much worse. What with the
time constraints and "not doable" comments and all. He steals a
glance at Liam. God, he's so handsome. It's not fair. Gid closes his
eyes and envisions Liam handing him the keys to Nicholas's
mother's car.

I wonder if this is another trick from *Journal of the Zen Hut*.

"Olivia Hill is looking good this year," Cullen says.

How, Gideon wonders, is he able to pick one out for compli-
ments? "A lot of these girls are really pretty," he says.

"They're not girls," Cullen corrects him. "They're opportunities."

Nicholas shoots him a look like, *Don't give anything away*.

Liam Wu picks up a glass of cranberry juice and drinks the entire thing. "I totally disagree on the Olivia Hill thing."

"What do you know, you have slanted eyes," says Cullen. "I bet
you can't even see out of them."

Devon chokes on his food, laughing. Even Nicholas laughs.
Gideon wants to laugh but isn't sure how to laugh at a joke like
this. He can't believe it's allowed. He liked it, but it scared him.

"Don't eat too much," Liam says. "You don't want to get filled up."

"Why not?" Cullen says.

"You'll want to save some room," Liam says, "for my cock." He
smirks and looks up from his tray. His handsomeness, the way his
cheekbones pulse as he talks, hits Gideon like a pool cue to the gut.

After the laughter dies down, Gideon gets up the nerve to ask
who Olivia Hill is. Liam Wu angles his head and says, "Orange
shirt, two o'clock."

Gid finds the orange shirt in a sea of shirts, blooming with
breasts and offsetting soft skin. Its wearer is a tall girl with dark hair
and eyes; she's getting a cup of tea. She looks English.

Gid wonders if this is perhaps just because she's getting tea.
But she has rosy cheeks and light skin, and she appears reserved, in
a sexy way.

"Jesus," he says, "I think she's gorgeous."

This hurts a little. I wish Gid would only look at me and think that.

"Start with something smaller," Nicholas says.

"You mean a smaller girl?" Gid asks.

"Smaller like a big cookie," Devon says.

"But not a chocolate cookie," says Liam, drinking another glass of cranberry juice.

Everyone except Gid laughs. There's clearly some chocolate cookie joke that Gid will never know about.

Liam guzzles another glass of cranberry juice. Cullen says in a girlish voice, "At first I thought . . . but then I thought," and everyone laughs again.

Except Gid.

Gid is hungry. What am I going to do without meat, he wonders.

"No," Nicholas says. "Seriously. What I meant was, a girl in your league."

What's really sad is that he kind of said this to be nice. He felt bad at all the inside joking, and he was trying to be briefly earnest about what he'd meant by starting with something smaller. Yes, that's what passes for nice around here.

On the walk back to the room, Cullen starts talking to some girl with her hair tied up in a red bandana. They fall behind. Gid looks back forlornly. He knows that neither Cullen nor Nicholas has really decided to be his friend yet, but at least Cullen is easy to talk to. Nicholas is cryptic. Nicholas is intimidating. But Gid has to think of something to say to him. Shit, even his father would be able to think of something to say right now. It would be stupid, but it would be something. He thinks about Nicholas telling him what to eat. Could he start a conversation with that? He looks out onto the quad for inspiration. He sees a lot of bare legs. That works.

"Hey," Gid says, once again going for that intangible tone, interested but not desperate. "Why were you so concerned with what I was eating?"

Then there is a sound of hard plastic wheels scraping concrete, and Gideon feels a rush of air at his arm and shoulder. He jumps to the side, terrified, then ashamed to see the object of his terror, a ten-year-old on a skateboard.

"That's little Cockweed," Nicholas explains. "Tim." Up ahead, Tim Cockweed stares at them with dead brown eyes. He looks like something off a horror movie poster. "It's okay if he scared you. He scares me."

That Nicholas gets scared sometimes is the most reassuring thing Gid has heard all day. "But what I was asking," he says, feeling more at ease now, "was why you cared what I was eating."

Nicholas nods. "Well, first of all, I care about the planet, which, and I really feel this goes without saying, is rapidly disintegrating before our eyes."

Gid nods wearily. Eco-freaks. They had these people at his old school too. For selfish reasons, he's glad Nicholas is part of this movement. There's at least a corner of his personality that Gideon can dismiss.

"But more important, you and I start our workouts tomorrow, and you need a healthier diet."

"But I don't want to work out," Gideon says. Up ahead, Tim Cockweed is going down a set of stairs on his skateboard. The focus of his eyes and set of his jaw is indeed demonic. "I'm not very athletic, so . . ."

Nicholas puts his hand on Gid's arm, effectively shushing him. He says, "I have three things to tell you. One, Liam Wu drinks cranberry juice because when he has too much sex, like he did this afternoon as soon as he got back here and saw his girlfriend, Jordan, he gets a bladder infection—like a fucking girl. Second, you want to use the word *gorgeous* very, very sparingly around here. Especially in your position. Third, I am going to make you athletic, or you will never, ever get laid, except by fucking accident, which is in some ways worse than never." He fixes his cool blue eyes on Gid's warm brown ones.

When Nicholas goes into his evil honesty mode, he has Scary Husky Eyes.

"Wait," Gideon says. "Don't you want me to not work out, because what if I get this really great body? Then I'll get laid fast, and you'll lose."

Nicholas laughs. I don't blame him. Gideon could certainly improve his level of fitness, but he's hardly in danger of becoming an Adonis. "Yes, I want to win the bet, but I mean, every single interaction I have with you can't be about the bet. I want someone to work out with. Cullen won't. So I'll do it with you."

Not exactly a declaration of friendship. But not nothing either.

sneaking
out

It's well past lights-out, and it just so happens that when Gideon is awake, I'm awake too. It's so quiet right now, and I can almost see his thoughts arcing through the darkness. Like most girls, I have spent so much of my life dreaming what it would be like to be close, really close, to a boy. And here I am, closer than I've ever been, and I'm not actually even there. I'm sure there's a lesson in there, but I'm not yet sure what it is.

Gid's thinking about Danielle. Not in a longing-for-her way. He realizes his story got only so far as his accident with the thong and never back to how it ended up in his possession in the first place. How, when Danielle said good-bye, she got herself looking all sexy in cutoffs and a little T-shirt and said things like, "Maybe you're too numb to cry," while Gid said things like, "Yeah." When all he could think of was climbing into the Silverado and peeling out down Christmas Park Circle, never to be heard from again, Danielle knelt down and fumbled in a black corduroy handbag (yuck) as Gideon (why not, one last time) looked down her shirt. Danielle stood up and handed Gid the brown bag.

"Don't open this until you get to school," she said.

It's not that Gid doesn't like Danielle. He does. And it's not that he's just not romantic. In fact, what I'm getting at is that he's very romantic. That's his whole problem. He suspects that there is someone out there who's way better for him than Danielle Rogal. He's even thinking that there's someone out there better for her than he is. So in the darkened quiet clarity of Room 302, Proctor Dormitory, he's cold not out of coldness but out of respect for the real thing.

Danielle really was a nice girl. But how did he know what was waiting for him out there? It wasn't as if he'd ever been anywhere. Well, except Florida.

He's still smarting from the twin bombs, the "doable" and "in your league" comments. In Gid's fantasies, *Sports Illustrated* swimsuit issue models fall in love with him because they have some transcendent mutual understanding. The bet has made official what he's always feared. Love is not about love. Love is a game. There are winners and losers.

Of course, he reminds himself, if he were definitively a loser, there would be no bet. No one would even pay attention to him.

This thought is comforting enough to put him, and thus me as well, to sleep.

A scant three hours later, he's being shaken awake. He's so far behind a wall of sleep that just the simple act of opening his eyes feels like crawling through packed earth. Cullen towers over him.

"What the fuck are you doing? It's 1:10." Gid could count on one hand the number of times he's been up after 11:30.

"Now it's 1:11, make a wish," Cullen says. If he notices Gideon's surprising tone of insubordination, he doesn't say so. "Here's mine. Fifteen minutes from now, I will be sitting in a girl's dorm with my good buddy Nicholas and my we-shall-see-how-he-works-out Gideon Rayburn, high as a kite and drinking expensive wine."

Outside their window is a sugar maple with a fat, straight, sturdy branch. Gideon watches as Nicholas crouches on the ledge. Holding on to the window frame for support, he extends one leg to the branch and anchors it there. Then, with one quick movement, he transfers all his weight out the window, setting down his other foot and grabbing another small branch, this one a little thin for Gid's taste, with his other hand.

Gid weighs the misery of a broken leg against chickening out. The campus looks beautiful at night, the buildings still and regal, the lawns and trees deep green even in the dark. Tingling with desire and fear, he eases himself onto the ledge and, with Nicholas's movements running through his mind, copies them exactly.

White is remarkably close. Plus the way the campus lights are set up, there's a dark patch of lawn from one corner of Proctor to a tree between them. A door on the back side of White has been left open.

Prep school has a lot of rules. But it has many more wily, horny, substance-abusing students who learn how to get around them.

They tiptoe through the halls. Cullen motions for him to crouch. "Mrs. Geller's apartment," he whispers. Mrs. Geller. She's the headmaster's assistant. Her name is on all his correspondence. It's incredible that she's a real person, with a dried flower wreath on her door.

In the boys' dorms, the doors are bare, or just carved up with words like *prick, blow me,* and so on. The girls' doors are covered, not an inch of wood remaining, with Polaroid photos, memo pads with messages like "I luv you," and magazine cutouts of hot young actors. Gid recognizes a guy from *The O.C.* and, weirdly, Mel Gibson. Cullen and Nicholas are as handsome as actors. I am normal, Gid thinks, I am regular.

Cullen taps lightly on a door marked 13. The door opens,

revealing Madison Sprague, who is, in Gid's estimation, about nine hundred times as hot as her phone voice.

Madison is maybe three inches taller than Gideon, and she's wearing jeans tight enough to make her look taller, low across her hips, secured with a brass buckle that reads RIDE ME. Her white wife-beater tank top clings to braless, medium-sized breasts. She's not exactly stacked, but she probably should be wearing a bra. That's my opinion, of course. Not Gid's, though he does manage to force his eyes upward to settle on her shoulders, sparkling under some iridescent lotion. Gid doesn't know about iridescent lotion, so he just thinks she's touched with magic. Her hair, short and dark, is glossy and tight against her head, like a perfect little hat. There's a dark curl hanging over her forehead, and she shifts her hazel eyes upward and blows it out of the way.

She cocks her head to the side, and Cullen kisses her cheek. Nicholas allows his cheek to be kissed but does not kiss her back. Gideon just stands there. He can't look at Madison anymore so he looks past her, into the room. It's not as nice as the boys' room, really just a rectangle with white walls and that lentil-soup brown carpet. Erica sits on a bed covered with a shiny green quilt; the wall behind her is a riot of clippings, medals, and pictures of girls playing soccer. Next to her is another blonde girl. "Hi," she says. "I'm Mija." Mija, despite her glorious name, is the least intriguing of the three. She's small and blonde, and full of European restraint. She has a tidy air about her and pink, pensive lips. She's not hot like Madison and she doesn't seem like she could break you in half, like Erica (Gid finds this attractive), but she's definitely cute. "Get in here," Madison says, her tone impatient. "My God." Gid takes a step, and then, afraid to venture much farther, deposits himself on the floor, right against the wall.

Cullen stretches out on Madison's bed, his head in her lap. Nicholas, whose sole purpose in life seems to be to prove that man is indeed an island, lies on the floor. He refuses offers of wine and stares at the ceiling.

"I can't believe you guys get out of your room by leaping off a fire escape and grabbing a tree branch," Madison says. "I would be so scared." Gid wants to tell her how, when they were jumping, he pretended he was in *The Matrix,* that he said to himself, "There is no branch, there is no tree." Instead, he says, as Madison goes to pour him some more wine, "You have the shiniest hair I have ever seen."

"Holy crap," says Cullen.

"You see?" Nicholas sits up. "This is what I mean. June, and not a minute sooner."

Now Cullen gives Nicholas a cautioning look. Gid feels a little flattered. The bet might embarrass him, but it's a big, powerful secret, a bond.

Erica, in the true spirit of a competitive athlete, is underwhelmed by the boys' escape tactics. "I went on NOLS last summer," she says. "We had to jump off stuff a lot higher than that." Well, good for you, little Heidi scholar athlete.

"What's NOLS?" Gid asks.

Mija smiles at him cautiously. "It's National Outdoor Leadership School," she says. "It teaches you how to survive the wilderness." Gid can't imagine why any one of them would need this skill. But he smiles politely.

Madison flips onto her stomach, pokes underneath her bed, and comes up with another bottle of wine.

"I'm wasted," Cullen says.

"Good," Madison says. "That's the whole point." Then she turns to Gideon: "Did you know that Cullen and I are cousins?"

"No," Gideon says, "I had no idea." He looks to Cullen for confirmation. Cullen nods.

"Her mother is my dad's cousin," Cullen says.

Gid immediately launches into a fantasy that he is older,

twenty-five or so, and he is tall, taller than Madison, and that the two of them and Cullen are standing on a dock drinking champagne and laughing into the pink light of a setting sun. But he wonders, Is Madison too fashiony, too indoorsy, to enjoy the sunset? He emerges from this to see Mija watching him. He wonders, Is this some kind of setup? She is the least pretty of the three, and he concludes, with no real gloom but a calm understanding of his limitations, that she has been set aside for him.

Mija gets off her bed and settles herself next to Erica, who, following an unspoken directive, begins to braid Mija's blonde hair. "They're in their little cuddly pseudo-lesbian phase," Cullen observes.

"They're like blonde Care Bears," Madison agrees.

Teenage girls are always grooming each other, like sexy little monkeys.

"Why don't you tell us about your summer?" Cullen says to Nicholas.

Nicholas says nothing.

Madison gestures at Nicholas with the wine. "This should make you ease up a little bit," she says.

"Fat chance," says Cullen. "He still doesn't drink." So he wasn't just not drinking earlier. He doesn't drink at all. I'd say it was an affectation, but let's see if he sticks to it.

"More for us," Cullen says, producing a Swiss army knife and uncorking the wine. He takes a sip from the bottle and passes it to Madison, who then passes it to Gid, who, while staring at Madison's mouth, takes a sip.

"That's good," he exclaims.

"It should be," says Madison. "Considering what I went through to get it."

Mija takes a sip. "It's very good," she says formally. She puts the bottle to Erica's mouth.

"I have double sessions tomorrow," Erica says, shaking her stubborn little blonde head. "No drinking."

"Oh, but you'll smoke pot!" Cullen laughs.

"Pot's natural," Erica insists. "Wine has all sorts of chemicals in it, and we only get organic pot."

"You sound just like Nicholas," Gideon says to Erica. "You two are made for each other."

"You're not the only one who thinks so," Madison says.

Nicholas twitches and frowns. Suddenly, Erica's face reddens. Cullen and Mija look slightly embarrassed. Madison, however, has a watchful smirk on her face and seems to be having the time of her life. Gideon tries to glance furtively at her, but she proves too captivating for such self-control. She catches him looking and stares right back. He can tell that even though she thinks he's kind of a dork, she doesn't have disdain for him, which, for a girl like her, is a huge compliment.

"Madison," Erica says, jumping up, abruptly dropping Mija's half-braided hair. "I need to talk to you for a second."

Madison checks the peephole, then she and Erica step outside.

"Jesus," Nicholas groans at the ceiling.

"Jesus is right," Cullen says.

"What's going on?" Gideon demands. "Did I say something wrong?"

Cullen leaps up, an unlit joint between his teeth. "You said something stupid, but it wasn't your fault. Madison said something mean."

"What a surprise," Nicholas says. He rolls over onto his stomach and starts to do push-ups. "All that rock star attention is making Madison a little too C-U-next-Tuesday-ish—even for my tastes."

Cullen places his hands on his knees and bends over, putting his face right next to Nicholas's. "And whose fault is all this, anyway?"

Nicholas is still doing pushups when Erica and Madison come back into the room. Erica appears to have been crying but also appears to have washed her face.

"We're going to go smoke this organic joint," Cullen says, wrapping his arms around Madison's shoulders. She squeals.

Gid loved the squeal. I thought it was a little unnecessary. But in order to ignore a squealing, pretty girl, especially wearing a belt that says RIDE ME, Gid would have to be so sophisticated that I'm not sure I would like him as much.

"I'm coming too," Gid says.

"Nah, nah," Cullen says, ushering Nicholas and Erica and Madison out the door. "You stay here and keep Mija company." With a wink, Cullen disappears.

Mija smiles shyly at Gid. The room, empty and quiet now, smells overpoweringly of girls, of scents both complex and strong and completely beyond Gid's power of description. In fact, what he's smelling is wine, Chanel 19, and Tide. Gid sits next to Mija on the bed.

"So, where are you from?" he asks.

"Where am I from, where are my parents from, or what do I consider my home?"

Gideon's going to be hearing that a lot from now on. At this point, he doesn't know enough to find it annoying.

"Where were you born?"

"Kuala Lumpur," she says. "It's in Malay—"

"I know where it is," Gid says. "I used to read atlases as a kid."

"But my parents are Dutch," she says, unimpressed with Gid's hint that he was a gifted child. "Well, my father is Dutch, and my mother is sort of Dutch. It's a long story."

Gid moves a few inches away from her. He's unsure what information to offer next. Should he tell her he has a girlfriend? He decides at this point that he's never, ever going to say more than he has to, and to always remember that the more other people talk and the less you tell them, the better.

I think he has a lot better chance of not eating chicken until he gets laid than he does of sticking to this rule. He's just a born confider.

"Is this your second year?"

"Oh no," says Mija, "it's my fifth. Another long story."

"I see," Gideon says, wondering why one of these long stories doesn't get told so he can stop trying to think of what to say.

"What was the deal with that thing with Nicholas and Erica? Did I say something wrong?"

"Oh, that." Mija waves her little hand dismissively, and one of her eyelids flutters. "That wasn't your fault. I mean, you would have no way of knowing, and I am sure they didn't tell you, because it's a giant secret, but Erica is in love with Nicholas. And apparently, they've had sex. But the thing is, Nicholas gets all close to her, and then she thinks he actually likes her, but once he's had sex with her, he's mean. But I'm not supposed to tell anyone." She frowns. "Last year, Erica didn't live with me and Madison. She lived with Marcy Proctor and Edie Bell, but then she became friends with Madison . . . so . . . she mostly just hangs out with her now. Erica is one of those people who was sort of popular. But when Madison started to like her, she became really popular." She blushes a little. She has huge green eyes, and her blonde bangs are so neat it looks like they were cut with a ruler. Gideon stares back but very pointedly does not stare at the waistband of her blue thong underwear, which protrudes rather aggressively from the top of her pajama shorts. "They left us together because they want us to hook up, you know," Mija says. "And we can, if you want." She moves toward him, almost imperceptibly. A symbolic gesture.

God, Gid thinks, I could win the bet right now. Or start winning. So why doesn't he feel victorious?

"Do you think we should try kissing?" she asks. "As long as we're here?"

"Sure," Gid says, glad to have a focus. They tilt their heads, and as they lean in toward each other, Gid realizes he's thinking not about the kiss but about what he's going to eat tomorrow now that he's sort of a vegetarian. His lips are on hers, and her mouth is opening slightly. He opens his eyes. Mija's looking right at him.

"I have a girlfriend," he says.

"Oh!" She jumps up, putting her little hands to her mouth. "I'm sorry!"

"No, no," Gid says, his mind still catching up to what he just said. "I . . . Don't be sorry."

He's freaked out by how relieved he is that they're not making out. Don't guys constantly want to make out with everyone? But Gid doesn't. He isn't sure about that concept, although he does find Mija attractive. He just thought that if a pretty girl was around, then you must want her. He thinks it's strange that he doesn't.

I think this is cute. Mind-blowingly cute. A teenage boy with real taste. I mean, not that Mija's gross. But she's not for him. And he's not trying to just hit it because he can. My heart is beating really, really fast.

Mija sits back down on the bed, pulling some of her blanket up over her feet. She seems totally over Gid's rejection. "Do you miss her?" she asks.

The phrase "not really" pops into his head so quickly that it's a wonder he manages to say, "Oh, yes. A lot." Mija nods sympathetically, her blonde pageboy swings next to her head in a smooth sheet. Gid realizes that he isn't attracted to girls who are too neat. But telling her he has a girlfriend—now other girls are going to think he's off-limits. And shouldn't he have just tried to have sex with her? And win? But he couldn't. He thinks back to that moment, where he was trying to move his lips against hers and physically couldn't will himself to do it, because he just didn't feel anything for her.

Wait a minute. That's a pretty unusual feeling for a guy to have.

Does Gid—dare I say this about him, about any sixteen-year-old sex-crazed boy—have a soul?

He's wondering that himself right now, but the words in his head take a different form: Why didn't I just jump her? What is my problem? Do I have a problem?

"This has been a really weird day," he says.

"Tell me about it," Mija ten Eyck replies. "This morning, I was in Amsterdam."

She doesn't seem at all upset that they didn't hook up. Gid wonders, fleetingly, if she feels as indifferent to him as he is to her. He does think she's a nice girl, though. She reaches into her night-stand and takes out some acne medicine. She puts a little on her chin, then dabs a little on Gid's chin. "You need to take better care of your skin," she says. "I have a lot of products that would help you."

They share a sincere moment of looking into the mirror, con-sidering each other's faces. Gid has made a friend.

The grass is wet, and the sky is just starting to turn pink over the hills as the boys walk home. Gid confesses to Cullen and Nicholas that he told Mija he had a girlfriend. "It just popped out," he says. "So now all the girls are going to think I'm already taken."

Cullen slaps him on the back. "You are the man," he says. "That's the best thing you could have said. Also, it's very good to re-ject girls. It makes you much more desirable. Wow, saying you had a girlfriend. What a stroke of genius."

Gid wants to say that it was just an accident, but I'm glad he doesn't. He should take credit for it, and besides, strokes of genius are almost always accidents.

Like this one. End up in some pretty weird kid's head and the more you see his weird thoughts, the more you . . . well . . . After tonight, I am most definitely somewhere very close to being in love.

Now definitely no one can know who I am. Whatever kind of confidence I might project to the outside world, my heart is very tender. Strange considering just a little while ago, I was afraid he could read my mind. Now that I know he can't, I almost wish that he could.

skinny_{fat}

For the second time in eight hours, Gideon Rayburn is awakened. This time, the agent of rudeness is Nicholas, and he has actually reached under the covers, scooped his hands beneath Gideon's underarms, and is now, causing not inconsiderable pain, pulling him out of bed.

Gideon moans. "I think you're digging into one of my glands."

Nicholas, strong despite his wiry frame, is dressed in a pair of navy nylon shorts and a T-shirt tight enough to say, *I have a nice body,* but loose enough to pretend that's not its goal. "We're going running," Nicholas says. "Come on."

"Running?" Gid has barely ever thought of the concept of running and certainly never in relationship to himself. He clearly remembers that whole working-out conversation but thought it was just theoretical. I knew it wasn't. Guys with posture like Nicholas don't usually bullshit. "Why?"

"Because you're skinny fat." Nicholas pinches a bit of flesh hanging from Gid's arm.

"Ow." It hurts more than it should.

"That hurts because it's skin, not muscle. You're not over-weight, but you have no muscle whatsoever. Skinny fat," he repeats.

Gid falls back onto his bed. Nicholas goes to his bureau and removes a pair of shorts and a faded yellow T-shirt advertising a corporate 5k race in Central Park. He throws them onto Gid's (sunken, skinny-fat) chest.

"Get up," he says, "or I will pull you up again."

"No, no," Gid protests, suddenly all obedient. "That hurt."

"It hurt because you're sk—"

"I know, I'm skinny fat. I heard you."

Five minutes later, they're running around the track. Or rather Nicholas is running and Gideon's propelling himself forward on desperate exhalations and sheer force of will.

Passing the reflective windows of a spanking-new field house, he gets a glimpse of himself. Sure enough, a pale lip of flesh dangles from his arm, like turkey wattle. He *is* skinny fat!

"I know I'm not supposed to talk, but I gotta know," he says. "Do girls really care if you're out of shape?"

"Girls," Nicholas says, "are even worse than guys about that stuff."

I'm not sure that's true. I feel like a guy would go out with a girl with no brain and, like, a totally ugly face if she had a nice body. Or even a nice body part. But Gid would do well to believe him. Because the whole skinny-fat thing—it's real.

Gid's lungs feel like two charred steaks. "It's incredible how much legs weigh," he says. A commuter train whistles from somewhere off beyond a wall of trees. He wonders if he could sneak off and get on it and find his way back home. Or maybe he could just fall down in a heap of girlish tears and simply refuse to go on.

"Your fight-or-flight mechanism is probably kicking in about now," says Nicholas, not even panting. "I'd bet you've chosen to fix-ate on escape."

Gideon wants to say that he's doing fine, but he can't breathe well enough to speak. He stifles the urge to vomit. He tries to turn off his mind. It doesn't work. So he tries to imagine that he's watching himself from outer space, that he weighs nothing, and finally, that he is in a movie about someone who has to run two miles. He finally concludes that there's no substitute for willpower. Each step of the last four laps is a distinct and memorable slice of hell. But he makes it. The moment he's done, he collapses into the grass.

"You're in horrible shape," Nicholas says casually. "I have you running to build confidence. In three weeks, it's going to be a whole different feeling. You'll have less fat, more muscle. You'll have a lot more respect for yourself."

I don't think that's fair. Just because Gideon is scared sometimes, or unsure, or even ashamed of himself doesn't mean he doesn't respect himself. But I guess it just depends on what kind of beast you're trying to build.

And, more important, what kind of beast does Gid want to become? As miserable as running was, Gid knows he will do it every day. Yesterday, he looked at Nicholas and Cullen and felt nothing but hopeless envy. He still feels envy, but it is a distinctly hopeful envy. He is not powerless over his own hotness. He has a destiny. One of those girls on the quad will be a part of it. Skinny fat will not.

Per Nicholas's instructions, Gideon is to do fifty push-ups—he can manage twenty, done naked on the cold tile—then shower for approximately seven minutes in a hot, hard spray and two minutes in a cold, soft one. During the hot part, he thinks about Madison and her perverted belt buckle and wide upper lip, like Julia Roberts. Gid imagines his body with large lats and biceps, and Madison lacing her fingers around them admiringly.

I don't like Gid thinking of her. Because no matter how pretty I am, I could never be pretty exactly like her. And it makes me a little sad that he thinks she is the apex of what he could achieve in life. I don't think he even noticed how she had so much base on, and that the iPod on her dresser was pink. Any girl who buys a pink iPod is, well, the kind of girl who probably gets a lot of attention and doesn't care how gay she is.

Afterward Gideon wraps his towel around his waist and stands in the window, letting the fresh air dry him off—he read (so did I!) that P. Diddy air-dries. Perhaps it invites success. He takes in the world below: backpacks carried on young, sturdy bodies, slow-moving shiny German imports, the tops of pretty trees. He feels his heart soaring out above it all. His mind-set is positive, defiant. Why not Madison? Why not any of them? Not only is he going to get laid before Halloween, he's going to get laid well before Halloween.

When he opens the door to the room, he's surprised to see Cullen and Nicholas seated in their desk chairs, waiting for him. Nicholas is already showered and dressed in khakis, a white shirt, and a red tie; Cullen's still in the ripped hockey shirt he slept in and a pair of plaid boxers. Their expressions are grave. Cullen flips his cell phone over and over in his hand. He's clearly just gotten some information.

"Madison," Cullen begins, in a tone mixing sarcasm and affection, "wants to have sex with you."

"Madison? Madison likes me?" Gid sits down on the bed, exhaustion forgotten, adrenaline flowing. "It's so weird. I was just thinking about her in the shower." Nicholas wrinkles his nose in distaste at this image. Gid's too excited to care. "She wants to go out with me?" he says.

"No, dumbass. She wants to sleep with you. She goes out with Hal Plimcoat."

"Very funny," Gideon says. Hal Plimcoat is the lead singer of the Rutts, a British rock band.

Cullen gets up and goes to the closet, pulling off his underwear. "I'm not joking, dude."

Gideon averts his eyes. "Afraid of facing the giant monster, huh?" Cullen says. "I dig it. Hey, it scares me sometimes." Gideon doesn't say anything. He isn't afraid of seeing Cullen's, as he calls it, "giant monster," but he definitely doesn't need any more proof of Cullen's superior being. But who cares about that? Madison's boyfriend is famous! Rich! And she wants Gid instead!

"So," Nicholas says, "what this presents is a problem."

"A problem!" Gid has visions of Hal Plimcoat collapsing onstage in grief. And would this make the papers? He opens the drawer to take out his brand-new khakis and in the back sees the little paper bag. Three days ago, he was lying on Danielle's canopy bed, surrounded by her "wipes clean!" flowered vinyl wallpaper, and now he's being pursued by a leggy brunette who dates rock stars and dresses like a rich hooker. "I don't see a problem."

Nicholas and Cullen have this shorthand when they don't know what to say where they make their lips disappear into their mouths and raise their eyebrows. In Gid's case, I think it means, What the fuck are we going to do with this country bumpkin? I feel bad for him. There's nothing worse than being around two people who don't even have to speak to understand each other, especially when you don't understand them when they're actually speaking.

Gid repeats, "I don't see a problem."

Nicholas puts his hands together and bows to Cullen. "I'm sure you will put it best," he says, meaning, I guess, that he might put it unkindly.

Gid is quick to detect Cullen's smile as a member of the blow-softening variety. "Nicholas and I agree we made a mistake in not making the bet specific enough," Cullen says, half-dressed now, his red tie in his hand. "You can always get girls to sleep with you. You can always fall in with this one or that one. What's difficult is getting a specific girl, setting your sights on someone, and getting her to sleep with you. Especially girls out of your league," Cullen says.

"But Madison is specific and out of my league," Gideon says. "Why can't I just sleep with Madison?"

Nicholas ignores the question and continues. "We need to find a girl tailored to you. A girl who really might sleep with you, who isn't below your level, but who isn't above it. A good challenge, but not an absurd one."

Hapless Gid still believes he just hasn't made himself clear. "I don't understand," Gid says, "why I can't—"

"If you say 'sleep with Madison,' I promise you, you will be killed," Nicholas says, now casting a dark eye on Cullen and a look that says, "Sometimes, no matter how painful it is, you have to spell it out."

"This campus is crawling with freaky girls who will sleep with you once just for the weirdo factor," Nicholas says.

"Wait a minute," Gid says. "I'm a weirdo?"

Nicholas waves his hands in front of his face. "No, no. I wouldn't fixate on that."

Everything Nicholas tells Gid not to fixate on is exactly what any sane person would fixate on.

"Anyway," Nicholas goes on, "when we made the bet, we forgot about all these freaky girls, so now we're changing it to accommodate this fact. It has to be one girl. And, until her, absolutely no other girl."

Cullen presents Gideon with a large maroon leather book. "Open this to page 132."

The large maroon book is *Timepiece,* the Midvale yearbook. Page 132 is a dorm photograph, with thirty or forty girls standing on a lawn, squinting into the sun, some hugging each other like sorority sisters, some aloof and angling for the glamour shot. One photograph is circled, a slim girl with dark hair and a perfunctory smile. He's seen this face before . . . was it at dinner? No. "Wait," he says. "I know her . . . that's the girl we stopped to ask for directions . . . Molly something."

"McGarry," Nicholas says. He runs his finger along the bottom of the photograph, where the names are listed. McGarry, Molly E. Second from left, row three. It's her.

"Her?" Gid says. "There are four hundred girls going to school here, and I have to have sex with a girl that curtseyed to my dad?" Why did they even dangle Madison in front of him, to what frustrating end? So he sleeps with her and becomes her funny story. He's totally up for it.

Cullen pulls his tie through his collar, grinning. "She curtseyed at your dad? Why?"

"It's a long story," says Gideon, miserable. "I only met her for, like, forty seconds, but she seems like she has . . . an attitude problem."

"That is such a totally excellent call," Cullen says, clapping him on the back. "I have never quite figured out what it is about her, and hey, you got it."

I can't tell whether Cullen's being sarcastic or not. Neither can Gideon. He's also trying to take a step back from Madison's hotness. Maybe they're really protecting him from her. She did drink that wine a little fast. Not that he'd have to marry her, but still.

"Look," Gideon says, "I can maybe understand the whole Madison thing, and I understand, she's off-limits. Fine. But can't we just have it the way it was?"

Both Cullen and Nicholas are fully dressed now, and back in their chairs, and emanating an imperious, tribunal quality. "Molly McGarry is the logical subject for this bet," Cullen says. "She's pretty enough that you wouldn't be grossed out to have sex with her . . ."

Gideon wants to laugh here, kind of. Because Molly McGarry, well, she is pretty. These guys, being around so much of it, have just gotten so warped about pretty. And being so pretty themselves.

Okay, that again. An extremely cute thought. Shit. I've had crushes before. But you know, I could, like, go for walks in the woods, drink schnapps, and get away from them. Ha. Not this time.

Cullen continues, "But not *so* pretty that it's ridiculous. That attitude makes her a little hard to get, but she's also available. She's our girl, no question. Of course, we don't have to do the bet at all, right, Nicholas?"

Nicholas stands up, smoothing his pants. "No, we don't. We could call it off."

Gideon doesn't know if they're calling his bluff. (I don't think they are, for what it's worth.) Here he was thinking he didn't like the bet, that if he was going to enjoy his life here it was going to be in spite of the bet. But could it in fact be true that the bet is the heart of his life here? After all, for better or worse, these guys are his life on this campus. And what other than the bet ties them to him? What else, since they made the bet, has been discussed?

"Don't forget about the car," Cullen says.

Oh, right, the car. What if Gid wins the bet, and a year from now he is driving me around in that car? Will he tell me where he got it? What if he borrows the car from Liam and wins the bet in it? Will he clean it? Will I be grossed out anyway?

Gid squares his shoulders and feels the pleasantly achy buzz left in his body from this morning's workout. He didn't think he was going to like running, and he actually did, quite a lot. Maybe these guys are on to something.

"I can get Molly McGarry to like me," he says. The boys cheer. He likes the sound of them cheering. But over it, he remembers trying to make a move on Mija, how his apathy turned his limbs and mouth to stone. He has a premonition. One that, having observed him, I share. The success of this bet will not only hinge on how much she likes him but also on how much he likes her. He just can't lie to girls the way some guys can. He considers this a fault. I, of course, do not.

"No other girl?" Gid says. "But what if . . . ?"

"Just get Molly McGarry to sleep with you," Cullen says with affectionate weariness. "Then you're free to do what you want. That's the story. You get it. I know you get it. It's not hard."

Cullen has loaded up the Vaportech for a smoky, pre-class send-off. Gideon steps up, hopeful. Nicholas waves him away.

"You can't smoke pot during the day," he says. "You're around too many people, and it will make you too paranoid."

Cullen nods and smokes more. "What about him?" Gid asks.

"I don't get paranoid," Cullen says. "Paranoia's just nature's way of saying, 'Hey, you really are a dork.'"

of the
buffalo
mcgarrys

So. Molly McGarry. Gid recalls the knowing way her smile slid to the left side of her mouth, the smug sparkle in her brown eyes. Gid didn't tell Cullen or Nicholas this, but she intimidates him.

Gid, *hello.* They know a girl like that would. It's why they picked her.

He strolls across the quad, head down. Nicholas gives him a bottle of green tea to take off to class every day—antioxidants, possibly fat-burning—and he's clutching it in his hand. Yesterday, he was glad classes were starting, because he wanted to have something to think about other than girls. Now, he thinks, she better be in one of my classes, because I can't spend all my time trying to subtly run into her. One, because I haven't got much time, and two, because I don't know if I know how to be subtle.

Gid's first class is English. It is in the basement of Hull Hall, an ancient building that smells of old books and disinfectant. The hallways are lined with sepia-toned photographs of old men frowning in three-button suits and young men with toothy, carefree smiles, rowing crew. All this makes Gid forget about Molly for a few minutes and feel serious and important and smart.

English is taught in a cramped basement-level room with wood paneling and a rim of windows looking out at the grass. Gid sits at the far end of the long oval table. His classmates are achingly pretty girls and infuriatingly handsome guys. The teacher is an austere black man named Jake Barnes. "I am aware," Mr. Barnes says, pacing slowly, deliberately, "that my name is the same as the main character in *The Sun Also Rises*. A character who has a certain . . . sexual dysfunction. So let's all laugh about that right now."

Gid, as I suspected, has no idea what the guy's talking about. He taps his pencil against his notebook. He likes this whole sitting-in-a-circle thing but not for pedagogical reasons. Usually in class you can look only at the girls next to you and the rather sexually uninspiring back of the head of the one in front of you. This way, you can look at all of them: Across from him, Edie, Molly McGarry's friend, sits with her ankles crossed and two fingers pressed to her mouth. Gid considers her. She might be pretty when she's older. The other girls in the class are more obviously arresting. One has a mass of dark hair piled on top of her head, held there with a red lacquer chopstick. Another has wide-spaced brown eyes and curly lighter hair tumbling down her shoulders. She's wearing pink boots, with thick platform soles. There's a dress code that says all girls need to wear skirts, but apparently it doesn't say anything about them dressing like total sluts.

Copies of *A Tale of Two Cities* are passed around. Gid weighs its heaviness in his hand. The girl in the pink boots shifts in her seat. Gid watches the shadow between her knees optimistically. Then he catches Edie looking at him and quickly averts his eyes and starts to thumb through the novel with great interest.

Mr. Barnes wants them to read seventy-five pages, which seems to Gid like an awful lot. He considers asking Lacquer Chopstick about Cliff's Notes, but something about the tilt of her chin and determined gaze makes him think she's not a Cliff's Notes kind of gal.

Art History is held in a small theater underneath the dining hall. The teacher, Mrs. Yates, is ash blonde and lanky and humorless, with large-lidded eyes behind giant glasses. The lights go out. The first slide is a winged woman with large breasts, no head, and no arms. Back in Virginia this would have been cause for some vulgar commentary, but here, everyone just nods and types into their smugly tiny little laptops. Gid just has a notebook. "In the year forty-seven B.C., Thrace came under Roman control," Mrs. Yates says. Gid tries to writes this down, but he can't see in the dark, and he knows he won't be able to read it later.

Lunch is like dinner was yesterday except Gid is less surprised by it all. No sign of Molly in the cafeteria. Pink Boots is there. I love her, Gid thinks. Relax, Gid, you're just hungry because you're living on beans. Once again, it is the five of them—Cullen, Nicholas, Liam, Devon, and Gideon. Gid sees that it will always be the five of them. Devon gives them pieces of a Toblerone candy bar. Liam doesn't talk to him, but he doesn't insult him. "Any sign of Miss McGarry?" Cullen whispers when the other three are embroiled in an argument about which, if either, of the tennis-playing Williams sisters they'd like to have sex with.

"No," Gideon says. "I'm a little concerned."

"What have you got next?" Cullen asks.

"Spanish," he says glumly.

"Hmmm." Cullen presses his mouth together. "Molly seems like a French kind of girl to me."

Yes. Gid was thinking the same.

But they are both wrong. Arriving in Spanish class, Gid takes a moment to be sorry that the chairs aren't in a circle, largely because in the second row sit several entirely straight-haired slim brunettes, all of the same pleasing species. He sits in the fourth—close enough to look but not too close. In the midst of this row of brown heads, Gid sees a flash of red. Molly McGarry's hair. Molly McGarry. The prize. The goal. Or whatever she is, other than, of course, herself. She turns around and looks right at him. She recognizes him.

Gid's having trouble interpreting the look on her face. At first, he thinks she's sneering at him. Then he decides she's actually trying to look sexy. I think the truth is probably somewhere in between. Meanwhile, Molly McGarry and her sneer/whatever have turned back around.

Liam Wu appears in the doorway and stands there for a moment, pretending to survey the room when he's really letting people survey him. And in fact, every girl present is looking at him. Every girl except Molly McGarry, Gid notes with satisfaction. Surely not every girl in the world would prefer Liam Wu to him, and maybe Molly is one such girl. But then, of course, Molly looks too.

Liam spots Gid and moves confidently in his direction. "Hey," he says, sliding into the seat next to him. "In about five seconds, the reason I take Spanish and the reason you're going to be glad you did too is going to walk in."

Gid looks up to see a preternaturally beautiful dark-eyed blonde woman with very large breasts, walking on crutches.

"Check that shit out," Liam says under his breath. Gid knows exactly what he means: The crutches are fantastic cleavage creators. She leans the crutches against the wall and hops to the teacher's desk. No way! She's the teacher? She's wearing jeans, a T-shirt, and an orange corduroy blazer, cut—and to Gid's credit, he knows even teachers are capable of such calculation—to show off her slamming body.

She hops up to her desk and smiles briskly. *"No te preocupes,"* she says. *"Estoy bien. ¿No creo que juege otra vez fútbol con hombres Americanos, sí?"* (Don't worry, I'm fine. I don't think I will play football again with American men.)

Everyone laughs. Gid has no idea what she just said. He took

Spanish for two years back in Virginia, but while he studied the textbook, all the rest of the class did was make piñatas and watch videos of people tangoing or tending goats. He passed the tests, but he's never actually conversed with another person in this language.

Her name is Laura San Video, and with her left eye one quarter shut in perpetual amusement, she takes attendance.

"Pauline Mellon?"

One of the players on the Hot Brunette team.

"Molly McGarrrrry?"

Gid tries to get a good look at her, but the angle is all wrong.

"Geedeon a-Rrrraaay-burn," she calls his name with one eyebrow raised.

"Yvonne a-wel-stead?"

This is the pixieish blonde.

As a book with a blue cover is passed around, Ms. San Video stands in front of the room, smoothing and resmoothing her blazer over her hips. "This class," she announces, "is not just about learning to speak Spanish but coming to comprehend the mind of the Spanish speaker, how this language has shaped the philosophies and culture of people from Spain to the Caribbean to South America."

Gid frowns. This sounds like a lot.

"I," Ms. San Video says with a flourish, "am from Venezuela."

I've heard that among South Americans, Venezuelan women have a reputation for wearing slutty clothes. I've seen sluttier clothes for sure, but truly never on a teacher.

She has them turn to a Julio Cortázar story. Each student reads a paragraph out loud. Gid is blown away. Five minutes into class, and they are already working? At his school in Virginia, there were at least two or three days, sometimes even a week, of throat clearing and orientations and covering your book with paper bags before you saw an actual assignment. For a little blonde girl, Yvonne Welstead has a fantastic Spanish accent. At the story's end,

Gid knows this: The guy in the story was at some point riding a motorcycle. That's it.

He understands that paying attention will be a constant battle for him. The girls, they command the front of his brain. And there's not that much left beyond that.

"Okay, what did we learn from this story?" Ms. San Video asks in Spanish. She stops in front of Gideon.

"Are you talking to me?" he asks.

"Hablemos español," instructs Ms. San Video.

"Okay," Gid says with a Spanish accent.

The class laughs. Ms. San Video's face barely moves, but Gideon (and, of course, I) feel her amusement expand.

"Tell us what you learned in the story," she says, in *español*.

"That cars are better than motorcycles?" Gideon says in Spanish, hopefully.

The class laughs again. Ms. San Video frowns. "You can't roll your *R*s?" she says, exaggeratedly doing exactly that.

"No," Gid replies.

"Why not?" she says. "You are afraid, Geedeon Rrrayburn?"

"It's because—" Gid knows what he wants to say, but he feels so much pressure, feels his face heating up, and all he can come up with is, "I think probably your tongue can do more stuff than mine." He says this in English.

Everyone laughs. Even Ms. San Video. Gid, at first stunned and confused, then ashamed, finally laughs too, partly because Liam, who terrifies him, is laughing the hardest.

Gid would never admit to himself how much it pleases him to make Liam laugh. Will I ever, he wonders, still laughing, stop wanting to impress people I don't even like?

When Molly McGarry turns around and proffers him the tiniest of smiles, Gid stops laughing and nods to her.

For a boy, a nod is, like, intimate. Molly colors slightly, and Gideon does the same. They both start to smile and then try not to.

He settles back in his chair as the class calms down, deeply pleased at having made progress, however small, this quickly.

There is chemistry between them. I can see it. Now, chemistry is good, of course, but for a boy like Gid, who examines his instincts a lot but has trouble trusting them, chemistry can be confusing. It can feel a lot like anxiety, and this, of course, is something Gid's always trying to avoid.

^{of} the bahía blanca benitez- joneses

Friday night, two weeks into school, Gid sits in study hall. He's annoyed. He understands prep school is about working, but Friday night study hall, well, it's stupid. (It's actually Calvinist, Gideon, and if you didn't spend all your time getting high and panicking about how you're going to impress your roommates by having sex with Molly McGarry before Halloween, you might develop the cultural literacy your hardworking blue-collar father sent you here to get.) He reads the first chapter of *A Tale of Two Cities*, where the lady is making the scarf. Madison was knitting last night. She was knitting a sweater that seemed to me to be mostly comprised of holes where she could show off her breasts. Gid can't help thinking about her. Molly McGarry, okay; she seems like a nice girl, but Madison . . . he can't explain.

I can. Molly's appeal requires some concentration. Madison's appeal is like . . . well, a sweater with lots of holes in it.

Outside, a pizza delivery car is circling the quad, probably for one of the faculty. On Friday nights, Jim Rayburn would leave Gid twenty dollars to order a bottle of grape soda and a sausage pizza.

After he ate his pizza, he'd call Danielle. Then they'd retire to his room for some . . .

Danielle. Holy crap, Danielle. In a damp, hot rush of sweat and guilt Gid realizes that he hasn't called Danielle, whom he spoke to every day for . . . well, he can't say how long (it was seven months, Gid, you went out for seven months) since he got here.

Gid secures permission to return to his dorm on the grounds that he doesn't feel good.

The pay phone is in the basement rec room of Proctor, where small alumni gifts come to die. I don't understand how a campus whose entire branding centers around cushy flawlessness allows such unchecked mayhem. The veneered furniture is damaged and splintered. The television, connected to a dusty old VCR, only gets UPN. On top of it is a dusty plastic fern in a tin pot covered with calico fabric.

A kid wearing a bathrobe and reading *The Turn of the Screw* lies on a cracked red vinyl sofa.

"I'm sick," he announces the moment Gid walks into the room. "Don't come any closer."

"Well," Gid asks, "why aren't you in your room?"

The kid shrugs. He has dark curly hair and small eyes and glasses. He still looks like a boy. He smells like pot and some gross illness smell. Gid guesses he's a freshman. "I came down to use the phone," he says. "But it doesn't work. And I'm too tired to go back up."

Gid puts the pay phone to his ear. Dead.

"I told you." The kid groans theatrically and sets his open book on his chest.

"You really don't have a cell phone?" Gid says, actually kind of happy about this.

The kid shakes his head. "My parents don't believe in cell phones," he says. "They hate the government."

Gid doesn't understand the connection. And he's never heard

of anyone hating the *whole* government before. It seems kind of extreme. "Your parents sound kind of crazy," he says.

"Probably," the kid says, totally unbothered by this idea. "I have an idea. Why don't you do me a favor?" He goes to sit up, and it seems he really is sick. He holds the book upright against the frayed arm of the sofa and kind of uses it to hoist himself up. "I can't leave. Go over and use the phone in the girl's dorm, White, and call this number." He reaches into his book and produces a number written on a ripped-off corner of a newspaper.

As Gid moves toward him, the kid makes a halting motion with his hand. "I told you I was sick," he says. He balls up the paper and tosses it to Gid. It lands at his feet.

"It's my brother," says the kid. "Call him and tell him that Grandma is coming tomorrow at four-twenty."

"You have your brother's number written on the corner of a piece of newspaper?"

When Gid doesn't move, the boy sets the book down again and looks at him. "Look, if you do this for me, I'll do you a favor."

Gid almost laughs out loud. The kid scowls at him. "You think I can't do you any favors, but I guarantee, I can do a lot for you."

The kid has a lot of self-confidence, even if he is annoying. "Okay, your grandma's coming at four-twenty, and what's your name?" Gid says, not trying to keep the irritated tone out of his voice.

"Mickey Eisenberg," the kid says.

"Nice to meet you." Gid waves, hoping to avoid another germ lecture. "I'm Gid."

"I know who you are," Mickey says. "You're the one who said that thing about your tongue to Ms. San Video." He clucks his tongue. "That Ms. San Video, she is all woman."

"You're fourteen," Gid says. "You can't say someone's all woman. It's ridiculous."

Mickey Eisenberg just shrugs. "Hey, I know what I like," he says. "Someday, maybe you will too."

I think I might have a little crush on Mickey Eisenberg too! Not really. But if he's this sexually decisive at fourteen, well, things can only improve.

The lounge in White is about as ugly as the one in Proctor, save for a poster of Edward Hopper's *Nighthawks* tacked above the pay phones. Gid stares at the poster, in particular at the man in his trench coat sitting at the lunch counter. Gid identifies with him. The guy just plain looks like he doesn't know what to do.

Gid asks himself what seems like a thousand questions at once. Has he effectively broken up with Danielle by not calling her? Does he need to actually break up with her, or could he simply behave as if they were never going out—i.e, do nothing?

His mind starts to take a strong liking to this notion. Then a phrase comes into his head that he thinks might be just what he's looking for: I've been feeling confused.

Guys think the word *confused* gets them off the hook. They are so wrong. All it does is give girls hope where there is none.

Wait, not confused. Oh, good, Gid figured that one out all on his own. *Confused* will lead to a conversation about what he wants. No way. He gets a brief image of his parents, fighting.

He has to call Danielle. It's the decent thing to do.

Even I think so. And I don't want him paying attention to other girls. Even if he's only doing it to be polite. What if he falls back in love with her from the sound of her voice? Doubtful.

He'll do the favor for Mickey first.

A guy, maybe twenty or twenty-five, answers. "I'm calling for Mickey," Gid says. "Your grandmother will be here tomorrow at four-twenty."

"Okay," says the guy. And hangs up. Gid stares at the phone, wondering if he did everything right. He's thinking about calling back when he hears a girl's low, snickery laughter. He turns around. Standing there dressed in a white T-shirt, white pants, and brown sandals, next to the world's biggest pile of Louis Vuitton luggage, is a girl who is somehow, impossibly, even more beautiful than all the other girls he has seen so far combined.

I can attest that she really is.

Gid gasps, as if the girl were on fire. The girl opens her mouth.

The girl says, "Four-twenty?" and raises one perfect brown eyebrow. "You know what that means, don't you?" Her hair and eyes are dark, and her skin is a uniform golden tone. She reaches around and lifts the hair off her neck, then winds it like a rope and ties it to itself so that it hangs in a heavy knot down the middle of her back. *"¡Qué calor!"* she says. "You'd think these people could pay for some air conditioners, no?"

She looks Gid up and down, realizing he hasn't said a word and is just staring at her. Girls are starting to filter back from study hall, walking quickly, heads lowered, though most eyes cheat upward for at least a quick glance at this girl. This creature. This apparition.

Gid's mind is going apeshit.

Her face lights up with expectation.

He realizes he will have to say something. "Do you go to school here?" he says.

She feasts on his incredulity. "You're new," she says, slowly, deliciously. Again with the eyebrows. Gid prays to God that she's flirting. "I have been here since ninth grade." Her accent is totally different from Ms. San Video. But he doesn't want to ask this girl where she's from, because he has learned that sometimes people with accents are just from the United States and they get mad when you ask them where they're from.

"My name is Pilar Benitez-Jones," the girl says. "I am late because my sister got married." Pilar Benitez-Jones laughs, Gid notices, with little humor. "My sister got married, which was a long affair involving two continents, a lot of air travel, which dried out my skin, and there was also an awful lot of my parents screaming at each other. Or, rather, my mom screaming and my dad trying to excuse whatever behavior of his had made her scream." Pilar sits down on top of one of her suitcases and, as if to shut it all out, clamps her beautiful hands over her beautiful ears.

"That's so funny," Gid says, happy for the first time in his life about his parents' acrimonious divorce. "I mean, I was just thinking about my parents' fights in exactly that way. I'm Gideon," he says.

"Gee-de-on," she says. He doesn't even think of correcting her.

"My mother and her new husband moved to Santa Fe," he says softly. "I call it Santa Gay because it's—"

His confession is interrupted by a soft ringing. Pilar reaches into her bra—oh my—and extracts a tiny silver phone.

Gid thinks it is appropriate that this information about his mother kind of went into the ether. He would like for it to stay there.

Pilar speaks excitedly, head bowed, in Spanish. Gid, who, appearances to the contrary, is not entirely clueless, realizes this may be his invitation to leave. But Pilar covers up the phone's tiny mouthpiece with one pink-polished thumbnail. "Wait," she whispers. She's off the phone in a few seconds. She looks around cautiously.

"What are you doing in here, making calls for Mickey Eisenberg?" she demands.

"You know Mickey Eisenberg?" Gid is amazed.

"Of course, he sells Ecstasy. He calls himself Four-twenty, some pothead reference."

"I thought he sold Ecstasy."

Pilar holds out a lock of hair and pulls it down so it bisects her mouth. I recognize this as a brazenly manipulative female gesture, but Gid just thinks it's the hottest thing he's ever seen. "He sells Ecstasy," Pilar explains. "He smokes pot."

Gid must look shocked and stupid, because Pilar starts to laugh. "Mickey Eisenberg has you in here making drug deals for him, and you don't even know it."

Pilar thinks this is very funny. Then her eyes soften with concern. She touches his arm.

That's when it happens. The slight weight of her finger on his arm feels like the whole world, in a good way. She's talking. Gid tries to concentrate on what she's saying, but he's dizzy. He's in love. This is why he left Danielle standing in the driveway without telling her what she wanted to hear. This is what he was waiting for.

Oh, and Gideon is forgetting the bet. Pilar has transported him from the cares of this world.

"Don't worry," she whispers. "None of the teachers here have any idea that Mickey Eisenberg sells drugs." She rolls her eyes. "And as long as we all keep getting our Ivy League acceptances, they wouldn't even think to care." The dorm is starting to buzz now, as more and more girls come back from study hall. Suddenly, Pilar's golden and perfect face lights up. "Madison!" she cries.

Madison Sprague's short hair is in little pigtails. Gid thinks they look cute, because he is a guy and doesn't know to be annoyed by the whole "I'm so pretty I don't care what I look like" aesthetic. She and Pilar give each other a big girly hug as Gid hovers, embarrassed. He should probably walk away, but he just can't. He knows he'll be at school all year, he hopes all next year as well, but as he looks at Pilar's sparkling brown eyes and perfect butt in her white pants, he can only feel this is the most important moment in his life.

"Hey, Gid." Madison gives Gid a flirtatious punch on the arm. She reaches over and kisses him on the cheek. Then she says, "He lives with Cullen and Nicholas," which makes Gid wonder, does she have to explain why she knows him? Couldn't she just know him?

"I gotta go, Hal's calling," Madison says, walking backward up the stairs, sending smaller, less pretty girls scurrying from her wake. "I'll come to your room later."

"Cullen and Nicholas," Pilar says when Madison's out of earshot. She shakes her head sympathetically. "That must be fun, but also"—she puts out one of her hands, turning it from side to side so her assortment of rings sparkles under the lights—"maybe a little bit not so fun?"

Yes, yes. This is exactly what it is like. This girl, with her beautiful white clothes and her sparkling jewelry, she deserves to know everything about him. He wants to tell her about his parents and the culs-de-sac and the kids playing in their driveways and Merle Haggard. About how the Vaportech is wonderful and awful all at once, and how when he runs, he dreams that a girl as absolutely perfect as she might one day think he's something other than skinny fat.

"Do you need help?" he says. "I could bring this stuff up to your room."

"You can't go there," Pilar says.

"Oh, right," Gid says. Perhaps the best thing to do at this point is extract himself before saying anything that would point to how he feels. "I guess I should get back to my dorm."

"But if you go back to your room," Pilar says, "you're not going to hear the secret I'm going to tell you."

So I'm not imagining things, Gid thinks. We connect.

He comes to this conclusion partly because he wants to and partly because he doesn't know that a pretty young girl will tell a secret to a fucking handbag. It's just what they do. What we do.

Pilar leans in. Gideon focuses all his attention on the light pressure of her mouth on his ear as she whispers, "Madison likes to record herself deflowering guys on her camera phone and then send the footage to her boyfriend. She says he gets 'bored on tour.'" Pilar says this last part in a not very good British accent, which nonetheless conveys her lack of sympathy. She's visibly delighted to share this information, and her already formidable glow intensifies. "Have you ever heard anything so crazy in your life?" Pilar gives the word *life* about fourteen syllables. Moments from now, the radiance of her smile will not shine on me, Gid thinks, and I will die a little.

"Yes," Gid says. "I mean, I don't know." Then he backs away, tries to smile. Oh, Gid! Get out of there.

"Maybe?" Pilar suggests. She says this over her shoulder, where her T-shirt has moved a precious few inches to the side, revealing a narrow pink ribbon of a bra strap.

Gid nods. "Maybe."

"Maybe I'll see you around," Pilar says.

"That would be great," Gideon says. He looks down at her pile of luggage. He can't help her take it upstairs, since that's against the rules. But he bends down, picks up the heaviest duffel from the floor, and helps to arrange it comfortably on her shoulder.

Then Gid, not one to resist the final gesture (this is why I adore him so), tucks her T-shirt under the strap so it doesn't dig into her pretty skin.

"I'll bet you had a crush on Madison before I told you that," Pilar says.

Gid blushes.

"Try not to make any more drug deals," Pilar says and walks away.

maybe
not
zero
game

Gideon has been at Midvale for three weeks now. He has settled into a routine: running, class, lunch, more class, dinner, sitting around, studying, and, most nights, sneaking out.

I've found a way to sleep through some of the sneaking out. There's only so much of Madison Sprague's wine guzzling and Erica's Nicholas-loving and Mija's, well . . . general *Euro*ness that I can stand.

Erica's Nicholas-loving is especially disturbing. There's nothing more depressing than watching a girl love a guy who doesn't love her back.

The morning runs no longer shock Gideon. Sometimes he takes it upon himself to brew the daily batch of green tea that he and Nicholas carry off to class. Nicholas says he uses exactly the right amount of tea. Ms. San Video doesn't get less hot, but Gid knows he's going to see her every day except Thursday, so he regards her with more restraint. He actually read *A Tale of Two Cities,* and Mrs. Yates has taught him the difference between a da Vinci and a Caravaggio, a Rembrandt and a Vermeer.

Perhaps more important, Liam still scares him, but he no longer feels the impulse to sob when he sees him.

I've seen Gid look at me. I'm not saying where I fall on the worth-looking-at scale, but I will say that when Gid's eyes fall on you, you can't help but feel kind of pretty. Even if you know, as I do, that Gid's head does little but run in a loop, as regular as a train route.

It starts off with Pilar. He sees her from afar, sometimes she even comes close to him and says hello, and this sends him into near-spasms of happiness, which almost as quickly turn over into anxiety as he realizes that he has not, since that glorious day in the girls' dorm, had an actual conversation with her, and that he must make that his very first order of business. But he barely has time to settle on that plan before he remembers his anxiety growing that he must step things up with Molly McGarry. He tried to talk to her yesterday. But she was with that Edie girl from his English class.

At this point, frustration makes Gid's mind go blank, but only for a second. Because then, inexplicably, Danielle pops up, not Danielle per se but a dark, stomach-churning feeling of guilt for not yet having called her, and the only way he can stop berating himself is to again think pleasant thoughts about Pilar.

You might think it would be hard to be in love with a guy and watch him lust after other chicks. The thing is, I am in for the long haul. I want Gid forever, and I can wait for forever to start. (Oh my God, who is channeling Mariah Carey?) Besides, I already know Gid and I are going to end up together, because I know him better than he knows himself. Remember what Mickey Eisenberg said about Ms. San Video? That he knows what he likes? Well, Gid knows what he likes too. He just doesn't know that he knows.

On this particular night, Gideon has just smoked a little pot, and although Cullen assured him this particular pot's effects would be soporific, he can tell that he is (we are) going to be awake for a long time. You have permission, he tells himself, to think only of

Pilar until you manage to fall asleep. But it's no good, because there's Molly McGarry, or the anxiety of the bet, weighing dark and heavy on his chest. He realizes with some surprise that he might want to win this bet more than he wants to sleep with Pilar. That means, he tells himself, stoned and fascinated, that I don't care as much about what I want as I care about what other people want for me. He beats himself up about this for a few minutes, but then, remembering that it's not likely that either girl will ever sleep with him anyway, he can't help but laugh.

He's amazed at his total absence of tiredness. The whole inside of his head feels white, sparkling, alive. He remembers that he didn't brush his teeth or wash his face. He brightens at having something to do. In the bathroom Gideon stares at his face, at his nut brown eyes, his graceful eyebrows, and his fantastic, well-orthodontured teeth.

The more he loves Pilar, the cuter he gets. It's like her beauty shines on him. And the Mariah Carey theme continues.

He's staring at his face when the door swings open and standing there—no, this can't be, is he that high? But no, it's really her: Pilar Benitez-Jones. She looks right at him, but her eyes are big and unfocused. She ducks around the corner. "You have to help me get out of here, Gee-de-on," she hisses. The way she says *help,* with no *h,* and a long *e,* even her mangling of his name, gets him right in the knees.

Gideon leaves his toothbrush in the sink and rushes to the shower, where she stands, her back pressed up against the gray-and-pink-tiled wall. She looks terrified but elated, her big eyes glassy around the whites and shiny in their black middles. Her teeth gleam. His insides feel as if someone is pouring cold water over them.

Is Pilar in his dorm because she's visiting a guy? Why else would she be there? So he shouldn't put himself at risk of getting in major trouble for no good reason, for Pilar and some other guy's benefit. But—did he really just think this?—he loves her. He has to help.

Gideon ushers Pilar farther inside the shower, taking his toothbrush with him. "You're lucky there's no one in here," he says, liking the way he sounds vaguely reprimanding.

"We're in here," Pilar says. Is she wasted? Gid doesn't yet know the difference between merely under the influence and wasted.

"Sit down," he says. She looks at him challengingly. "Sit down," he says again. "You're going to fall over. Okay. You came running in here. Why?"

"I was in Mickey Eisenberg's room," she says. Gideon's eyes widen. Pilar laughs, a delightful bubble, with a warm vodka vapor. "Not like that," she says, poking him with one finger. The entire range of skin around the poke turns hot. She reaches her other hand inside her bra. God, a beautiful girl who is always pulling things in and out of her bra . . . it's too good. "Like this," she says. She holds a small packet of white pills and smiles proudly.

"Oh, right," Gid says. "The drugs that I got with my phone call, which was no doubt a felony."

"Anyway, Mickey was pissed I came over. He told me at dinner there was going to be a meteor shower tonight, and that your dorm head would be outside watching it."

Gid runs to the left-hand bathroom window and, careful not to stick his head out too much, looks down to the dorm steps. The meteor shower! Mickey Eisenberg was right! Captain Cockweed sits on a lawn chair five feet from the dorm's front door, his head tilted slightly to the heavens, moonlight shining on his bald spot. At his feet, his son, Tim, looks to the sky, his head tipped back at the same reverent angle. Gid knows the kid's faking it, that even at age ten, he's figured out how to pretend he likes things like stars so his dad will think he's a good, curious kid and not just a budding hoodlum who only wants to slam into people on his skateboard while muttering choruses from Blink-182 songs. Gid's about to wonder if he should feel sorry for Tim Cockweed when Pilar peeks around the edge of the shower wall. "Gee-de-on," she says, louder than necessary.

"Shhh," he says, shoving her back in the shower. The drugs have made her pliant and unstable, as if her body had been loaded onto a giant spring.

She giggles. "You're hurting me!" Her tone is mocking; she's not really saying *You're hurting me,* Gid realizes. She's imitating someone who might play damsel in distress this way. She can joke all she wants, but seriously, honey, you don't just accidentally find yourself stranded at midnight in a guy's prep school dorm without kind of wanting it to happen.

But Gid—in love, seeing nothing really beyond the velvet softness of Pilar's brown eyes and the satin of her skin—is incapable of such a critique.

Very incapable. "Pilar," he says, tenderly, bravely, putting his palm on her head, stroking her hair as if she were a child. "Why'd you go out tonight? Even when Mickey told you it wasn't a good idea?"

Pilar shrugs, and Gid, poor Gid, just watches the play of light on her shoulders as it moves up and down. "I ran out?" she says.

Pilar Benitez-Jones was an Ecstasy fiend! She was getting more and more interesting by the second. At this moment the bathroom door opens. Gid thinks about clapping a hand over Pilar's mouth, like he's seen in movies. Then he does it. Wow. He's enjoying this.

"Gid, are you in here?" It's Cullen. Pilar looks at Gid: What should we do? Gid shakes his head: Don't say anything. She nods.

"You know, Gid's pretty tight-lipped about who he really wants to nail." It's Nicholas talking now. "Surprisingly tight-lipped for someone with zero game." Gid wants to die. The sound of running water and vigorous toothbrushing. "I mean, I see Gid looking around at girls. But you know how we always tell each other who's in the hot seat? He says nothing. For a dork . . ."

"Don't talk about Gid like that," Cullen says. "He's our brother."

"Just telling it like it is. I like the guy, but he's not that cool."

"Personally," says Cullen, "I think that's what makes him cool. But what would you know, because you're completely cool, and that's what makes you so uncool."

"Suck it," says Nicholas. "We're not talking about me. Anyway, for a guy who doesn't seem to have a big game, he's real casual when it comes to the girls. Is he into Kelly, the sophomore with the big earrings and the matching butt? Rose May, that southern girl? Or maybe he's after Pilar Benitez-Jones?"

Cullen laughs. Gid would love to interpret the laugh in a different way, but he knows that a laugh like that—loud, quick, totally sarcastic—only means one thing: not in a million years.

"He probably just went down to the basement to sneak a Coke," Cullen says. "It's a funny world where you can smoke all the pot you want but Coke is off-limits."

"Coke is poison," Nicholas mutters.

"Yeah, well, my dick is poison," Cullen says. "But everyone still wants it." Nicholas manages a tolerant snort.

Pilar takes a deep breath, obviously about to speak. Gid shakes his head vigorously and clamps his hand over her mouth. Her lips worming against his palm, the wall of her teeth. Why do girls get so excited whenever their name is mentioned? He looks right into her eyes. She bites the skin between his thumb and pointer finger, and Gid moves against her. He is aroused. They stay this way until Cullen and Nicholas leave.

But when he goes to take his hand away she grabs it. She doesn't stop looking into his eyes. She grabs his hand, and she puts it—well, the fact that I don't want to say where she puts it should let you know where.

And what does Gid do? For those of you who said he grabs her and they make passionate love under the running water, well, you overestimate him. For those who say he sets his hand on her cheek and says, "Not here, Pilar. Not like this," well, that would make for great television. But it's not what happened. Because even though Pilar might have what it takes for primetime, Gid is pure after-school special.

Which is why I like him. And why he struggles.

sleepover

Pilar eventually sank to the floor. Gid made sure she didn't break any bones.

Gid stands there for at least ten minutes, watching her drift in and out and asking himself all sorts of moral questions about alcohol, girls, and sex. The yellow underwear flashes into his thoughts. When Pilar's eyes flutter open and she murmurs, "Let's do it," he thinks he will die of joy. But she's wasted. She doesn't mean it. But she doesn't not mean it. Her eyes are open. She's definitely awake. He holds up two fingers.

"How many fingers am I holding up?" he says.

"Peace," she says. Her eyes close, then open, then close.

He undoes a length of paper towel from the dispenser, folds it, and sets it under Pilar's head. "Just let me sleep for fifteen minutes," she says. She's awake. So she does know what she's saying! He peeks out the door. Nothing. He dashes back into his room.

The guys are asleep, though their personalities are still very much with them, even in repose. Cullen's on his back, mouth wide open, his whole upper body tipped backward on the white bank of pillows he stole from a four-star hotel in Tokyo. His head angles ever so slightly to the left, as if even asleep he knew this was the proper way to display his neck and shoulder muscles to the column of light coming in from the streetlamp. Nicholas lies on his side, his body in a perfect *C*, his hands clasped between his knees. Cullen's mouth grabs the air noisily. Nicholas doesn't make a sound; air just flows through him.

Gid hears the soft but deliberate sound of feet on carpet. It's not Pilar. The steps are too . . . angry.

He looks out the peephole. That pink head, that purposeful walk. It's Captain Cockweed, alert, suspicious, his powerful torso and hips propelling him toward their door.

Gid leaps onto his bed. He hears a tiny metallic sound, Cockweed's wedding ring against the doorknob. Then the room floods with light. The door shuts. It is dark again. Gid waits.

Should he let Pilar sleep in the shower?

Yes, Gideon, that would probably be best for everyone.

Then he has a bizarre fantasy. That Cullen wakes up before he does and goes in to take a shower and that he finds Pilar there, and that Pilar sits up, gives him a slow, sexy smile, and begins to slip off her clothes as Cullen reaches to remove his shorts . . .

Gid plays out that whole fantasy as an excuse to risk going back into the bathroom.

Pilar's still asleep. A clear ribbon of drool hangs out of the pink corner of her mouth and is spreading in a moist circle on the paper towel pillow. Gid slips one arm under her knees. She's wearing corduroys. They are soft. And then one arm under her neck. He bends at the knees and lifts her up.

He has to open the bathroom door with his foot. He pushes it with a little too much force, and it swings back too fast, lightly knocking Pilar on the side of the head.

She doesn't flinch. The hall is empty. It's only about six paces to his door, but Cockweed could emerge at any time. Gid leaps, his forward motion moving into the door so that he lands inside the bedroom.

He feels very *Matrix*.

Cullen and Nicholas sleep as Gideon eases Pilar onto his bed and gently straightens out her limbs. She opens her eyes. "Everyone thinks I am from Buenos Aires," she says, "but I am from Bahía Blanca." She stretches and rearranges her body so that she leaves only about a six-inch-wide strip, which Gideon, grateful he is skinny fat and not fat fat, eases himself into. His arm is scrunched up underneath him. Would it be weird or bad if he kind of laid it on top of her body?

He closes his eyes and imagines that Pilar Benitez-Jones is his wife, and that falling asleep next to her is the most natural thing in the world.

He wakes up to Nicholas and Cullen standing over him.

"Hi," Gid whispers.

"Holy fucking shit," Cullen says. "This is awesome."

"It's not that awesome," Gid says.

That makes me laugh.

"You're not going to believe what happened," Gid says.

Cullen wags his head from side to side. "You found her wandering around drunk and brought her in here. Happens all the time. Or it's not unheard of. Did you know Aztec warriors used to sleep next to naked virgins to increase their resistance to pain?"

Pilar, still asleep, is fully clothed. And I would be very surprised if she were a virgin.

"Can you believe how beautiful she is? I mean, isn't it just heartbreaking?" Gid says. He dreamed about her all night.

"Mother of God," says Nicholas. "Beautiful and about to get us fucking expelled." He goes to the peephole. "Mrs. Cockweed is out there with the damn ironing board. Oh wait, she's packing it up, she's going. Cullen, get your hockey bag out of the closet."

Cullen winks at Gid. "She is pretty hot," he says. "You're such a champ for not nailing her, what with the bet and all."

"I want to call it off," Gid says. "I really think that Pilar likes me. She said . . ."

Cullen is coming toward him with a human-size red bag.

"No," says Gideon, horrified. "You're not going to put her in a bag."

"What are you going to do, carry her out in your pants?" Nicholas asks. He cocks his head at Gideon. "You wake her up."

"Wait," Cullen says. "Gid wants to call off the Molly McGarry bet because he's in love with Pilar."

"No, no, no," Gid says, "I didn't say I was in love with her. I said she likes me, and—"

"Both of those things are equally absurd," Nicholas snaps. "More absurd, in fact, than the fact that one of us has to carry this one-hundred-twenty-pound girl out of our dorm in a bag."

Pilar opens her eyes. She sees Gideon, Nicholas, Cullen, then the bag. She knows what it's for.

"One hundred fifteen pounds," she says. She laughs. She closes her eyes again.

"You don't have to," Gid says. "We can probably . . ."

Pilar opens her eyes. She rolls onto her side and hoists herself on her elbow. She sits on the edge of the bed, then puts her head between her knees.

Cullen opens his mouth. He's about to make a gross joke. I don't need to be inside his mind to know that.

"Shut up," Nicholas says. "It's too early for your stupid fucking . . ." He rolls his eyes, too world-weary to complete the sentence.

Pilar, woozy, lowers herself onto the floor. She looks up at Gideon, her eyes huge and moving in her head with intoxicated instability. She crawls into the bag. "Leave me in the woods behind my dorm." Her tone is dull. She is a practiced misbehaver.

Gid savors every inch of Pilar's face as the bag is zipped up and it disappears.

Gid insists on carrying the bag. It's not too heavy. He can handle it. But walking through the doorway the bag swings out and some rather hard part of Pilar's body hits the molding. "Sorry," Gid says. A few steps down the hall, the bag swings the other way. There is another thud. "Geez, sorry again," Gid whispers, kind of caressing the bag.

Cullen and Nicholas have been watching from the doorway, and Cullen comes barreling down the hall, exasperated. "You can't fucking talk to the fucking bag," he says.

With little effort, Cullen takes the bag and hoists it onto his shoulder. "If you're totally fine in there," he hisses, "don't say anything."

The bag is silent. Gid would feel bad that he wasn't the man for the job, but he makes himself feel better by remembering it's because he cares too much. After all, he did carry her last night. Under the right circumstances, she is not too heavy for him.

crates
aren't
inhumane

Days pass, and Pilar doesn't talk to him. She always says hi, which in a way makes it worse, because it's not that she doesn't see Gid. She totally sees him and chooses to restrict the terms of their interaction.

He hates that Nicholas is right. I kind of hate it too. This whole "in your league" idea is very unromantic.

Though, like most unromantic things, it could very well be the way life works.

Gid resolves to get used to the dull pitch of life, down from the whirring frenzy when Pilar was sort of around more, and resolves to set his sights on Molly.

For three straight days, he studies the back of Molly McGarry's head all through Spanish class. Not surprisingly, this provides no insights.

He's going to ask Cullen. This whole watch-and-learn thing, while less desperate than actually being schooled, is also less effective.

Gid finds Cullen just as he's walking into the dining hall with Fiona, the calculating babysitter. Fiona Winchester, black-haired, pink-cheeked, pert in front and behind, stands a whole foot shorter than Cullen. She looks up at him with adoring eyes. Her eyes have a natural softness to them. It's easy to see why she might cultivate motherliness to pursue boys. She's wearing shortish pants which are fashionable but to Gideon seem merely too short, a vintage paisley shirt, and a pair of high-heeled boots that look purposefully odd with it all. Even her outfit is sort of weirdo-cool mom-ish, though she's only fifteen.

"People don't understand that crates aren't inhumane," Gid overhears her say as he reaches them.

"Oh, Gideon," Cullen says, taking his arm. He puts his other hand on Fiona's back. "Will you excuse us?"

"Sorry," Gideon mutters as Fiona walks away.

"Please," Cullen says, "she was telling me how to train Irish setters. You did me a favor. What's up?"

They make sandwiches in the dining hall. Gid wraps his in a lot of napkins. Cullen doesn't bother. They settle against a maple tree. Gideon has to force himself not to maniacally scan the quad for a glimpse of Pilar. "Okay," he says to Cullen, "I've gone over this, and I just don't even know where to begin with Molly. I mean . . . you can't just make a girl like you. Can you?"

This is an excellent question. A hard question. And even though Cullen's not usually up for the hard questions, this one is made for him.

Cullen leans his head back against the tree trunk and closes his eyes. Gid eats his sandwich. He took the opportunity of a lunch away from Nicholas to get salami with cheese, mayonnaise, and mustard. It's only cafeteria quality, but it's incredible.

Cullen opens his eyes and sighs with some impatience. "I am trying to imagine what it might be like to get a girl if it was, you know, not ridiculously easy." He closes his eyes again.

Cullen really only means to state the facts. Still, it's got to hurt.

"Okay," Cullen says, "I think I have something. Girls—we all just think of them as, you know, nice tits, nice eyes, this and that, but the thing they are into is their personalities."

I thought it was this bad. But I always sort of hoped it wasn't.

At least I can hear Gid thinking, "Wow, I know what Cullen means, but isn't that a bit extreme?" Though he's still taking Cullen's advice. Well. I hate to admit it, but he probably should.

"We need to think about who Molly is, what she's into. When you know what chicks dig, it's a lot easier to get them to like you. Give me your notebook." He starts writing. After a minute or two, he opens it so Gid can see. He has written a few categories: *habitat, interests, friends, food*. At the top, in large letters, he's written M^2. He grins and nods at Gid. "Pretty cool!" he says.

"Food?" Gid asks. "Who cares what kind of food she eats?"

Cullen just smiles. "Okay, what does Madison eat?"

Gid rolls his eyes.

"Go ahead," Cullen prompts. "You know."

"Uh, wine? Cottage cheese?" Gid throws up his hands. This is stupid. A new wave of students pours out of Barrett, one of the classroom buildings, onto the quad. Gid can't resist looking. No Pilar.

"What kind of wine?"

Okay, he'll play. "Red."

"What kind of cottage cheese?"

"Fat-free?" Gid has seen it. Little blue plastic containers that she brings to the dining hall in her backpack. Sometimes she eats it plain, sometimes with Ry-Krisp she gets off the salad and soup bar.

"Okay, you're doing very well," Cullen says. "So. What does the wine tell you?"

"That she likes being drunk?" Gid's happy.

Cullen nods encouragingly. "And what else about the wine? What makes this wine different—the wine Madison drinks, the special wine, for special Madison . . ."

"She wants to be . . . French?" Gideon really wants to get the right answer.

"The wine's . . ." Cullen's eyes expand, as if he could somehow lead Gid to the word.

"Expensive!" Gid says, knowing he's gotten it.

"Okay, so let's put it all together," Cullen says, clapping his hands. Gideon sees that he's having a very good time. "Cottage cheese and expensive wine."

"Madison is interested," Gid begins carefully, "in being drunk, glamorous, and thin."

"Exactly," Cullen says. "And so how do you get to sleep with Madison?"

"By making her feel all those three things," Gid says.

"I think two would probably do it," Cullen says.

"That was just food," Gid points out, consulting the list. "We didn't do . . . habitat, friends, or interests."

Cullen shrugs. "Habitat, she's from Park Avenue. Okay, friends. Okay, she pals around with her roommates, reluctantly, they don't count. She's friends with . . ."

"All the pretty girls," Gid says, getting it. "And her interests . . . I think she's most interested in magazines. We could have stopped at food. Wow."

"I wonder if Hal thinks Madison is a pain in the ass or not." Cullen muses. "Whatever. Here we go, Molly McGarry!" He claps his hands together. "Let's start with what we know. Habitat." Cullen taps his pen efficiently against the notebook.

"She's from Buffalo," Gid offers, glad to have an answer.

"Good, good." Cullen nods. "Did she tell you this?"

"It was the first thing she said to me. When I met her, she introduced herself as Molly McGarry of the Buffalo McGarrys."

"No way!" Cullen is very excited by this. "That means she's on to it, well, on to it and over it."

"On to what? Over what?"

"The whole prep school 'thing.'" Cullen makes quotes with his fingers. "The whole 'Oh, no way, my dad went to the Strawberry

Shortcake Cotillion with your mom's border collie' thing. The first thing she tells you, the very first thing she wants you to know about her, is that she's from this shithole where most people here will never set foot, much less live."

"What's the Strawberry Shortcake Cotillion?" Gid asks.

"Forget it. Write down 'Over prep school.'"

Gid writes it down.

"Write down 'Outsider.'"

Gid writes it down.

"Okay. Moving along. Friends."

"Okay, well, I've seen her with Marcy Proctor."

"Former roommate, assigned roommate." Cullen is dismissive. "Incidental."

Gid wonders, am I incidental to Cullen and Nicholas? He really doesn't feel that way. Cullen seems to be genuinely enjoying himself.

"Mostly, though, she goes everywhere with that little girl, Edie."

"Right, right . . . ," Cullen says. "Edie was assigned to live with Erica and Marcy last year, but she and Molly chose to live together this year. So, write down 'Champion of the underdog.'" Cullen shakes his head. "That girl is in my History class. She is weird. But kind of sexy in a little-girl-with-too-big-eyes kind of way. Like kind of so innocent-seeming you want to defile her, but you know that you are also kind of a little afraid of her? I know you know what I mean."

One of the things Gideon likes about Cullen is that he gives him credit when he doesn't deserve it. Nicholas barely gives him credit when he does.

"Anyway," Cullen continues, "despite my occasional weird forays and creepy sexual thoughts, Edie is a serious nerd. So you might want to put in parentheses, maybe with a question mark, 'Loves nerds.'"

Fiona Winchester, now done with her lunch, walks toward

them with a comely mixture of shyness and sex appeal. "Who loves nerds?" she asks, shielding her eyes from the sun. Not waiting for an answer, she walks backward, away from them, all the while watching Cullen.

Cullen has never, not once, had to make a plan about a girl. Girls just appear to him, and all he has to do is decide which one he wants.

Cullen stabs the notebook with his finger. "Okay, forget Fiona," he says. "Concentrate."

"Who in the world would want to see themselves as a nerd?" Gid asks.

"Who the fuck knows why anyone does anything?" he asks. "Why do we have a stupid bet to see whether you can have sex with some girl? Because it's enjoyable. It gives us something to focus on. Because we will laugh when that douche bag Liam has to give you the keys to Nicholas's car. What have we got now?"

" 'Over prep school,' " Gid reads. " 'Outsider. Champion of the underdog. Loves nerds?' "

"It's a pretty good start," Cullen says. "So here's the thing, when you talk to her, you have to make sure that the stuff you say, like, confirms how she sees herself. I'm going to make it real simple for you. Say one thing, just one thing, for each one of these things we've figured out about her."

"That's weird," Gideon says. "I don't know if I get it."

I get it.

"Sure you do." (Trust me, Cullen, he doesn't.) Cullen stands up and brushes his pants off. "You'll figure it out when you talk to her." He looks across the quad and smiles. "How convenient."

Sure enough, here come Molly and Edie, their heads bowed over the books they're carrying. Edie's tucked inside a giant scarf that makes her look even smaller. At one point a tail of it starts to trail down Edie's back, and Molly catches the end of it and winds it carefully back around her neck. As they get closer, Gid sees Edie's tiny, grateful smile and her eyes, saucer-round with what seems like perpetual bewilderment. Or maybe, Gideon thinks, she's really bored and trying to stay awake.

"Champion of the underdog, loves nerds, et cetera." Cullen gives him a good-luck shoulder clap. "And most important, you want to see what she's having for lunch. I think we've proven that's very helpful information."

antifreeze

When Gid enters the cafeteria, Molly and Edie are already sitting. This was not what he wanted. He wanted to give them the choice to join him. How did they do that so fast? He looks around for another place to sit down, but there are only about eight other people there, and he only knows two of them: Luke Miles, a linebacker on the football team who eats five full meals a day. (He once drew a chart on a napkin to show Gid the number of calories he ate per day in order to, as he put it, beefy thumbs pointing at his chest, "keep this machine running.") Sitting maybe twenty yards away is Sergei Rofganif, who, Gid happens to know, eats lunch late because he takes physics at MIT. Not freshman physics, like, "find out how dense this sphere is," but crazy advanced physics, like, "find out where the universe ends—and what comes after it." Sergei Rofganif is transfixed by what appears to be a blank piece of graph paper. Gid imagines they would not have much to discuss. Luke Miles has consumed two hot dogs and is staring down a third. As maybe off-the-beaten-path as it would be to go sit with Molly and Edie, it's so much less so than his other options.

It's time for a little positive visualization, à la *Journal of the Zen Hut*. Gideon stands facing the soda machine, closes his eyes, and imagines sleeping with Molly. Interesting that he goes not to the actual sex part but getting up afterward. When she's asleep—oh yes, Gid, no doubt your prowess took her unexpectedly by storm—and he puts his clothes back on and goes to tell Cullen how he has done what he set out to do. He imagines Cullen's filial pride and Nicholas's initial disappointment in losing, followed by more filial pride.

Good. This tactic works. He puts one foot in front of the other, and then he's there and it's time to start talking. He thinks about saying "May I sit down?" but changes this at the last minute (smart play, Gid) to "Can I sit here?"

Molly turns around. Smiles. Looks him up and down. "Well, hello," she says, making a show of checking behind him. She's wearing a plain brown cardigan, a white blouse, jeans, and some kind of fuzzy boots that look like little animals. "Where are your friends?" she asks. Is that sarcasm? Because her tone made it sound like she was saying, "Where are your ubiquitous friends?" But her smile really is intense, really . . . ugh. Warm. Gid doesn't feel that bad as he sits down. He thinks, She's a person, I'm a person, how bad can this be? She smiles more. He thinks how Pilar's smile makes him stare. Molly's doesn't make him stare. It just makes him feel like he's not afraid to sit down. Staring's fun. Not feeling like a stupid jerk isn't bad either.

That's when he notices that Edie is staring at him. Her eyes are really giant. Do small people have giant eyes, or do they just look giant? How, he wonders, would this fascinating puzzle in special dynamics strike Sergei? Edie is dwarfed by a rather enormous plate of macaroni and cheese, which she shakes salt over and begins to eat. Gid's anger flares a little that she doesn't say hi. She should be nicer. Her haughtiness is not in proportion with her hotness.

Now, this is Gid listening too much to his roommates. I don't like this Gid. I mean, I still like/love him but not at moments where his insecurity makes him lash out.

Molly is eating salami and American cheese, with mayonnaise and mustard on white. "Incredible," he says. "I ate the exact same thing for lunch today."

He is immediately overwhelmed by the banality of this observation. But Molly warms to the salami conversation. "I didn't know, you know? I stood up there for a while," she says. "I was tempted by the macaroni and cheese, but then I was like, who wants to eat one flavor over and over again? No offense," she adds to Edie.

Edie shrugs.

What does it mean for a girl to eat a salami sandwich with American cheese? Gid wonders. She's drinking what appears to be a Coke. But maybe it's diet. He imagines this would be an important distinction. He's going to have to consult with Cullen on the food, its hidden message. Is she just saying that she's regular, that she's like a guy? He says, "I like salami." Again. Cursing himself.

"I get the salami whenever it's available. You're not going to make any 'hide the salami' jokes, are you?" she asks.

"If I were sitting with the crowd I usually sit with," Gid says, "I would have made a 'hide the salami' joke. But I didn't really think you were the type of person who would laugh." Molly, almost imperceptibly but without a doubt, inches a little toward him. Receiving the small compliment, getting the fact that Gideon saw her as slightly outside of things, just as she wanted to see herself. Cullen was right. This made sense. It wasn't that hard at all!

"You're from Buffalo," he proceeds, buoyed with success. "What's it like there?"

Molly looks pleased to have been asked. "I can't describe it. But I can tell you a story."

This is great. She's going to talk. It's going to take up time. He's going to relax a little and think of what to do next. It would be enough just to pay attention. But of course, as a guy, he has to think about his next move.

Edie sets her fork down and smiles as Molly begins. "A while ago, like maybe twenty years ago, there was a guy who sold hot dogs in Delaware Park in Buffalo. It's a park that was designed by Frederick Law Olmstead."

Gid has no idea who that is, and his poker face sucks.

Molly frowns. "Frederick Law Olmsted designed Central Park," she says. "Central Park is in New York City."

Edie smiles, presumably enjoying Molly's smugness a degree more than Gid.

"Anyway, he is the only guy licensed to sell hot dogs and stuff at this park. And he's been doing it his whole life. But one year, there's a new mayor. And this mayor decides he's going to take that license and give it to someone else, you know, probably his cousin, or his sister's stepkid or something. So the guy, he's out of a job. Just like that. So in the park, there's a pond where kids skate in the winter, and that's how this guy made a lot of his money, selling hot dogs and hot chocolate to all the kids who skated there, right? So, you know what the guy does? He puts antifreeze in the lake, and the new guy, well, he goes broke. End of story."

"Oh my God." Gid feels himself forgetting his agenda. That was a really good story. "Like, how much antifreeze?"

"Who knows?" Molly says. "Who besides a freak from Buffalo knows how much antifreeze it takes to keep a pond from freezing?"

"I bet he does." Gid points to Sergei, who, as if on cue, is trying to balance a spoon on top of a water glass. To Gid's absolute delight, Molly laughs. Out loud. Edie laughs, into a napkin, like she's going to get in trouble for it. Gid is so pleased with himself. He sits back, very satisfied, but then sees that Sergei is no longer playing with his spoon but looking uncomfortably at the ground.

"Oh no," Molly says.

Gid isn't sure what force takes ahold of him but he walks over to Sergei, who turns to him, his giant eyeglasses first flashing at the light coming in the window. "Sorry to bother you," he says, "but you know, we're, uh, not laughing at you. We didn't want you to feel bad." He takes a quick glance behind him. Edie and Molly smile grimly, supporting him.

"Fuck off," Sergei says quietly.

Gid feels anger surge in him. He almost says, "Hey, I was trying to be nice." But as Sergei rushes to gather his things, Gid notices the weird patchy hair on his chin and the rough black plastic of his eyeglasses. Gid realizes that as stupid as he feels, this kid probably feels even stupider. He realizes that if he wants the fact that he apologized to actually make the kid feel any better, he'll just take the fuck-off and move on. Gid kind of deserves it. And he can handle it.

"He said, 'fuck off,'" Gid mouths as he nears the table. He sits. They all shake their heads and just sit in the silence for a few seconds. There's the clang of coffee cups being washed in the kitchen, a whistle sounds sharp and close over the dull, distant throb of the commuter train. Gid wonders if he might be starting to get why people say New England is cozy.

"Anyway," Molly shrugs and smiles, "that's what Buffalo is like."

Gid imagines the hot dog guy, in a tiny little ranch house with cars in the yard, sitting at his kitchen table, maybe repairing old toasters, as he came up with his grand plan. How much he must have savored the feeling of adrenaline in his veins, the excitement in his heart as he ventured out to Milt's Garage and spent the last two hundred dollars he had on antifreeze. "It's really kind of great," he says. "You have to admire a guy like that."

Molly smiles. "I agree," she says. "You could make it in Buffalo."

Later, he finds Cullen, and Cullen wants to know what happened. He's been all geared up to give a full report, but suddenly, he can't remember a thing. He just says it was fun.

it's
fiona's
party,
and you'll come
if she
wants you to

Gid's fourth Friday at Midvale is one of those fall days with a menacing violet-gray sky. Gid's walking to Spanish with Liam Wu, enjoying their odd camaraderie and feeling a slow-burning anxiety he attributes to the weather until he realizes what his real problem is. Yesterday was Danielle's birthday, and he still hasn't called her. "Danielle," he groans involuntarily, forgetting he's not alone.

"Who is Danielle?" Liam asks.

Gid hesitates. Smart on his part. The Danielle Road can't be a good one to travel with Liam Wu.

"She's . . . a friend from home. I forgot her birthday."

"Whatever," Liam says, scowling. "My mother doesn't even remember my birthday." Liam's mother, Gideon knows, is a banker in Hong Kong. "I thought she was some chick you wanted to ball. Birthdays, I don't give a fuck. But balling . . ." Liam nods. "We can talk ballin' all the livelong day, son."

Gid winces. Not because of Danielle, but because of Molly. That if he does have sex with her, it will be spoken of as *balling*.

"Liam," he ventures, "this is kind of a stupid question . . ."

"I expect nothing less from you," Liam replies. Unlike Cullen and Nicholas, there's never even the slightest glimmer of affection in Liam's insults. Maybe when your mom forgets your birthday, you get hard like that.

"What do you think is sexy? I mean, how do you define *sexy*?" He's thinking of Molly and Pilar and his different feelings about them.

Liam Wu stops short in the middle of the quad. "A chick you want to ball," he says. With an exasperated shake of the head, he resumes walking.

Liam frustrates Gideon. He's not sure why. I think it might be because he can't decide whether to direct his hostility at Liam himself or at the system that rewards Liam for being a handsome, mean, intimidating asshole.

And here comes, or rather, waddles, Devon Shine. Gid might be skinny fat, but Devon Shine is fat fat! He keeps tugging his T-shirt over his stomach. And he's wearing barrettes! "What's up?" Devon says to Gid, not looking him in the eye.

Gid nods politely, thinking, Why isn't anyone on your case? While he huffs and puffs his way around the track in the morning, Devon sleeps, cozy under layers of blankets and blubber. And he loves himself. And girls like him. And he wears barrettes, for Christ's sake. It's not fair.

Devon pulls Liam away from Gid, into the middle of the quad, where they begin to whisper and gesture. Gid waits in the path for a few seconds as a parade of girls walks around Liam, adjusting their book bags on their shoulders, tucking their hair behind their ears, and casting sidelong glances, hoping to be noticed. Gid has tried to catch girls giving him sidelong glances but so far, nothing. To maintain his sanity, he has convinced himself he's never looking at the right time—not entirely untrue, since I look at him that way all the time.

Suddenly he realizes he's blocking the path. He feels stupid, vestigial, and stands on the grass watching Devon and Liam. Their conversation shows no signs of ending. He continues along to class, watching his feet, trying to convince himself that he wasn't just abandoned. He takes some comfort in the Birkenstocks Cullen gave him last week, along with orders to dispose of his white sneakers. Gid admires the way they look against the cuff of his khakis. When he first got here, he didn't think there was any way he could achieve the look—rumpled formality is a good description—but he's got to admit he's kind of nailed it. "Definitely," he whispers, feeling soothed.

"Definitely what?"

It's Molly McGarry, bundled against the cold day in a red hooded coat, her hair smooth and flat against her pink cheeks.

Molly repeats, "Definitely what?" Her smile is mischievous. She knows he was talking to himself.

Fine, but there's no way he's admitting to it. "Oh, I was just continuing the conversation I was having with Liam," he says, pointing at Liam as if to prove it.

"What does one talk to Liam about?" Molly asks, laying a con-spiratorial hand on his arm. Gid counts the girls who have touched his bare skin. Danielle, Pilar, Molly, Svetlana, his next-door neigh-bor's cousin from Ukraine, whom he kissed in ninth grade in a garage smelling of cat litter and crowded with cases of diet cola. Five girls in his whole life. Not counting, like, clerks handing him change.

"Liam seems like a freak to me," Molly continues, glancing quickly over her shoulder. Her touch isn't as crazy making as Pi-lar's. Pilar, though, seemed so aware of the fact that she was touch-ing Gid, as if her hand on his arm were a piece of art she was arranging on a wall. Molly's hand is just a hand. Small, with plain nails and a gold ring. When they walk up the steps into Thayer Hall, she removes her hand and puts it on the black iron railing. But it was on his arm for a good long time. And once they are past the railing, she reaches out and touches him again, saying as she does so, "He seems not entirely human."

"Not entirely human like an animal or not entirely human like a space alien?" Gid asks.

Molly presses her lips together and nods. Gideon can tell this is an important distinction for her. He likes it that she understands him, that what he says means something to her. He hasn't been feeling that much lately.

"Space alien all the way. Sure, he's good-looking." She shrugs. "That's probably a matter of fact, not opinion. But I don't, like, fantasize about him."

Gid's ears flare up. He looks around nervously to see if anyone heard this, but everyone around them is moving, rushing, turning off cell phones, and hurriedly reading the last words of their assignments. Is Molly talking about masturbation? My God. Why would you ever tell anyone anything like that? But maybe it's just an expression. And she's still touching his hand, he notices.

There's movement on his left. Mija and Madison pass by. They saw Molly touching him. Couldn't they have just come by a second later? Madison is dressed in prep school couture—high-heeled boots, a belted sweater she probably picked up off the floor but cost what Gid's dad makes in a week, and jeans so low that as one of her long legs swings forward, Gid sees the knot of her hip bone. He notes that actually, Mija's dressed similarly, but that she just looks neat and moderately stylish, and it's the come-on of Madison's long-legged walk that dresses up her look. Madison and Mija have stopped off to the side and are huddled near the window, ostensibly reapplying lip gloss, but watching. This pursuit of Molly is more uncomfortably public than he'd like it to be. He tries to imagine how he and Molly look walking together.

Molly notices the girls. "What's their problem?"

"I don't know if they have a problem," Gideon says. "They're actually pretty nice." He's aware his tone gives away his pride in knowing these girls, understanding what's behind the expensive sweaters and high heels, but it doesn't make him feel any less special.

The first thing he notices upon entering the classroom is Ms. San Video's butt. She's wearing leather pants and writing verbs on the board. The pants are tight, brown, and shiny. He wants to sit down and look at them and talk to Molly later. So he does.

When Liam comes in and spots Ms. San Video's pants, he shoots Gideon a thumbs-up and says, "Oh, yes, I definitely *habla español*!"

Gid smiles and nods, forgetting all about Liam's running off with Devon outside, their excited, exclusive whispering. Even Mija and Madison's attention takes on a new cast. I'm part of things, Gid thinks. I'm in a groove. I'm happy. No study hall tonight—the first Friday of every month is a free night, one of those weird little rules designed to trick you into thinking prep school's really not that bad. Tomorrow's Saturday. Gid has it all planned out, he is going to go to the library, to the basement, where a certain kind of girl who lives in Emerson—the bookish and slightly sexually interesting because of, and not despite, it—is known to study. He will find Molly, making it look, of course, like an accident, and he will talk to her. They will talk for hours. And then . . .

Liam leans over. "Hey. What time are you guys leaving for Fiona Winchester's party?"

"Party?" Gid says, immediately concentrating on his own face, on lifting it, instead of letting it cave with disappointment.

Oh, Gid. For five whole minutes life seemed to be coming together. It's all falling apart now, but didn't you enjoy it?

"Whoa," Liam says. "Well, maybe Nicholas and Cullen didn't tell you about it yet."

Nicholas, maybe. But Cullen. Cullen never shuts up. No. This was withheld. Gid closes his eyes and can't think.

Two minutes before the end of Spanish, Gid mumbles, "*El baño*," and hightails it out of there. He jogs over the granite floors and down the tiled steps and, blowing off a little steam, heaves himself against the heavy door to the outside. It was sunny and clear for about half an hour during class. Then the wind came up again, and now the sky's rapidly clouding over, all the little patches of blue shrinking to nothing. The leaves fall steadily. He sees a figure in white coming right toward him. Gid's a little nearsighted, but even before the form takes shape he knows—that teetering-on-heels walk, that bouncing hair—he is looking at Pilar Benitez-Jones.

Incredible how, as Gid's anticipating total defeat, he's brimming with some kind of stupid happiness. As she gets closer, he sees she's wearing a belted white coat and light tan suede boots. Sort of slut meets sophisticate meets slut, one more time, just in case sophisticate forgot her. Pilar's got sort of twitchy hips. As she gains on Gid, the twitches pick up speed. Just as she's approaching, she puckers up and kisses the air. He stops in his tracks, but she blows past him. She's carrying a weekend bag. "I'm in a hurry," she says, smiling. "See you around."

Gid breaks into a sprint, determined to make it to his room before anyone can see him crumble in a heap of mortification and self-loathing.

Not going to the party was one thing. Not going to a party where Pilar would be—he doesn't know for sure, but he just knows—that was quite another.

He has the room all to himself. With great effort he removes his shoes and, still fully clothed, eases himself into his bed. Absolutely every single person on this campus that he wants to impress will be at this party, laughing, drinking, talking about things he'll never understand. Meanwhile, he will be at this dry brown leaf of a place, loitering outside Molly's dorm.

He pulls the covers over his head as if he could hide from his own shame. Maybe the fact that everyone's going to this party is good. In fact, maybe they didn't invite him because they knew he needed this weekend for the Molly project.

That doesn't work. Gid knows that people either want you around or they don't.

Cullen and Nicholas burst in with energy, and Gideon can feel the cold fresh air come in with them. Over his blazer, Cullen is wearing an orange down jacket patched with duct tape, and Nicholas wears a bright blue scarf. Their robust perfection is humiliating.

"Dude, what are you doing in bed?" Cullen asks.

Gideon mumbles, feigning sleep.

"We're leaving for Fiona Winchester's party in, like, fifteen minutes."

"Have fun," Gideon says glumly. He rolls over on his stomach and tucks his hands under his shoulders. This feels nice. Maybe he can stay in this position all weekend.

"Dumbass!" Cullen grabs a handful of Gid's bedding and whips it off him. "Did you think we were going without you?"

Liam and Devon are waiting for them outside Proctor in the white BMW. Liam's driving. Cullen points to it and nods meaningfully to Gid. "This is *the* car," he says. "This is the car that's going to be yours."

It's a beautiful car. I can see Gideon becoming more beautiful in it.

A few miles from school, Liam stops for gas. As he steps up to the pump with what is very likely his mother's credit card, Gid leans out the window and says, "Hey, you better put the high-test in. I hear any engine pings, and I'm going to be a little upset."

"What the fuck do you care?" Liam snaps, and Gideon is overcome with a happiness unlike any he's ever experienced when Cullen and Nicholas burst out laughing. Their laughter is mean. There is a secret from which Liam is excluded! Gideon is usually nicer than this, but at the moment, he likes the fact that Liam's face is growing red. That he looks wounded and will never admit it. I might be sitting in the middle of the backseat, Gid thinks, but next year, I'm going to be driving. And Liam can put his feet up on the transmission hump. And like it.

vicodin
makes you
love
yourself

The Winchesters' family house—in the hip, artsy, but, make no mistake, thoroughly expensive Cape Cod town of Truro—is a cross between an airplane hangar and the Lila Acheson Wallace wing at the Metropolitan Museum of Art. The furniture, all either beige or black or light mint green, is spare but lush. The art is giant and genuine. The front of the house is private and a little understated, but the back is a wall of thick glass that looks out on the white dunes and choppy blue of the Atlantic. Gid's blown away. Personally, I prefer something that feels like it's actually inhabited by people.

The ocean is right there. We both feel we could touch it.

More incredible, however: There are rock stars here. Real ones. Just hanging out like normal people.

Soccer star Erica, who generally favors T-shirts, is shockingly mod and sexy in a pink-and-purple paisley halter top, giggling, teetering on Jett Injuns guitarist Neils Tolland's bony British knee. Gid's a little more used to—we all are—Madison in suggestive clothing. And here she's wearing a bikini. And chugging champagne. Some of it runs down her chin, and Hal Plimcoat grabs her by her tiny tan waist, buries his neck in her chest, and licks it off. Even Mija is tarted out, for Mija, wearing pants so low-slung they need that special low-slung-pants thong.

Naturally, Gid doesn't know about special low-slung-pants thongs. If I could, I would tell him that when good girls put them on, bad things happen.

Cullen and Nicholas melt into the party, throwing no lifelines. They shake hands with Hal and Neils, then head over to a glass bar in the corner where Yves Mountjoy from the Rutts (Gid and I recognize both of them from MTV2) pours various liquors into a chugging blender. They finally settle in another seating area, where Neils's brother Dennis hovers over a glass-topped coffee table, covered with drugs. "The three Ps," Cullen says approvingly, kneeling down and examining the spread.

"Pills, powder, and pot," Dennis says. He reaches up and engages both Nicholas and Cullen in some kind of elaborate handshake, vaguely rock and roll, vaguely black. "Right on, great to see you cats again." To Gideon's credit, he's annoyed by this, wondering why everyone has to be so cool all the time, and also, whether white people will always have to act like black people to avoid looking like dorks. At the same time, holy shit, Dennis Tolland—a man Gideon has seen in magazines and on television—is friends with his roommates?

As exciting as Gid finds this proximity to stardom, he's wary of the competition. Getting Pilar to pay attention to him is one thing. Getting Pilar to pay attention to him in a sea of rock stars is quite another.

Now Dennis Tolland himself extends a hand to Gid. His clothes are cartoonish, bell-bottom brown polyester pants and a red tie-dyed shirt with a big green collar. His hair is dark and springy. "Hey, man, you must be Gid."

Gid's bowels contract. He shakes Dennis's hand.

"Pull up a chair, have a drink," Dennis says. "And let's start you out with one of these." He hands Gid something large and white. "It releases large amounts of serotonin into your brain all at once. It makes you feel really good."

Gideon is very interested in this. Who wouldn't be?

"I'll take that." Nicholas swoops in. "We have to be prudent about Gid's drug consumption."

"Maybe Gideon should be prudent about my drug consumption instead," Dennis says, cracking a wry smile, crossing his legs, and tossing a motley assortment of tablets onto his tongue.

"Too late for that," Gideon says. Dennis washes everything down with a swig of beer and smiles with appreciation. Gid likes this guy.

There's a loud thump, and Gid turns around to see that Neils, in the process of standing up from the couch, has unceremoniously dumped Erica off his lap and onto the floor.

Dennis sees it too. "Best to get fucked up," he says with a wink.

Gid thinks this is excellent advice and retreats to the empty kitchen. Everything is giant, stainless steel, and shiny. The refrigerator is full of beer and bottles of white wine. He takes a beer. Budweiser. Defensively, Gid thinks he's not so keen on the Rutts. Too loud but not exciting loud. Just loud. But he loves the Jett Injuns. In fact, the lyrics to "Vine Worthy" (yes, it's a Tarzan parable) are written in their thorough and humiliating entirety on one of his notebooks from last year. Thank God he knows enough not to mention this.

Fiona Winchester, barefoot and hostessy in pink satin pajamas, enters the kitchen and gives Gid a surprisingly inviting smile. The back of her pants is totally smooth against her butt. No underwear. Gid stops himself before he gets too excited about this. Whatever she's trying to project, it's not for his benefit. Now Cullen comes in. Okay, that's who it's for.

Cullen reaches out and touches Fiona's back, a quick swirling motion with the back of his hand. And you know what he says?

"Silky." Because it's all he needs. Because he can. Gid notices Cullen noticing the lack of underwear. "See you guys later," Gid says, with a cool nod that he hopes indicates he knows what's going on. As he leaves the room, he hears a snap of elastic and a giggle.

And when he walks back into the living room, there is Pilar, dressed in a brown velvet warm-up suit, lounging in an overstuffed chair. She is casual, perfect. "Hey, Gid," she says, winking. Gideon's relief that she is not sitting on a rock star's lap is, sadly, short-lived when Yves Mountjoy saunters over to her, holding a cocktail shaker, and pours a healthy measure of something appealingly blue-green and frosty into her open mouth. "That's good," she says. "Very good." He pours more in a glass, and she takes it from him with a languid, practiced hand.

"Let's make one for my friend Gid." Pilar waves at Hal, who is manning the blender. After tucking a greasy lock of dark hair behind his ear, he waves back. "Oh, by the way, this is Yves." Yves nods at Gid, who does not say, "I've seen you on TV," or "Why do you guys dress like first-graders with special needs?"—though he would love to.

"You know what," Gid says. "I don't want one of those. I'm just going to drink beer." Pilar pats the seat next to her. Did he win it with his confident refusal? His stick-to-it-iveness to beer? Who knows? He sits.

We can both feel the softness of her butt next to his thigh. He likes it more than I do.

"Tenemos que charlar," Pilar says.

"That means 'to chat,'" Gideon says, excited.

Pilar nods warily. "You Americans, you are so happy to know just one word. I want to tell you that the night when you helped me in the bathroom, it was very nice of you."

"Thanks," Gid says. He contemplates adding, "I live for opportunities to please you," but then, thankfully, Nicholas appears with the white pill. He breaks it in half and hands both halves to Gid. "Wait before taking the second half," he says. "Remember, you're not going to have a better time with more."

"*Hola, Nicolito.*" Pilar exaggerates her accent. "*¿Cómo estás?*"

Nicholas nods. "What's up, Pilar?" He walks away.

"Oh my God." Pilar turns toward Gideon and seizes his chin with her perfectly manicured thumb and index finger. "Why is he always so serious?" Her giant brown eyes look right into Gideon's. If Gid passed out from sheer joy, she would just keep holding his chin, and his head would dangle from her fingertips.

"Nicholas is just like that," Gid says. "He doesn't really mean it." Pilar finally lets go of his chin. Gid busies himself with the pill, puts half of it on his tongue. "What am I taking here, anyway?" he says, trying to talk around the pill, but its rough bottom part, where it's been broken in half, touches the roof of his mouth and then drips onto his tongue. It tastes like bad lemons and dust.

Pilar reaches into his mouth and takes the pill off his tongue. Gid fairly soars on a sense of victory. Pilar knows that there's another half of this pill in his pocket. So she could have looked at that if she wanted, right? This can only mean one thing. She wanted to put her hand in his mouth, which, Gid thinks, can only be fantastic news.

"Vicodin," she says. She opens her mouth, indicating Gid should do the same. She sets the pill back on Gid's tongue, and for a heavenly second, Gid inhales her smell of soap and lotion. He pours a good shot of beer over it and swallows. "It tastes bitter, but trust me, it makes you feel amazing. In fact, I wouldn't mind taking the other half."

After the chin grabbing and reaching into Gid's mouth, Gid hopes wildly that Pilar's going to help herself to Gid's pockets. He shifts a tiny bit, just in case this is her intention. It doesn't seem to be.

Pilar takes the pill with a hefty dose of her blue-green drink.

"Are you guys taking Vicodin?" It's Mija. She's wearing small, flattish white shoes. They're ugly. Gid's never been to Holland, or even to Europe, but he's right to associate her clothing problems with her nationality.

"Tell him how it's going to feel," Pilar encourages.

Mija jams her hands in her pockets and thinks. "Well, first you're going to feel a little light. And then you're going to feel like you really, really like everyone."

He liked Dennis's general promise of feeling good, but this makes him nervous. Liking Pilar more than he already does could lead to embarrassing confessions. Maybe this isn't a good idea. The memory of the pill is still in his throat. He has time to stop this. In eighth-grade health, they were forced to watch a film strip on bulimia, and Gid's pretty sure he remembers how to make yourself puke. He saw a bathroom near the kitchen with a nice, solid, soundproof door. He gets up.

"No," Pilar coos, "don't go anywhere. You were making me warm!"

Wow. Gid sits back down.

"More important," Mija adds, "it makes you feel like you really, really like yourself."

Now, this is something he can get behind. Gid settles into the seat, inching even closer to Pilar than he was before.

"I thought you would like that," Pilar says, pursing her lips seductively.

The drug is working on her! Gid thinks.

Or Gid is. Probably a combination of both. She seems to be softening up, like butter left out.

"You know, I wonder about your relationship with Cullen and Nicholas," Pilar says. "The three of you have a secret."

"No secrets," Gid says, feeling as easy as his tone. "I mean, aside from the usual."

"What is usual between guys?" Pilar asks. "You're part of the, how do you say, sewing circle? What do you think of yourself, you, Cullen, Nicholas . . . the three amigos?"

But Gid's not listening. He's watching—and who can blame him?—Cullen and the no-underweared Fiona Winchester making out on the couch.

Fiona's leg lifts up in the air and wraps itself around Cullen's waist. Cullen picks her up, walks across the room kissing her, and carries her up the stairs. "Jesus," Gid says.

Pilar says, "If Fiona falls for him that easily, then, you know, you really can't blame him." No softie, that Pilar.

I can't say I feel sorry for Fiona, but I don't think she's an idiot for believing Cullen really likes her. Why shouldn't she? She's a beautiful girl. She's smart. Her parents have a fantastic collection of modern art. And up until now, most of the information she's received about herself has proved to be more or less true. How's she supposed to know that the lying starts now, with Cullen McKay and his great smile and his love of all things silky?

Pilar knocks back the rest of her drink and saunters to the bar. Gid observes Liam, Devon, Hal, and Nicholas as they all watch her. She's sitting with me, Gideon wants to yell. Pilar says something to Devon Shine, and he blushes. The kitchen door swings open and Dennis Tolland appears, holding a playing card over his head. "Yes," he shouts. Pilar walks by him and smiles. "I'm winning at poker," Dennis says. "Do you feel lucky tonight?" Pilar keeps moving. Dennis stares at her while she walks away, mouthing the word *lovely* before ducking into the kitchen again.

Pilar returns. "What's going on at the bar?" Gid asks. They are snuggled into the chair now.

"Oh, everyone's getting wasted and talking a lot of shit. Nicholas isn't saying a word. Or drinking." They look over. Everyone nurses cocktails; Nicholas has his bottle of water.

"That's why I think it's so weird that you hang out together,"

Pilar says. "Cullen is a schemer. Nicholas is quiet and sort of mean. And then you, you are just, you know, chatty and nice." Pilar shrugs. "I see you talking to Molly McGarry sometimes," she says. Gid looks around to see if anyone else heard. There's no one even remotely close to them who's not talking frenetically or woozily glass-eyed.

"She's a friend," Gid says, watching her face. She seems to accept this. The light on her cheeks is fucking poetic to him, so much so that even as he senses himself careening toward audacity, he is powerless to stop himself. "It's so loud here I can't think," he says. "Let's go upstairs."

He watches her face as she considers this, more terrified than he's ever been in his life. Is she smiling? And if so, is it out of happiness, or derision? "Let me go up first," she says. "Then we won't have to answer any questions."

The moment is so incredible Gid can't quite occupy it. He's never in his life even dreamed of being this thrilled. He watches Pilar hustle up the stairs, thinking, Those feet, those legs, that butt, that hair, are all going upstairs because of me! He guesses he should wait about five minutes and wonders how he will make it. Madison, Erica, and Mija are all huddled on a couch in the corner, whispering. Erica looks sad but hopeful; Mija, sympathetic but wary; and Madison—ubiquitous bottle of wine at her side, her pretty face wild-eyed and pink—she just looks drunk. The guys are a roving pack of blender duty and various loud arguments about guitars, guitar players, marijuana quality, and the relative appeal of various tropical vacation destinations.

Gid decides to bide some time in the kitchen. A little side trip, to throw everyone off the scent, then upstairs. Madison bounces in behind him. "Sorry," she says. "Girl crisis." Hal grabs Madison's arm, pulls her roughly in, and kisses her. Madison giggles. Gid notes that Hal Plimcoat doesn't really have a chin, and that his front teeth, which are the size and shape of Chiclets, are concave, almost at right angles. The stretchy, stripey little-kid clothes don't help. No wonder Madison wanted to have sex with me, he thinks; I'm way hotter than Hal Plimcoat.

Gid, let's not forget that Hal has something very important called extreme sexual confidence. And also, if you tried to grab a girl the way Hal just grabbed Madison, you'd probably wind up falling over.

Dennis, with a sort of wobbly hand, offers him a cigarette. "I don't smoke," Gid says. "I run." Laying claim to his athleticism makes him puff out his chest. Outside, the BMW waits. But not for me, Gid thinks. That's okay. Pilar, he thinks, is better than the BMW.

"That so?" Hal Plimcoat says. "I run too."

Gid has never been to England and wonders what running is like there. He pictures Hal padding slowly around a muddy field dressed in an old suit, smoking, with waterfowl scattering in his wake.

"You don't really run. You sort of shuffle along," Madison says, encouraging Gideon's vision.

Hal shrugs and taps an ash. "That's right," he says. "Jog. Didn't say I sprinted like bloody *Chariots of Fire,* did I?"

Madison ignores this. "We're playing strip Scrabble."

Gid asks how this works and is told that the high scorer at the end of every round has to take off his clothes. "So, like, see, you get punished for being smart," Dennis says. "Like in the real world."

Gid's dad always says this. It's pretty banal, right? Less than you'd expect from a British rock star.

"Or," Madison says, "in my case, I get to show off my brains and my tits."

Gid's trying to decide if Madison is smart in an idiotic way or idiotic in a sort of smart way. She raises one of her eyebrows. "So, Gid. You looking for your roommates? Don't quite know where Nicholas is, though I have a good idea. I think Cullen and Fiona are taking a walk on the beach."

"Actually, they're taking a walk upstairs," Gid says, happy to be in the know.

At this, Dennis stands. He's wearing a leather cap, several turquoise necklaces, and a pair of Bruce Reynolds-y sunglasses. And that's it. No one—no one except Gid, that is—blinks as he crosses the room and peers out into the living room. Cullen and Fiona are indeed nowhere to be seen. Mija's lying on the couch, thumbing through a coffee-table book on Helmut Newton, and Yves is passed out on the floor, a red towel under his head.

Dennis sits back down and shakes his head at Hal. "That Cullen. Can you imagine a bloke like that, not even seventeen, doesn't even try with girls, but gets it all."

Neils nods. "When I was in high school, girls threw things at me."

Everyone goes back to the game except for Dennis, who stands up again and, to Gid's delight and surprise, walks over to Gid. He drapes an arm heavily tattooed with Asian writing over Gid's shoulder. "You like that Pilar, don't you?" He nods, not waiting for a response. "I think she's perfect for you."

Gid looks nervously over his shoulder.

"No one's listening, kid, this is about you," Dennis says. "Look, your buddy Cullen, I love that dude, but you've got soul. I'm serious. Go put it to work."

upstairs

As Gideon ascends the back stairway of the Winchester summer home—in fast pursuit of the future so optimistically promised by Dennis Tolland—the Vicodin turns to molten silver. The molten silver decants itself into a deep pool, and Gideon tells himself, Pilar digs me. By the time he's stepped inside this pool for a long, hot soak, he's arrived at, Why wouldn't she? I'm awesome.

Through the closed windows Gideon can hear the ocean crashing. To the left is a door, and then a long hallway that, Gideon guesses, leads to the master bedroom. He walks down the narrow, high-ceiling hall, past a wall covered with photos: Fiona on a horse, Fiona climbing a hill, Fiona in a bathing suit, her eyes as bright as the sea around her. Gideon's parents each have a few pictures of him, but they're all posed, impersonal—not, he thinks sadly, unlike his attitude toward both of them.

At the end of the hall, there's another, smaller hall off to the left, and a door, open about an inch. Gid senses this is the place. He opens the door into an alcove. Straight ahead he sees the foot of the bed, and Pilar's bare, manicured feet, crossed demurely over each other, and the wide cuffs of her velvety brown sweat suit. Gid moves forward, still floating on Vicodin and Dennis's encouragement.

Pilar's hair is laid out in a silky rope on the pillow. (I know it's really gay to call hair silky, but her hair is silky, okay?) A wineglass, half full and balanced on her stomach, throws red shadows on the far wall. She smiles as if she were expecting him. "Come in." She moves over. So he's supposed to lie down, next to her. "What are you doing up here?" she asks playfully.

She's a great flirt. I am jealous.

Gid can feel Pilar's expectant smile in the dark. "Well, I was just in the hallway, looking at photos of Fiona, and I was thinking about only children. I'm an only child, you know."

Pilar smiles. "I know. You told me that the first day I met you."

The fact that he has a life inside of Pilar's mind, even a small one, deepens his bliss. I wonder how he would feel about his situation with me. Sure, everyone wants to be listened to, to be understood, but perhaps not this well.

"I mean, obviously, she looks perfect and pretty in all those photos."

Gid lies down. Then he sits up again, takes his shoes off, and lies down again.

"You think Fiona's pretty?" Girls are really unbelievable! This is so not the point of the story, but of course Pilar can't resist.

"Of course," he says. "I don't think Fiona's prettiness is up for debate. Anyway, moving along [Good for you, Gid, not to indulge Pilar in this], Fiona just looks so . . . adored. In my photos, I look . . . well, I'm just there. Taking up space. Anyway, it's clear Fiona's parents see her, their only child, as their crowning achievement. I am just the weird remnant of a big mistake."

"That is so depressing!" Pilar exclaims.

"Is it?" Gid asks. He's thinking that maybe it's not, that if your parents were obsessed with you, they would never leave you alone. Being left alone is not that bad. Fiona Winchester's mother probably calls her three times a day. "Being a weird remnant is kind of fun," Gid says.

Then the most amazing thing in the world happens. Pilar rolls over so she is facing him. Gid rolls over toward her too. Their bodies make the exact same shape, knees bent up, hands folded and pressed against their chests. Where their kneecaps and elbows almost touch Gid can feel heat, not just from her but between them.

Pilar giggles. "I feel like we're stowaways on a ship," she says. "Close your eyes."

Gid closes his eyes. He opens them to see if Pilar's are closed. They are. He closes them again and listens to the waves breaking outside. He peeks again. Pilar's eyes are still closed, and she's smiling.

"So," Pilar says. "Gee-de-on. Do you want to know what else I was thinking?"

This is abrupt but exciting. Gid's eyes fly open. "Sure, I want to know."

Pilar props herself up on one elbow and with her free hand traces invisible patterns on the white bedspread. She looks exactly like a wife talking to her husband in a movie, in the part where she gives him levelheaded, loving counsel and says things like, "I think you'll be a great father," or "Don't worry about the election. Worry about the people. The election will come." Gid imagines himself running for office. He's wearing a blue suit and a red tie. At the end of the day, Pilar serves him a sandwich and some chips.

"Pilar," Gid says, making no effort to hide the desperation in his voice. "Do you ever think that we could go out?"

She laughs. Big. Loud. Mocking. Weirdly, his first impulse is annoyance: A smaller laugh would have been sufficient for making her point. What should he do now? Roll over in the other direction? Too petulant. Argue? Creepy. Even stalkerish. He decides not to do anything. If he's quiet long enough, maybe she'll say something that makes him feel better.

"Actually, I have thought about it."

Gideon had hardly been expecting that!

Pilar is so close to him that he can see the reflection of the Winchesters' ABC Carpet & Home sconces in her eyes. He reaches out with a finger and strokes her shoulder. Pilar doesn't move away, but she doesn't move toward him. The Vicodin has softened his mind but strengthened his resolve. His hands move toward her face, and his mouth to her lips. He gets very, very close—close enough that as she exhales he can almost taste that blue-green blender drink.

She doesn't exactly push him away. Her eyes lower just a little, almost demurely, and she puts her hands on his wrists and brings them down so she's holding them near her waist. "Let's not," she whispers. "It's not that . . ."

"Not that what?"

Pilar shakes her head. Gid's heart is beating so fast he's afraid she can hear it. "We can sleep like this, though," she says, sliding her hands down from his wrists and wrapping his fingers in hers.

Gid's heart slows down, still excited, and relieved not to be totally rebuffed. The Vicodin tells him that he is loved.

In the silence that follows—a good silence, thinks Gid, who, as a child of divorce, really knows his silences—he dares to let his eyes take her in. Yes, Pilar is the most incredibly gorgeous thing he's ever seen in his entire life. He wasn't making it up. He resolves then and there that he will make getting her to be his girlfriend the most serious priority of his life. Well, he will try to do well in school and so forth. But other than that, it's all about Pilar. Which is fine. It might take a long time. He might have to actually become a state senator or whatever before he can get her, but that's okay. Out the window, the sky and sea are both black; one shines, the other stretches on, dark, studded with diamond-hard stars. I have nothing but time, Gid thinks. And, incredibly, Pilar, drifting toward sleep, inches closer to him, as if, Gideon reasons, her body would allow her things her mind would not. Basking in this possibility and the incredible warmth coming off Pilar Benitez-Jones's elbows and knees, he falls asleep.

And I, wherever I am, fall asleep too.

bonding

Late the next morning, driving back to school, Gideon slouches in the backseat as a stern Nicholas drives and a carefree Cullen chain-smokes, alternating between joints and cigarettes. A small but concentrated ache presses against the top of Gid's head, but that's nothing compared to his depression. When he woke up, Pilar was gone and every remnant of her—wineglass, cute little slip-on athletic shoes, shiny hair clip—was gone too. The tyranny of her absence, he thinks, was almost not worth the magic of her presence. But that can't be all of it. He feels scraped out, utterly hollow. The yellowed nowhere of southeastern Massachusetts slips by, a deserted Ames's, a row of split-level vinyl-sided houses, then a Cumberland Farms where guys in quilted flannel shirts with mullets blow on cups of coffee.

In short, God's country.

"I'm depressed," Gideon says.

"It's the Vicodin, dude," Cullen says. "It uses up all the serotonin, the stuff in your brain that makes you feel happy and good about yourself, and then the next day, you don't have any left."

Someone might have told me that *before* I took the thing, Gid thinks bitterly.

I think someone did. I think he was high when they said it.

But the reason Gid's really mad is that when Cullen came up to the room where he knew that he'd slept with Pilar, he didn't ask him a single question. He wasn't at all excited for Gid. It was just like he assumed nothing happened. All he said was, "Get your stuff. And don't talk in the car. Nicholas slept with Erica by accident, and he's in a bad mood."

How do you sleep with someone by accident? Of course this annoyed Gid too. Here he is, trying to sleep with people on purpose, and well . . . oh . . . never mind.

They stop so Nicholas can use the bathroom at a Shell station. Gid decides to give Cullen one more chance to ask him a question. "Pretty amazing house," Gid says. "Lots of space. Totally quiet last night considering . . . all the people that were there."

Not a word.

Gid decides he can either get apeshit mad or become his own Pilar cheerleader.

Pilar. Pilar. Pilar! She did sit for a long time with her butt pressed up against him. She did share with him a strong, mind-altering prescription drug. She did spend the night next to him. These thoughts are velvety smooth and soothing and beautiful. He curls up to them and falls asleep.

He dreams that he and Pilar are swimming in the ocean outside the Winchesters' house. He has the sense, in this dream, that the house belongs to them, that it is the future, that they are adults, that they are rich but playful. Pilar whoops and laughs and pelts him with colorful shells. They're having a great time until one of the shells turns out to be a big gray rock. It cuts his head. He bleeds. Pilar shrugs and slips into the surf.

When he wakes up, the car has stopped. Out the window, he can see the square top and spindly tower of the Prudential Building. He smells pot. Cullen sits in the driver's seat now, and he passes a lit joint to Nicholas. "It's not going to be as weird as you think," Cullen is saying to Nicholas. "You shouldn't feel so guilty about girls. They don't do anything they don't want to do. And they're not as innocent as you think, okay?"

"Okay," Nicholas says, his voice surprisingly childlike.

Nicholas's tone surprises Gid; it surprises me too. Even more surprising to Gid is Cullen's consoling and advising Nicholas. Gid feels himself start to soften, just a little. Cullen truly seems to want Nicholas to feel better. And Nicholas truly seems to be hanging on Cullen's assurances. A guy like Cullen must be a great comfort to a guy like Nicholas. As much as Nicholas prides himself on being in control, Cullen reminds him that he might still survive if he lost it.

Up to the right, Gid sees an apartment window decorated for Halloween, with orange and black ribbons sprayed with some sort of synthetic, cobwebby stuff. He groans. Isn't September 27 a little early for Halloween decorations? "I can't believe I have to go back to school and get some girl to fall in love with me, even though I'm in love with some other girl," he says.

Cullen and Nicholas turn around. Their faces light up when they see Gideon's awake.

"Did you guys go buy pot while I was asleep?" Gid asks. "Because this car smells like pot really seriously. I mean, I know you guys are smoking it, but it also smells like we're growing pot in the car."

Cullen hangs over the seat and cups Gid's face in his hand, the way Pilar did last night. He reaches into the pocket behind his seat, producing a baggie bulging with marijuana. "This," he says, "awesome pot. We just got from Mickey's brother at B.U."

He puts the pot back. "And what you've got coming is some of that"—he hands Gid the lit joint—"and some guidance."

Gid accepts the joint and puffs, listening.

Cullen continues, "The time has come to go to the place where men who have lost their way can find it in the wisdom of men who have gone before them."

"What?" Gid asks. "Are we going to a museum?"

"No, stupid," Cullen says. "And let me assure you that I mean 'stupid' in the nicest possible way. We're going to a bar."

They walk across a mostly empty parking lot full of sad-looking cars, the undercarriages rotted brown with salt and rust, most of the back windows decorated with Patriot and Red Sox decals. Cullen leads them through the metal door of a squat, brick, industrial-looking building. There's no sign on it, but a small faux brass plaque in the brick vestibule reads DEMPSEY'S TAVERN: SERVING THE COMMUNITY SINCE LAST TUESDAY.

The bartender, a broad-faced, fortyish Irish guy, comes toward them with such a swagger that even as he moves forward the upper part of his body still seems to be moving backward. He looks Cullen straight in the eye and asks, "How old are you?"

Cullen takes a bill out of his wallet. On the brown Formica bar top is a coffee can bearing a hand-lettered sign: TWENTY-SIX PLUS SIX EQUALS ONE. (I know what this is! It's about Southern Ireland and Northern Ireland becoming united.) In the corner of the sign is a little shamrock. Cullen stuffs the bill into the can. "I don't know how old these guys are," he says, "but today is my one hundredth birthday."

The man grimaces. He reminds Gid of Cockweed, except that where Cockweed is the kind of guy who shakes with rage, this guy looks like he'd snap you in two with one hand and pour a shot with the other. "Go sit over there. And try not to be too loud."

Gid's dad doesn't drink. He's in AA because he used to drink about seventeen giant Coors Lights a day and do cocaine. (Gid doesn't know about the cocaine thing, but I do, because Gid knows somewhere in his mind about it, and I am a lot better at sifting through that stuff than he is. Another thing Gid doesn't know: Pilar was late to school partly because of her sister's wedding, but mostly because she had to fly to London to be fitted for a custom pair of Costume Nacional boots.) As far as the bar, Gid likes being here. There are no windows. The door is upholstered in red vinyl and so are the booths along the wall. Gid feels a million miles away from everything—almost as wonderful as being up in that room with Pilar. Up in the far corner is a smallish color TV broadcasting a Red Sox game. Ten customers, all well over fifty, contently drink and watch the Sox win. If any of them give a shit about the three prep school kids settling into the corner booth, they don't say so.

Nicholas goes off to get them drinks. Cullen leans in and looks right into Gid's eyes. "I knew you wouldn't nail Pilar," Cullen says. "That's why I didn't say anything."

So Cullen's not completely clueless. He knew that was bugging Gid.

"I know you wouldn't let me down. I know that even with Nicholas pulling his little Vicodin trick on you, you'd stay cool."

"Trick?" Gideon says. "I don't understand."

Cullen leans back on his arms, surveying the bar as if it were his hangout and he weren't five years underage. "Yeah, trick. He thought you and Pilar, all mellowed out, all groovy, would get it on. I knew you'd resist."

They thought he resisted?

Nicholas walks up. "You have to admit it was a pretty good idea," he says, setting down three pints of black beer. The glasses say *Guinness*. So Nicholas is drinking too. "I mean, I deserve some credit."

"Dude, when it comes to you, I am Señor Credit," Cullen says.

"I always say you are smarter than me. You're just not as lucky. I know a thoroughbred when I see one." Cullen takes Gid's arm and raises it over his head. "My man."

They thought he resisted?

This outpouring of support and confidence from Cullen about Pilar—the idea that Gid didn't have sex with Pilar was because he was behaving himself for the bet—should Gid actually believe it? Did Cullen actually think Gideon had dictated the terms of how things with Pilar had gone, or rather, not gone? Or was he pulling a self-serving flattery thing?

Fuck it. He feels comfortable enough to ask some questions. "So," Gid begins, "I just want to get your . . . input on something. There's the whole bet thing with Molly, right? But then what about . . . I really like Pilar a lot. And I know I have to put all this energy into Molly, but it's kind of hard to commit to it when . . . you know. Pilar."

Nicholas snorts. Cullen shakes his head. "I'm losing you," he says.

Nicholas, who generally gets things about an hour before Cullen does, laughs and says, "When you do get it, you're not going to believe it."

It's difficult for Gid to proceed in light of this comment, but he manages.

"Because," Gideon says, "once I have sex with Molly, I'll be going out with her, for a while, and . . ."

Cullen looks at Nicholas, sharing his pain. Then he shakes his head at Gid.

"Why?" says Cullen.

"Well, because," Gid says. He feels like he's being asked to explain why you get wet after jumping into a lake. Across the room, the old-timers shout, raising their arms weakly over their heads. The Red Sox scored. Wonderful. Gid sighs and goes on. "You have to, like, work up to the whole thing, and you know, get the girl to like you, and then, you know, after you do it, you can't just be like, 'Oh, I lied.'"

Cullen smacks Gid's head with his hand. "You don't have to say that you lied. You just say you're a guy."

"Okay," Gid says, like that all makes sense to him. Shit, he thinks. I can't do that. I mean, I guess I will, but I'm not looking forward to it.

Cullen must sense Gid's lack of caddish resolve, because he gets up, places his hands squarely on Gid's shoulders, and focuses on him the full force of his winning personality. It's truly overwhelming. Gid takes in the light in Cullen's eyes, the glint in his smile, and the glow of his skin. He feels taken care of, adored, even though he knows deep down it's partly an illusion. "My friend," Cullen says, "how would you like to know the terms of the bet?"

"It could be a great relief to you," Nicholas says. "Because if you thought you were the only one putting yourself on the line and—"

"You're not!" Cullen interrupts.

"Right. And if you know a little more about what's at stake," Nicholas adds, "well, maybe you won't think we're such total assholes."

"I would like to know," says Gideon. "But I'm probably not going to stop thinking that you're assholes."

They laugh. The tide is changing here. The love grows. Almost makes you think male bonding is really sweet and innocent. Ha.

Shots are purchased. Cullen and Gid drain the shots. "Okay," Cullen says. "If I win, I get to have sex with Nicholas's sister." He nods at Nicholas.

"If I win," Nicholas says, "Cullen has to go out with one girl for an entire year. And she has to go to our school, so that he has to see her every day. He can't cheat. If she breaks up with him for any reason, he has to find another girl and start again. At day one."

The terms of the bet—which involve Cullen's having sex and Nicholas essentially only bearing witness—are of course painfully homoerotic. Of course, this is prep school. So where's the big shock there?

"We're not just talking school year either," Cullen says. "An entire calendar year. Which means behaving in the summer—the season in which I'm accustomed to doing my best work."

Gid doesn't know what to say. He's in shock. He's flattered that the stakes of the bet are so high.

Cullen and Nicholas nod gravely.

Totally unaware that I know they are so incredibly gay.

Cullen leans across the table. "We're telling you this so you realize that this whole thing . . . it's all a game. I mean, the whole thing is so crazy, how can we not make a game out of it? Girls get caught up in the moment in their way—romance, love, whatever—and you get caught up in the moment in your way. With sex."

"How? How do we get caught up in sex?"

Cullen raises an eyebrow. "Because you're fucking? Girls get caught up in the love part, and we just get caught up in the thing itself. And the game part, the bet, and then, getting back to what you were calling lying and what I would just call being a guy, well, it's just part of how guys and girls just do this whole *thing*."

"Oh, right. Okay." Poor Gid thought he was about to get some useful advice. Maybe next time. At least I find Cullen and his occasional philosophical sidetracks fascinating.

"Anyway," Cullen says, "I may have said some things to Fiona I won't mean forever . . ."

What an incredible turn of phrase to get around the word *lie*!

He continues, "But Fiona's going to be *fine*. Erica's going to be *fine*. Honestly, and I really mean this, we are preparing them for life. I mean, in a way, a girl meets a guy like you, and she could actually go through the rest of her life thinking guys are sweet and caring and nice. And what kind of good is that going to do them?"

You know, in a really disgusting, morally bankrupt way, Cullen's got a point.

And maybe it's just the weird stupid clarity of two Guinnesses and a shot of whiskey gorgeously killing his Vicodin hangover, but it's all making incredible sense to Gideon.

On the walk back to the car, more doctrine on the subject of girls is drilled into Gideon's head. It's not about a girl; it's about girls. You don't worry about one specific girl, because there are always more. Molly can just be part of a master plan, which involves putting off Pilar, and then having sex with her. And maybe he could even have sex with both of them. "Remember how you refused to fool around with Mija, and immediately, Madison was on your jock?" Cullen points out. "When you start having girls hit on you and you turn them down, or better, when other girls see that you have sex with other girls and then blow them off, you totally increase your chances of being able to get anyone you want. Dig?"

Gideon decides Cullen is snowing him a little. For sure. Cullen makes it sound as if Mija had been really into him. And Madison, well, wanting to have sex with Gid so she could show a video of it to her boyfriend, that's a far cry from being on his jock. He's going to have to talk to someone about this.

"I would like to say something about Pilar, if you're ready to hear it," Cullen says.

"Yes," Gid says. "Of course." This is his dream. He wishes she were all they talked about. Anything to make it feel, even if it's only in his mind, that she is part of his life.

"I can see why you're so into her. She's really smart, but she totally has the body of a stupid person," Nicholas says.

Cullen nods. "It's a lethal combination."

The campus they pull into is the campus of Gid's daydreams, cozily dark, yellow lights twinkling in the dorms, fresh-faced students bundled in fall layers just starting to trickle from their studies to dinner. Among them, coming up the campus road three abreast, just as they did on Gid's very first day of school, are Molly Mc-Garry, Edie Bell, and Marcy Proctor.

Gid spots them first. Molly's wearing a blue pea coat and a black wool hat, with her hair tucked up underneath it. Her head is bowed with an air of scholarly duty. I'm jealous of her, Gid thinks, surprised. She looks so self-contained, so unconcerned with anything but her own thoughts. He closes his eyes and intones a short, fervent prayer that Cullen and Nicholas won't see her.

But Cullen's eyes light up. "Ho, ho! What have we here!"

Nicholas looks out the window and nods. "You should probably talk to her," he says.

Gid wants to say something about how now doesn't seem like the right time, but it seems even less like the right time to say that. Nicholas slows down.

Edie, her giant saucer eyes framed by lank hair, stares at the ground. Bright, cheerful, direct, Marcy says "Hello" and "How are you?" perhaps a little too friendly, probably blushing at Cullen's interest, however indirect. Molly looks suspicious. Not only that, she walks right up to the car, leans down, and sniffs. She sniffs again. Gideon looks down her shirt. She's wearing a white bra. Padded? He can't tell.

"Hi, Molly," says Gideon. What should he say next? How was your weekend? How are you? What's going on? He's weighing his options when Molly speaks up.

"Your car smells like pot," Molly says. For a split second, Gideon feels proud of himself. Attractively outlawish. Though there's nothing in her tone to suggest she's impressed. Girls have to be impressed with you, Gid knows, in order to have sex with you, but you can't try to impress them. Cullen and Nicholas are sort of laughing. Not too hard. Not denying anything, not admitting. Gid imagines he should laugh too. He's about to start when, a hundred yards or so up the road, he sees a figure coming toward them. The figure is tall, with a serious, adult gait.

Marcy notices the figure at the same time. "Oh, God!" she says. She smoothes her blonde hair with a flat hand, and, grabbing the strap of Edie's ubiquitous book bag, takes off with her.

"Oh, great," Nicholas says. He squints up the road. They all do. There's definitely someone coming, a large person.

"Holy shit," Cullen says. "Captain Cockweed."

The figure is still pretty far away, but when he raises his hand as if he wants to talk to them, no one misses it. Now they can't just take off. It would look weird. It would look like they had pot.

"Your car stinks," Molly says matter-of-factly. "I mean, I wouldn't be surprised if he could smell it from up there. Not that he would ever put two and two together and suspect a nice group of boys like you." Her smile blazes with sarcasm. But when she turns to look at Gid, her face softens into concern. Maybe she's affected by the terror in his eyes. Maybe it's just a burst of altruism, or one of those weird sensations that seemingly comes from nowhere that makes you want the next minute of your life to be really, really exciting.

"Give it to me," Molly says. "Hurry up."

Gid unzips the compartment. Now the smell is stronger, so dense it almost seems to have weight and texture. How could they not have noticed it before? "Hurry up," Molly says, "before he can see who I am." But before he can hand it to her, Molly reaches into the car and grabs it from him with considerable force. The momentum makes her stumble back a few feet, but then she pivots and takes off running through the dark patch of the quad.

Gid's heart beats in his chest and his throat. His stomach tingles. Gid can vaguely make out Molly racing toward the deeper shadows alongside the classroom buildings at the top of the hill. Mr. Cavanaugh must be able to see something too. As he walks toward the car, swiftly now, he keeps glancing up that way, as if he isn't sure what to track. He approaches the window and motions for them to put it down.

"Can't we refuse?" Gid whispers. "What about our rights?"

Nicholas rolls his eyes and starts tucking his shirt into his pants. "You douche bag," he says. "We're in prep school. We don't have any rights."

pork
butt

Dr. Frye, the headmaster, is at a chamber music concert in Brookline. So Cockweed left them in the care of his wife, Mrs. Frye. For two hours, Gideon, Cullen, and Nicholas have been sitting at the foot of a large wooden antique dining table covered with dried flower cuttings, watching her putter about and braise a roast. Her kitchen is wood-paneled, and copper pots and baskets of garlic and tomatoes hang from hooks on the low ceiling. "Pork butt is such an excellent cut," she says. She's very breezy considering how much trouble they're in. But maybe she's just British and batty and consumed with her pork butt. "Inexpensive, yet succulent," she continues as she shuts the oven with a satisfied smile.

She's watching over them like a mother hen. There's nothing prison guard-y in her manner, but it's kind of clear that she's not going anywhere. So neither are they.

She opens a sizable bottle of white wine and pours some over a tall glass of ice.

"Jesus," Gid whispers to Cullen. "It's not fucking Sprite."

"Hey," Cullen whispers back, "I got a question for you."

Gid nods gravely.

Cullen narrows his eyes and makes his face very serious. "If there's a God," he says, "then why does my anus itch?"

They laugh the laughter of the condemned.

Mrs. Frye dumps her first glass of white wine into her mouth and immediately refills it. She adjusts her bun with a hairpin, dries a blue glass vase, and sets it down on the table. "Feel free to try your hand at arranging some of those ranunculus, roses, and lavender," she says. She cocks her head at Gideon, and her loose bun tips over to the side of her head. "You're new, aren't you?" she asks.

The telephone rings. It's the only vaguely modern thing in the house, and its space-age alert sound is sort of a surprise.

"Excuse me!" Mrs. Frye cries out and whips the phone off the wall with a flourish. "Oh hello, dear," she says. "Yes. Yes, they're here, awaiting your judgment. Nicholas Westerbeck, Cullen McKay, and . . . I'm sorry, young man, I don't know your name. Funny, I know how you like your tea, but I don't know your name." She laughs, again chugging her wine down to the ice cubes.

Gid—it is about time—realizes at this moment that she is insane. "Gideon Rayburn," he says.

"Gideon Rayburn," she repeats. She winks at him. "You got the story from Gene, then?" Gene is Captain Cockweed's real name. Not surprising. She cradles the receiver under her chin and fiddles with her hair with both hands, producing several pins. She puts one of them back in, tucks the rest into her mouth, and speaks over them. "Certainly. Certainly. So you're going to fix the tire and then be over. I will call him, yes, by all means get off the phone if you're running out . . . Whoop!" She hangs up and sets her hands on her hips. "Lost him."

She dials. "Hello," she says. "This is Mrs. Frye. Just fine. A little excitement, indeed. Anyway, the doctor wanted me to tell you he'll be there in about forty-five minutes? All right. Good-bye." Mrs. Frye's brown eyes hover above them, the whites round and glassy like boiled eggs. Gid's insides pulsate.

"Well, boys," she says, "the headmaster and commander will be back in an hour." She checks an old wall clock that makes hideously hollow and ominous ticking noises. "I'm going to go watch my program, and you . . . are going to sit here." She drapes her apron over the cabinet door and, grabbing her tumbler and the bottle, walks out. They hear the stairs creak and a door shut.

"I can't believe there's a television in this house," Cullen says. "I feel like we're in Colonial Williamsburg."

Nicholas is on his feet. He picks up the phone and hits REDIAL. He taps his foot. "Come on, come on," he mutters. Then his eyes light up. "A machine." Cullen rushes over to hear and Gideon, having no idea at all what's going on, does the same. Nicholas holds out the phone so they can all hear the message. "Hello, this is the constable. Leave a message or, if this is an emergency . . ."

"I knew it," he says, hanging up. "The constable."

"Who is the constable?" Gid asks. It doesn't sound like anyone good.

"The constable," Cullen says, "is a town policeman. A real old-school kind of guy. Anyway, when drug stuff goes down here, they call him. He shows up, with this dog that he's got. And they walk around the dorms. And they find it. You better believe they find it."

"What kind of dog is it?" Gid asks.

"What kind of dog? Who cares what kind of dog it is?"

"I think it's a yellow Lab," Nicholas says.

A yellow Lab? A special, drug-smelling golden Lab? God, I love New England!

Cullen blows air out of his lips, a sort of defeated half-snort. Nicholas paces a little, hoists his foot onto a window ledge, stretches a hamstring, then paces some more. He opens the refrigerator again. He takes out a grape and eats it.

"So," Nicholas continues, "here's what's going to happen." He's now removed the entire bowl of grapes from the refrigerator and is sitting cross-legged on the headmaster's kitchen floor, eating them one by one. "The constable will get here. Molly McGarry, who has no idea that anything is going on, and has more than likely hidden the pot in her dresser or under her bed or some other incredibly obvious place, gets caught with it, and et cetera, et cetera, et cetera. I mean, you know, if it comes to that, we won't let her hang, but she'll get in trouble too."

"No, that can't happen," Gid says. "One of us has to go find her. I can't let Molly go back to Buffalo."

"If Molly gets kicked out and you don't," Cullen says, "we can fix the bet."

Oh my God! Evil!

Gid is standing up, putting on his coat.

At this moment, Mrs. Frye pops in, shuffling in sheepskin slippers. "Just checking in on my friend," she says. She bustles around the oven with a baster, poking the pork butt. "That's fine," she says, and pads back upstairs.

Gid zips his coat and, rather nerdily, checks his shoelaces.

"You can't go anywhere," Nicholas hisses. "She'll be back."

"We're all going back home, courtesy of the constable," Cullen says. He lies down on the floor and rests his feet on the oven door handle. "This is surprisingly comfortable," he says.

But Gideon's not ready to give up. The outlaw spirit starts to burn in his chest. "Maybe you won't mind going home," he says to Cullen. "You'll have your own car that you'll be driving to a posh day school full of new, naive girls. But if you knew what I was going home to, well, you would know that I would do anything to keep that from happening."

Cullen and Nicholas are certainly surprised by Gideon's bravery in the face of danger, prep school style. I, for one, always knew he had it in him.

impulsive
gid

Gid figures the dining hall is the best place to start. He makes his way there in what he hopes is a stealthy manner, low to the ground, ducking behind a bush, hovering near a tree whenever possible. He takes a wide angle on a seldom-traveled campus road behind Emerson, and cuts through a small patch of trees behind the dining hall to find himself standing in front of a picture window, looking right in at their regular table, where Liam Wu sits, alone. He's trying to look as if he's staring into space, but Gid is almost sure he's looking at himself in the window.

Gid waves. He thinks, God, I'm not even scared of him. He waves some more, with two hands. Liam continues to stare. Gid waves faster. It is only when Gid is jumping up and down like a shipwreck victim seeking the attention of an airplane that Liam leans forward, his brow furrowed, and mouths what appears to be the word *me?*

Gid stops jumping and shakes his fists in the air. He mouths, "Yes, you, you moron!" Shit. He squats down against the edge of the building, breathing hard. By the time he's gotten the courage to stand up again, he sees Liam storming down the hill toward him. To Gid's ever so slight pleasure, Liam looks annoyed.

"What's the big friggin' deal? Where the fuck is my ride, yo? And where's the weed? It's half ours."

"Liam, please just do what I tell you, and don't ask me any questions. I want you to go inside. I want you to find Molly McGarry and bring her to me. And if you can't find her, find out where she is."

"Are you joking?" Liam asks. "Why can't you go inside and do it yourself?"

"Liam," Gideon says. "We have a big problem. And you can go find out where Molly McGarry is or you will be extremely sorry that you didn't."

"Molly McGarry?" Liam asks. "That sounds familiar. She's, like, brunette . . . has a little friend with sort of freaky eyes?"

"Liam, I really don't have time for the whole 'let me try to place her on my exclusive radar' routine."

This statement is a miraculous distillation of the exact way in which Liam is an asshole. Liam, despite not being all that bright, knows this. His whole body deflates. Even his lips get small.

"I actually think Molly McGarry is kind of a stealth babe," Liam says.

Oh, okay, Gid thinks. He knows what Liam's trying to do. He's trying to turn the balance of power back in his direction. He knows that Gid wants Molly. Liam doesn't know why but he knows that, and he's trying to make it clear that what might be a real babe to Gideon is just a qualified babe to Liam. A stealth babe. What a dick. Well, fuck Liam. Molly would never fall for him.

Not so fast, Gid. Look at all the annoying hot girls that you want. Girls may be less susceptible to sheer beauty than you, but we're not immune to it. Besides, just because Liam Wu doesn't share his charming side with you doesn't mean he doesn't have one.

Gid wisely doesn't respond to Liam. They face off in the dark, cold quiet of a New England night. Finally, Liam says, "Dude, if you're going to make me go do something for you, you have to at least tell me why I'm doing it." He crosses his arms.

"I really want to punch you in the face," Gid hisses.

That was immature. Suburban. Gay. As soon as the words are out of his mouth Gid is mortified. But Liam's face grows instantly red and mottled. Gid knows that look. Liam is feeling shame. His ego is big, but it's fragile, and the fact that Gid, the new guy, is suddenly no longer terrified of him has rocked Liam's world.

Liam stalks off without saying a word.

Gid watches as Liam moves through the cafeteria. He's back with appropriate speed. Good, Gid thinks. He seems to understand. "Molly's in the library," Liam says. "What's this all about anyway, dude? Where are Cullen and Nicholas?"

"Where in the library?" Gideon says, ignoring the rest. "Come on, where?"

"In the carrels. In the basement. Jesus. I had to talk to the little weird girl. She's probably going to think I'm into her now. Great. Thanks."

Gid puts his hand on Liam's shoulder. He looks him straight in the eye and says, "Do you have any idea what a totally ridiculous person you are?"

He's gone before Liam can process what's just happened.

Gid giggles to himself all the way to the library. He might be screwed, but at least he knows who he is right now. What he's doing. The campus clock, a stately, Roman-numeraled thing above the chapel, reads twenty after seven. Forty minutes to find Molly, and a good hiding place.

Gid enters the library through the basement to avoid detection. He steps carefully through fiction, A–D, E–H. Finally, from behind the row of Henry James novels, he sees her nestled in a carrel with *Moby-Dick* and a red pen. "Hey," Gid whispers. She turns. And Gid's heart—like it's a tiny frog in his chest—inflates and jumps.

The thing is, he can't help but think of Pilar, that Pilar is, like, really, four hundred times prettier than Molly, four hundred times prettier, really, than anything he's ever seen. He's even thought of her, embarrassingly, as lit from within by a thousand candles. But Molly looks so knowing. Amused. The way her lips curve like that, it's not that it drives him crazy with sexual desire, but it does make him feel curious.

He's staring at her for some time before she says, raising one eyebrow so that she makes herself even more curiosity provoking, "May I help you?"

Gideon puts a finger over his lips. Beckons to her. She tiptoes over, the wry smile deepens. "My, my," she says. "This is very James Bond. You have this mysterious injury . . ."—she alludes to his eye—"and my pen doubles as a sword, you know." She pokes him lightly in the ribs, her knuckles brush against a bare strip of skin between the buttons of his shirt. Gid's aware of every stage of her fingers touching him, the light scratch of her nail, the warmth of her skin, the cooler metal of her ring. He finds himself, as if guided by a force greater than himself, taking her hand.

To his immense pleasure, and surprise, he sees that she's trying not to smile. He thinks this might be even better than if she smiled outright. Yes, Gid . . . this is indeed correct. "You're worried about the pot," Molly says. "But it's hidden. It's in my room. No one will ever look there."

"They have a dog," Gideon says. "And they are coming to look." He thinks he can put her hand down now. This is serious.

"What?" Molly says. "Who is 'they'?"

"A dog," Gideon repeats. "This guy has a big yellow dog, and it can smell things, the constable . . ."

Molly scowls and waves a dismissive hand. "That whole constable thing, that's just some dumb prep school myth. Like the ghost in the chapel."

Gideon tells her about the headmaster's kitchen. How, out of sheer boredom, he arranged a bouquet of roses, ranunculus, and lavender that the headmaster's wife seemed to be rather impressed by. He tells her about the phone call. "You can't redial a myth," he says importantly. "The constable is very real, and he's on his way."

Molly puts on her coat but leaves *Moby-Dick* and the red pen behind. "I'm coming back," she says. "This is my little way of telling myself I'm not getting kicked out of school tonight."

Molly insists they walk right through the middle of campus. "Hiding in plain sight," she says. "Didn't you see *The Fugitive*?" Gid still walks as fast as he can, with his head bent into his chest. "Oh, you don't look guilty at all," Molly says.

"I could hold a newspaper over my face," Gid says. "Would you like that?"

"No," Molly says, "because then I wouldn't be able to see how handsome you are."

Sometimes girls make comments that are so transparently flirtatious that guys are supposed to think, "Wow, that was way too flirtatious to actually be flirtatious." I think this was one of those.

"We do have to cut behind Morrison," Gid says. "Your hide-in-plain-sight plan was a good one, but there are limits." He likes the way she lets him take her arm to guide her into a small patch of woods, and when he lifts her over a tiny stream so she doesn't get her big black boots wet, she doesn't protest either.

When they arrive at Emerson, they agree that she will take the back entrance and he will wait outside, behind the Dumpster, under the fire escape.

Waiting for her, Gid stares up at the stars and remembers he's in trouble. He reminds himself that he's insignificant, that it won't matter at all in the grand scheme of things if he gets kicked out of prep school. I spend a lot of time trying to convince myself that nothing really matters except being alive. It never works for me, and I'm not surprised when Gid gives up on it too and just starts praying.

"Jesus," he whispers, into the brick wall, which feels like a holy thing to do, "I know that it's not a big deal to the rest of the world, but please don't let me get kicked out of prep school." He adds, "Because someday I want to help people and it will be easier to do that if I have gone to prep school. Whatever. Jesus. Or God, I guess. If you don't want me to get kicked out of prep school, send me a sign." And at that moment, an airplane flies overhead. No kidding. And then another one. Then Molly appears at the top of the back landing. "Check it out," Gid says. "I prayed to God to send a sign that I wasn't going to get kicked out of school, and a plane flew overhead. And then another one."

Molly puts her hands on her hips. "Look up." Gid looks up. Another plane flies overhead. "Behold, the celestial event so incredible it happens every thirty-four seconds." Gid stares at her, uncomprehending. "It's called a flight path," she says. "You're a moron."

Molly lowers the fire escape ladder and climbs down. She walks right up to Gid and, smiling her cryptic smile, plants a kiss on his cheek. "Thanks," she says. "As much as I respect the city of Buffalo, I have to say I'm not too keen on going back. Not like this."

"Thanks? It was my fault in the first place. I . . . just wanted to do what was right." Molly nods at this. But her expression, which he would have expected to be reverent, is instead somewhere between guarded and amused. "Do you always do the right thing?" she says.

Gid thinks of his Molly/Pilar plan. Which can hardly be classified as saintly. But is it wrong? "I mean, the right thing in the sense that letting you hang out to dry for our problem, that would really, definitely have been the wrong thing."

"What about other wrong things?" Molly asks. "When things get ambiguous?"

This question makes Gideon nervous.

Then it hits him: Molly just kissed him. Without him even trying.

He smiles at her. Inexplicably, he says, "Hi." But Molly smiles back. He thinks he might want to kiss her again. They're kind of standing side by side, and he takes a step so he's halfway to facing her. It's a very natural step. Another step would not seem so. He stares at her hipbone. Then he looks at her jawline. She is thin but strong and sturdy. He likes her body. He can't think of a really good reason to move his foot again.

"Gid," Molly says, her voice low and intimate.

"Yeah?"

"You've got to take the pot and get out of here," she says. She hands him the bag. She holds it by its corner, as if it were a dead fish.

The kissing moment is past, but he still wants to touch her, somehow. He grabs her wrist and looks at her watch—which, although he doesn't realize it, is perhaps as good a tactical gesture as kissing her back. Molly blushes at his hand on her wrist. What do you want? She's from Buffalo.

"I'll go with you," Molly says. "I'll help you."

"No, no. Just give it to me. I don't need any help." Molly opens her mouth in protest, but he puts a hand up. "Go back and read your book," he says. She smiles, and he sees that she knows he remembers that she left the book for herself. He sees her anxiety melt away. He sees that she believes he can take care of this.

He sprints across the field, hiding in plain sight, thinking, Molly McGarry calling him a moron, playfully, and then leaving her entire future in his hands . . . It's almost as fun as sleeping chastely in a bed with Pilar Benitez-Jones. By the time he reaches the car, he's elated, high on adrenaline and possibility.

Did you know that if you stuff marijuana into a gas tank, the gas overpowers the smell of the marijuana? Gid did. He saw it on the Discovery Channel, sometime last year when he was home from school with strep throat, on a special about bloodhounds. They aired it three times in one day, and Gid, too racked with fever to move, saw all of them. At the time, he was bored out of his mind but now, holding the roll of duct tape he filched from Mrs. Frye's potting shed and tucking the neatly rolled bag under the gas cap of the BMW, he can't believe his luck. Perfect. But now it won't quite shut. The bag is too full, by just a little bit. He takes it out, pulls off a bud, and on second thought, another. But what's he going to do with them? He can't throw them in the woods. As Nicholas said earlier, they're prep school kids, they don't have any rights, and any pot found in the vicinity of this house is going to be blamed on them.

Okay, well, he's got to do something. Mrs. Frye could have come down at any point, and they would have told her Gid was in the bathroom, but they can't get away with it twice. He tiptoes up to the kitchen door and peeks inside. Nicholas is at the kitchen table with his head in his hands. Cullen paces. Gid opens the door quietly, remembering to reach in and put his hand over the little bell ornament hanging from a leather strap. Cullen sees him first and shakes his head. "Excuse me. Hello, what are you doing, you asshole!" he whispers fiercely. "Where the fuck have you been?"

"Just shut up," Gid says.

"I sure hope no one saw you," Nicholas says.

"Please," Gid says, "just shut up and listen. The pot is hidden. Let's not talk about where right now. The problem is, I still have some." He opens his hand. "And I don't know where to put it."

Upstairs, Mrs. Frye stirs.

"Run out into the woods, dude!" Cullen says.

"Won't work," Nicholas says. "The dog will find it."

Mrs. Frye's steps sound in the upstairs hall. She's coming toward the stairs.

"Yoo-hoo," she calls. "Boys?"

"Oh my God," Cullen says. "What if she wants us all to come upstairs and have a four-way with her? Do you think you could get hard?"

I'm all for trying to live life in the moment, but Cullen takes it a little too far.

"Gid, she likes you," Nicholas hisses. "Go see what she wants." Gideon moves slowly into the hallway, noticing that this is a very nice house. Was it only this morning that he was at the Winchesters'? He likes this place better. He sees with some satisfaction that Mrs. Frye set out his arrangement, succulent pink and dryer purple blossoms in a cut-glass vase, on a dark-wood side table. He wonders how much money the headmaster makes. "Gideon!" Mrs. Frye stands at the top of the stairs, one hand fiddles with her bun, the other holds a cigarette that's almost all ash. "I'm wondering if you could do something for me?"

Gideon can't help but think of Cullen's fear about the four-way. But that's stupid. Mrs. Frye doesn't seem like she'd be interested in that sort of thing. Cullen probably just wants to have sex with an old lady.

"Of course," Gid says, stepping forward. "Whatever you want. I'm at your service."

"There's a jar of rosemary in a little dish above the stove. I plumb forgot to put it in the pork. . . . Would you be a lamb and toss in a tablespoon or so for me?"

hero

When Gid and Cullen enter the mail room on Monday, Gid recalls in vivid detail his first day at Midvale, walking to the dining hall with his roommates and that very distinct rush of being a part of something special. Today, he's not only part of that specialness, he *is* that specialness. His schoolmates filter in and out and, bringing with them their various pleasant smells of perfume, soap, and detergent, all of them, Gid can see, are totally tuned in to his presence.

Inside Gid's little wooden mailbox with its ancient combination lock is a note. It's written in black ink on a light blue card reading:

FROM THE DESK OF MOLLY E. MCGARRY

> Hi Gid,
> *I appreciate what you did for me, even though of course*
> *the whole thing was basically your fault. But seriously.*
> *You didn't have to do that, and it was very nice and not*

what I would have suspected of you or necessarily any-
one at this place. What I'm trying to say is it was very
Buffalo of you to stick your neck out like that for me on
Sunday.

Sincerely,
Molly E. McGarry
(The E stands for Ellen.)

The *E* stands for Ellen. That is nakedly flirtatious. So forward, if in a nonforward way.

"Very Buffalo." Cullen is reading over his shoulder. "My God, you're so going to make this happen," he says.

Gid thinks he is too. His heart was singing from the moment he opened his eyes. He loved Midvale. He loved feeling that he was going to win the bet and that maybe afterward, he and Pilar . . . well. Better not get too ahead of himself. Also, he likes this note. He reads it again. He tells himself it is for clarity, but it is for pleasure.

Does he like Molly, possibly a lot? Does he like Molly and love Pilar, and what does this mean?

He can't think about this at the moment. It makes him feel a little sick. He feels good and at ease when he just thinks about what he did last night, how he won. Best to stick to that for now.

"Why didn't you do anything yesterday?" he asks Cullen, seizing on his girl confidence. "I mean, why did you and Nicholas . . . ?" He wants to say "just sit there and do nothing." But that's a little too harsh. "It seemed like you were just resigned to letting whatever happen."

Cullen spreads his hands wide in a rare gesture of surrender and humility. "Dude, I was honestly racking my brains for how we could get out of there. And then I saw it was our role to just stay behind and, you know, let you be the man. Which you have been. And look where it's gotten you." He indicates Molly's note.

Now, this sounds like bullshit to me, and Gid's not quite buying it either. He scowls good-naturedly at Cullen.

"Fuck you," Gid says. "You guys were being pussies."

Cullen smiles back. Gid was feeling good, but now he has a certifiably gigantic crush on the world . . . about half the size of my crush on him.

Gid's first impulse, on seeing Liam Wu at lunch later on, is to apologize. He comes toward the table, his mouth open, words like, "I know I was a little harsh last night," or "Hope I didn't insult you" ready at his lips, but as he draws closer he sees that Liam's face wears an expression he's never seen before. Liam is eager to see him. Liam *likes* him.

Incredible that the best route to winning friends is not necessarily kindness or flattery but letting them know you won't tolerate their bullshit. I learned this a while ago. Gid learned this last night.

Gid holds court at lunch that day, and the next, giving Liam and Devon a full account of their lengthy brush with campus authorities. He describes how he slipped the pot into the headmaster's stew along with the rosemary. How the constable showed up with his dog not five minutes after Gid returned to the headmaster's house. How Cockweed showed up at the house and sputtered around, red-faced, insisting that the constable try harder to find the never-to-be-found pot. The constable, wearing a yellow rain slicker despite the absence of rain, and his dog, indeed a yellow Lab, had the same brown baleful eyes. He finally slouched home to bed, as did the headmaster, who, naturally, slept through his regular Monday morning meeting and turned up in his office around eleven, moving slowly, guided by a stunned, unfocused gaze.

Of course, everyone also has to hear about Pilar. "Tell us about spending the night with her," Devon pleads. Liam leans in close as well.

Gid loved telling them about the headmaster's house only slightly less than he is going to love *not* telling them about this.

"I'm going to take the Fifth on that one, guys, if you don't mind," Gid says. Devon and Liam laugh, but he can see little shadows of left-outness on their faces, especially as Cullen gives Gid the high five, then leans in and whispers, "These guys are not worth your secrets."

The truth that there is nothing to tell doesn't matter. What matters is that these guys think Gideon knows something that they would like to know, and that makes them want to be with him. And it makes them like him.

"Hey." Molly appears at the table. She looks over Cullen, Nicholas, Liam, and Devon, settling her gaze on Gideon. "What secret?"

Have you noticed Molly's German shepherd hearing?

"Gid had a hot night this weekend," Liam says. "Or so it goes."

"Hmm," Molly says. "No word of this up in the nosebleed seats."

Cullen pokes Gid under the table and mouths, "Outsider status."

Gid slowly nods to show that he understands.

"Anyway," Molly says, "I just checked my e-mail, and Ms. San Video wrote us all that we have to do these dumb Spanish projects. We're on a team: me, you, and, uh . . ." She looks at the floor and bites her lip. "Liam." She can barely look at him. He looks at her, quickly, almost annoyed, and goes back to talking to Devon. Gid's never seen her like this before.

Is she *afraid* of these guys?

She looks up, then looks at the floor again. There's a grim set to her mouth, a bit of a lack of focus in her eyes that Gid has not seen before, like she's trying not to see anyone but not wanting to appear to look away. She *is* a little afraid. "Sure," Gid says, standing up, ushering her away. He knows they're all watching him, but he doesn't feel self-conscious. He feels paid attention to.

"Why'd you do that?" Molly says. They're standing near the soda machines.

"Because I could tell you were uncomfortable," Gideon says. He might be getting a little cooler, but he's still unable to do much except tell the truth.

Molly puffs out her chest a little. "I'm not afraid of them," she says.

"I didn't say afraid, I said uncomfortable," Gid says.

A small, rueful smile starts to spread across Molly's face. "Okay, you got me," she says.

Gid knows then that she likes him. Because, well, it's obvious. She just lit up the second he called her out like that. Maybe she knows that he knows, because she says, "Who did you have a hot night with?" No attempt, not even a half-ass girl attempt, to hide the vulnerability in her curiosity.

"Oh, gee," Gid says. So many ways to play with this one. He knows it might not be bad for Molly to think he's got something else going on. In fact, that might make her like him more. Or, conversely, it could scare her off. "I'm not sure I even know what Liam's talking about."

He can feel everyone in the cafeteria looking at him. Gideon is *the* topic of conversation at Midvale. People he barely even knows—among them the orange-shirt girl from the first day and a parade of short, scruffy underclassmen who are all henchmen of Mickey Eisenberg—sidle up to him in the gleaming hallways and on verdant campus paths, whispering, "Good job." Now their curiosity turns to the intimate whispering between Gid and Molly McGarry. He hopes too that there are rumors about Pilar, although he knows that winning this bet with Molly is his first priority. Gid realizes that he only hated the bet when he thought he could never win. Now the bet feels like a little engine inside him. I am standing here for the world to see, Gid thinks, but there is also a reason that only me and my two closest—yes, he thinks he can use that word right now—friends know about. The feeling is delicious, Christmas morning-y.

"I think you do know what Liam's talking about, but that's okay," Molly says. She checks her watch, that big man's watch that takes up most of her wrist. She's medium-size, but he notices her hands, wrists, and feet are kind of small. He likes her. He likes her enough to convert, as Cullen might say, on the bet. And that's what is important. "I have to go," she says.

"No, I have to go," Gid says, trying to make a joke.

"Is that supposed to be funny?" Molly says, and walks away. Gid can't help but look at her butt. It's nice. Pilar's butt is epic. But Molly's is nice. Just fine. Good. Should never have to be compared with epic. He wonders if *epic* is a dumb word.

Later on, Gid goes to English class and is given back a paper with a C-plus and the comment "not so great." Geez, he thinks, it is one thing to feel steadily mediocre, another to feel awesome and then be taken down a notch. Disappointment and low-level shame lodge in his throat for the duration of class, and afterward, he visits the drinking fountain. It's broken.

"Hello, thirsty Gee-de-on." It is Pilar.

"That thing breaks all the time," Pilar says. She looks absolutely perfectly gorgeous in a pair of black pants and a tight orange T-shirt, which, naturally, makes Gid think of Halloween.

"Do you want some of this?" She holds out a can of Diet Coke, which Gid accepts. It is still cold and full. He forgets all about his paper. He sneaks a look at Pilar's ass.

And decides: *Epic* is exactly the word.

"We haven't talked since the party," Gideon says.

Pilar smiles. Gideon is dazzled. I see that it's not a real smile. It doesn't reach her eyes. "No, we haven't. But I have been . . . thinking a lot, and I finally made a decision."

At this moment, Edie comes out of the English classroom. Gid thinks he should follow her, find Molly. "Thinking?" Gid says, his heart a fluttering mess. "About what?"

"Well," Pilar says, "I decided I wanted to move from White to Emerson. I told them I had post-traumatic stress because I was near where that Citibank exploded in Buenos Aires a year or so ago. Did you read about that? And White is more quiet? They let me." She offers a pretty smile of triumph. "But really it's because my new room has a fire escape." She winks at Gid. "So . . ."

The fluttering intensifies. Is she inviting him over? Not quite, but she means to let him know there are means for sneaking out, and in, and that's why she changed rooms.

Gid nods knowingly. "I get it," he says. "In case there's a fire. You want to be prepared . . ." He trails off. Is Edie kind of lingering at the top of the stairs, watching him? Or is she just enjoying the burst of fall foliage through the circular window over the staircase? Gid can't tell.

"Exactly," Pilar says. "You have to be prepared when things get hot."

Now, again, here we are with the overt female flirtation. Gideon follows the twinkle in Pilar's eyes for a sign that its source is him.

"I have to go to Français," Pilar says. "*Mon* Diet Coke, *s'il vous plaît.*"

and
the
other
one
dies

It's a little cold out the next day while Gid walks to Spanish. Liam is not with him. Abruptly, they no longer accompany each other, but Gideon knows the desertion is his doing, not Liam's. Company would be fine, but he does not require it. His mood is pensive (Molly) mixed with agitated (Pilar). He alternates between trying to convince himself that Pilar's balcony wrangling meant nothing and that he should give up forever with deciding that it meant everything and that he should devote his life to her. He digs his hands into his pockets, remembering that these are the pants he wore that night with Pilar and that he hasn't worn them since. They are special. And in the right pocket is a thick square of folded paper. Naturally, Gid's felt his share of thick squares of folded paper. But this precise thickness and texture he's never felt before. It feels exciting.

It is a note. From Pilar.

Dear Gideon,
I had so much fun sleeping in this bed with you last night.
Isn't it weird the way things can work out? Anyway, it is

funny, don't you think, how we met? I think we have a lot
of things in common. I feel a little stupid saying it because
you could be like, What would I have in common with her?

This last line blows Gid away. It is so awesome, the idea that he
could have an impact on the feelings of a girl that hot. And that he
found this note at this moment—a moment in which he was about
to possibly abandon all hope?

Uh, Gideon . . . that is every moment. Every other moment
that you're not having a romantic fantasy.

My cell phone number is 305-555-5555. Okay? Pilar

Gid sees that he's standing in the middle of the quad, on a
path, in everyone's way. The post-lunch foot traffic parts around
him; Gid reads the note again, his heart pounding with anticipation. And a little shame, as he thinks. He absolutely must get things
moving with Molly so he can just start concentrating on Pilar.

Why had he agreed not to sleep with other girls until he slept
with Molly?

He has a short memory: It hadn't occurred to him such things
could be possible.

I can't help but wonder if such deviousness makes him a bad
person. But I think that all people are devious. Is there any other
way to make it through life, given what life presents?

Gid walks into Spanish five minutes late. The entire classroom
has been rearranged. As he's slipping into an empty seat in the front
row, Ms. San Video approaches, tapping her acrylic red nail against a
pen cap. "*Buenas tardes,* Gideon," she says, and continues on in
Spanish, "Have you noticed a change? We have paired off into
groups, and we will all be doing a group project." She puts her hand
on Gideon's desk. "Molly said that you spoke about being partners.

And Liam Wu volunteered to join your group. How do you like that?"

Liam? That's bad. Liam shouldn't be allowed near girls that you want or, in this case, must sleep with to win a bet. Even Ms. San Video's mere mention of his name and the girls in the class are perked up, smiling, preening in his direction.

Gid sits down with Molly and Liam. Liam's smile is giant and lascivious. He's seen Molly and Gid talking. Gid's instinct, and one I think he's probably right on, is that Liam wants anything anyone else wants. He better not screw this up for me, Gid thinks, his eyes narrowing unconsciously.

"Hey," Liam says, breaking in, "why are you giving me a dirty look?"

"Sorry." Gideon blinks a few times. "I, uh, was just thinking about something else." And then he forces himself to look at Molly, right at her, for three full seconds. This is a campaign, he reminds himself as he wants to break his gaze. You show up every day and work until you win, and now, especially that you have that note from Pilar, you have to make it your number one priority, every day. Molly reddens slightly. It's almost embarrassing, Gideon thinks, how well it works, just pouring on the intensity a little.

Intensity! Gid, you are sixteen. But the thing is that he is intense. It's just that he's only recently learning what to do with it.

"I think," Liam says, looking from Molly to Gid with a smug smile, as if in the entire history of class projects, no one has ever thought of such a thing, "that the three of us should put on a play."

"A play?" Gid says slowly. "That seems kind of hard." What he doesn't say is, You don't have to be a genius to know what generally happens in a play. One guy gets the girl. And the other guy dies. Plus, God . . . Gid must be a terrible actor. He can barely even lie.

"Not a long play," Liam says. "Just a one-act."

"A one-act?" Molly says. She lets the cardigan sweater she's been wearing fall off her shoulders. Liam immediately registers the presence of her bare skin. His eyes take on a predatory glaze. "That sounds doable." Molly nods.

"Doable," Liam repeats, still staring at Molly. "Definitely." He raises an eyebrow at Gideon, trying to share this joke with him. Gid won't share. "Ms. San Video suggested it."

"Whatever," Molly says. "It's all bullshit. Meredith and Yvonne are repainting *Guernica* with finger paints. And Richard Mass and Dan Drury are building a diorama of a prison cell in the Inquisition."

"Ms. San Video told them their idea was brilliant," Liam says. Let's take a moment to feel sorry for Ms. San Video. A beautiful cosmopolitan South American woman stuck in a staid suburb, surrounded by giggling sixteen-year-olds just counting the minutes until they can smoke pot again.

"So I guess the famous Midvale rigor doesn't apply here," Molly says. "Let's just get it over with and get A's and go to the colleges of our choice."

"I'm glad we're on the same page," Liam says, looking at Molly longer than necessary, letting his eyes not so casually linger on her chest. Which is small. But is still a chest. For guys, there is always something to see.

There is no doubt in Gid's mind that Liam wants Molly now. Not really. But preemptively. Yep. He's still looking at her, with those crazy almond-shaped blue eyes, those sparkling incisors. Oh, this is not fair.

"Okay," Ms. San Video is saying. "If you want to go to the library and get started, I will let you out a few minutes early."

"Well." Liam stands up. "I guess if no one has any objections, I'll go look into some drama *en español*! Do you want to come?" he asks, turning in such a way that the question is clearly directed at Molly.

This is when Gid sees evidence of what he was worried about that night outside the dining hall. Molly's brown eyes actually get kind of starry. They get kind of *moist*. She looks down to hide the blush seeping across her face.

"Sorry," Molly mutters, still unable to meet Liam's eyes. "I always have lunch with Edie after this class."

Thank fucking God for that little weirdo! Gid wants to scream.

But Molly watches Liam walk away. Not the way a guy would watch a girl walk away. Not the way a dog looks at a wet bowl of Alpo. But almost.

As soon as he's gone, she puts her sweater back on. Gid's paranoid now. Did she have it off for Liam? His mind races for a compliment. He's got to take advantage of every moment.

"You have nice arms," Gid says, as he realizes he has been looking at them, admiring the firm, small muscle of her bicep, the shadow of her tricep. Then he looks at the floor. Why did he say that? She's going to think he's some kind of arm freak.

But instead she says, "You have nice arms too."

"Really?" He holds his arms out and looks at them.

"Too bad you're wearing a long-sleeved shirt," Molly says. "You can look at them later."

Gid blushes. He actually held out his arms and looked at them. I would be embarrassed too.

"Anyway," Molly says, "should we go help Liam? I have a lot of other work to do and am more than happy to let him run the show, but if you by any chance have some pre-1945 Spanish one-act you've always been dying to stage, now is your chance." She smiles.

"The only thing I've ever seen in Spanish was *Selena*," Gid says.

"You are so hopelessly suburban," Molly says. "You know that, don't you?"

"I guess I do," he says. "I guess that's my whole problem."

That's part of your problem. Your other problem, for the moment, is Liam.

That night, Gideon's finishing his dinner when Liam struts up to him, a paperback curled in one hand.

Why do guys who think they're cool always have to hold books that way?

After sharing his little handshake with everyone, he sets the book down on the table. It's actually a play. *"El Perro que Compartimos,"* Cullen reads aloud. "The Pear in the Compartment?"

"Okay, douche, it's called another language." Liam swats Cullen on the head. "It's *The Dog That We Shared.* It's a play about a couple breaking up, and their dog is in the room."

"Oh, silly me." Cullen stands up. "Here I thought it was a high-stakes caper about produce packaging. I'm out of here. Nicholas, you coming?"

Nicholas, deeply ensconced in an organic chemistry textbook, shakes his head.

"So, dude," Liam says to Gid, "I really want you to read this. It's awesome! Ms. San Video is going to love it."

Liam makes a beeline for the cranberry juice machine, and Gid flips through the play for a minute.

"Hey," he whispers to Nicholas, "I'm only skimming, but I gotta say . . . this play seems kind of perverse . . . or perverted. And you know that we're in it with . . ." He lowers his whisper to a mere breath, "Molly."

Nicholas puts down his textbook. "I feel bad for you," he says, sounding truly sincere. Gid lets his gaze settle for a moment in Nicholas's blue eyes, seeking out and finding what he thinks is some real softness. However, all Nicholas has to add is "Perverse and perverted are the same thing." Then he goes back to his book.

Gid begins to read in earnest. By the time Liam returns, standing over Gid, grinning broadly and crunching on an apple, Gid's perspiring a bit. I don't blame him. This play's not just about a couple breaking up with their dog in the room, it's about a couple alternately breaking up and making out, with their dog in the room.

The stage directions read *Lucía y Oscar se besan con fuerte pasión,* or "Lucia and Oscar kiss with fierce passion," more times than Gid cares to count. The dog does not have any lines. In most circumstances, Gideon would lobby hard for the part of the dog. This is not most circumstances.

When Gid finishes, to the never-ending tune of Liam's self-satisfied apple crunching over his shoulder, he has no idea what to say. Nicholas flips through some photos in the back pages of the text, taken at the Teatro Experimental in Barcelona in 1967 and depicting the original cast of three. A petite, serious-looking woman with a dark bun at the nape of her neck embraces a short, bearded man around his waist. At her feet, another man lies on his side, his hands and feet bare, his knees curled into his chest. He's dressed, like the man in the couple, in a dark three-piece suit, but he's wearing a plastic dog snout.

"So," Nicholas says to Liam, "how are you going to decide who plays who?"

Liam crosses his arms over his chest and sits back with practiced casualness. "Good question, bro. Got any preference? How should we handle this?"

Gid hesitates. This is a risky move. It could, very easily, blow up in his face. But if things go in his favor, it could prove to have been his best move yet.

"Molly McGarry," Gid says. "She's the one who's in the play. So let her pick her leading man."

Liam reassumes his arms-crossed, casual, it's-all-good stance. "Lady's choice," he says. "Sounds like a plan. I brought Molly a copy of the play earlier. She suggested we meet tomorrow night."

"Tomorrow night?" Gideon thinks this can't be great news.

"Guess she's eager to get to it," Liam says. "And you know, we are on a bit of a deadline. It's the end of the first week of October. And we're doing the play right after Halloween."

Gideon has a paranoid fantasy that Cullen's having an affair with Ms. San Video, and he told her about the bet and she arranged to put him together with Molly. He knows deep down it's ridiculous. Not the Cullen sleeping with Ms. San Video part. That's totally possible. But he would never tell her about the bet. Cullen's sense of decency is warped, but it does exist.

image
rose

Cullen's giving a presentation in American History on the Battle of Bunker Hill. He's going to make a model of the barrier the American army made across the beach in North Charleston that ultimately led the British to defeat.

He and Gideon have in front of them one thousand plastic toy soldiers and several bottles of black and red nail polish. "We need to paint a black *B* for 'British' on half, and then a red *A* for 'Americans' on the other half."

Some of the soldiers stand at attention. Some stand and fire. Some are crouched and firing. Gid picks up one of the shooting soldiers and looks hard at its face. Whoever makes these, he thinks, does a good job of fitting that expression of determination and courage on such a small area. "We should do a black *A* and a red *B*," he says. "I think that with the whole redcoat thing, people will get confused."

Cullen claps him on the back. "You're a genius," he says.

They get to work, Gid on the *A*s, Cullen on the *B*s. "You have to stop thinking about Pilar so much," Cullen says.

"But I just can't help it," Gid says. "She gave me a note, you know. I really think she might like me."

I think she really might like him too. And while it's easy for me to see why I like him, I don't know if I get why she would.

Gid says, "I don't think I could feel this strongly for her if she didn't feel something for me."

Poor Gideon. Cullen has it so easy with girls. He doesn't understand Gideon's fear that if he doesn't immediately capture whatever scrap of attention Pilar might throw his way, he will lose her forever.

Cullen hangs his head back and groans. "I want you to be single-minded, determined. Look, in order to get a girl . . . I mean, for you . . . for the time that you're trying to get her, you have to be a little bit in love with her."

Wait a minute. Maybe Cullen does understand Gid's problem. That makes me like him a little more.

"Is Nicholas a little bit in love with Erica every time he has sex with her?" Gid asks.

Good question. I think that if I understand Nicholas at all, when he has sex with Erica, it's in that small window of time where his generally repressed capacity for tenderness and generally repressed horniness converge.

Cullen makes a guttural noise of frustration and annoyance. "Look," he says, "it seems to me that you're more upset about that than Nicholas is."

"Hmm." Gid wonders if this is true. "I guess it just fascinates me a little."

And he's been noticing that when he sees Erica, she looks a little damaged. Maybe he's just projecting. Imagining causing the same kind of damage.

No . . . she definitely looks damaged. But there's something to be said, as a girl, for that heartbroken look. I guess I'm a little sick.

Even with sunken cheeks and eyes, Erica, with absolutely no baby fat, well, she's kind of working it.

Cullen ignores him and says, "I've been thinking a lot lately about Pilar and you."

"You have?" says Gid, flattered and almost as thrilled as if he actually were with her.

"I feel like Molly McGarry is the good starter girl for you," Cullen says. "I used to think that she was the kind of girl for you, you know? But I see you with Pilar now, and I think, why not? And I don't mean this in a mean way about Pilar, but she's very vulnerable. Someone like you . . . well . . . she could use you."

"Wow," says Gid.

Uh, yeah, wow. This is nice and all, but Cullen must be having some kind of serotonin overload in his brain right now, because this kind of optimism, well, it sure smells chemical to me.

"At the same time, I feel like you need to just pick something, one goal, in your mind, or you create real problems for yourself. Some people can be thinking of a lot of shit at once," Cullen says. "But it's usually because they're not really thinking of anything. I can do that. You can't."

This is the closest thing to a tender moment Gid and Cullen have ever had.

Gid's nail polish letters are a lot neater than Cullen's. "Cullen," he says, gently, "you need to watch what you're doing."

On the window ledge, Cullen arranges a standing British soldier so it is being shot at by a crouching American soldier. "Don't you just feel like you're actually *at* the Battle of North Charleston?" He rolls his eyes. "Some girl in my class is writing a fucking diary of Betsy Ross, when she was making the flag. Isn't that stupid?"

I think Cullen's project is stupider, actually.

"If my parents had any idea how incredibly art-faggy this

school was, they would shit," Cullen says. "Hey, how did you end up coming to school here, anyway?"

"My dad was building a house for this rich guy, Charlie Otterman. And right before he finishes the house, Otterman gets a DWI coming home from a Northern Virginia Lawyers' club meeting. So he gets disbarred. Can't pay my dad all he owes him. But he went to school here, and he told my dad he could get me in."

Cullen laughs out loud. "No shit! Dude, you could have gotten in here anyway, I bet. You should make that guy give your dad his money."

Gid smiles. "I think I should just let my dad continue thinking he got a good deal."

And really, the skills Gid's developing—pot smoking, manipulation of innocent (possible) virgins—how can you put a price on that?

"Shit," Cullen says, "we're out of red. Hey. I have a good idea. Go find Pilar, and get more from her. It's a great excuse."

"Pilar? You want me to talk to Pilar?"

"If you can bring back a bottle of red nail polish and solid proof that Pilar likes you—not just 'Oh, she told me she had a dorm room she could sneak out of,' or 'Oh, she gave me her phone number,' but something that proves beyond a shadow of a doubt that she likes you, then I will talk to Nicholas about changing the bet around. It's my little thank-you to you for helping me . . . and also, that story about your dad kind of made me sad. I don't know why."

Gid knows why. Because it was white-trashy. No one with as charmed a life as Cullen wants to be reminded of the dark side. Nice that Cullen said he would have gotten in on his own. He thinks he would have too. C-plus notwithstanding.

Gid starts with the library periodicals room, where Pilar is known to go, generally under the influence of a Xanax or two, and maybe some vodka slipped into her watermelon Vitaminwater, to read foreign fashion magazines.

The library is shaped like a concrete egg. Madison and Mija sit in the two orange vinyl chairs by the entrance. Madison's reading Italian *Vogue,* and Mija, who is in Gid's English class, is reading *Moby-Dick.*

Mija holds up *Moby-Dick.* "This book is super boring."

"Tell me about it," Gid agrees, pacing to the edge of the room and peering through the door into the periodicals room. No Pilar. "I feel bad saying that, but I really can't read it."

Madison imitates a model's pout on the page she's open to. Mija and Gid exchange amused glances.

"I saw that," Madison says.

The sun sets early now, and the darkening room is snug. Gid stretches and then lies down on the floor under the table. "I forget sometimes," he says, "that we're supposed to be in prep school to learn."

Mija lies down on the floor perpendicular to him. "Me too. You know, I think sometimes that I would just like to be back in my village in Holland, you know, riding my bike around with my friends, playing broom hockey in the street. Every year my parents would have their *Het Nationaal Dictee* party." Her cute little canary face is soft and wistful. "My mother would make *spekulatius,* these Dutch cookies."

"What's *Het Nationaal Dictee*?"

"It's a Dutch TV special. It only happens once a year. Famous Dutch people and some people selected from a competition compete at live dictation."

Gid nods politely and looks toward the door again for a sign of his beloved. He looks the other way. Madison's eyes flutter. Even Italian *Vogue* can't hold her attention for very long.

Mija frowns, very grave. "*Het Nationaal Dictee* is hard, you know."

"Oh, I can imagine," Gid says quickly. "Dictation. I wouldn't even know where to start."

"The winner gets a golden pencil," Mija says. "I mean, real gold."

"Well," Gid says, "it certainly must be an honor to have something so beautiful bestowed on you by fellow Dutch people."

Now Gid's afraid he's going to laugh. But he doesn't want Mija to know he's making fun of her. So he turns his head to the side. A pair of high-heeled boots advances over the low-pile blue carpet. He'd know those feet anywhere.

Mija sees her too, pokes her head out from under the desk and smiles. "Don't you think so, Pilar?"

Heart beating, expectant, he thinks he was right to come here. And now all he needs is some red nail polish and an admission that she is in love with him.

She is always like an apparition to him. He never imagined until he met her that such beauty could exist. Pilar's wearing a jean skirt with her black boots. She really is always dressed perfectly—it's just what the young, on-the-go international student *should* wear to the library on a Thursday night. Even though it's freezing outside, her legs are bare. There's a patch of hair above the boot, below her hem, that she missed shaving. It's kind of dark. Gideon marvels at the power of Pilar's sexual allure, that this mistake—this remnant of what I know is a serious hirsuteness kept at bay with gallons of wax and jarfuls of razors—only enhances her appeal. I bet for a graduation present she's getting laser hair removal.

"What's with her?" Pilar asks. Madison is asleep, with a copy of Italian *Vogue* over her face. Of all the poses Madison could ever fancy herself in, I like this the most.

"I actually have to get out of here," Mija says. "That chick Edie has *Moby-Dick* on CD, and I'm going to go eat and then I'm going to her room to listen to it."

Pilar purses her lips—still luscious even without their patina of

Diet Coke. "Doesn't Molly McGarry live with her?" She points a playfully accusing manicured finger at Gideon. The half-moons on her nails are perfectly white and oval. "I see you talking to her a lot." Her eyelid does that half-closed flutter that always breaks Gid's heart. Mija has gone now. Gid didn't even notice her leaving.

"Molly and I are doing a Spanish project together," Gid says. He feels a little guilty saying this. Not because of the romance aspect— well, maybe a little—but because he feels he's selling Molly out socially. He doesn't want Pilar to think they're involved, but he hates acting like the guy who can't even admit they are friends.

"Hmm . . . ," Pilar says. "I suppose it has to do with Spain. You should do something to do with Argentina. It is way more interesting."

Gid blurts out, "Do you have any red nail polish?"

I am not surprised when Pilar opens up her Louis Vuitton doctor bag and takes out a small bottle of red polish. Gid reads the bottom. It is called Image Rose.

Pilar smirks at him. "Are you on a scavenger hunt?" she asks. "You are, aren't you?" She holds out the bottle to him. Gideon is so fixated on her that even though the generosity she's extending toward him is minimal, he's absolutely floored by it. When she holds out her arm, it presses against her chest, advancing her breasts forward a precious and fascinating quarter inch.

Gideon, you are so cute I almost wish you could disappear into an Italian *Vogue* fashion shoot with her and live there forever. But I'm glad you can't.

"No," he says. "Cullen needs it for his American History project."

Pilar puts her bare feet up on Gid's chair. How did he miss her taking off her boots? Does she not wear socks? "American History. You know, I don't have to take it because I am not American? It's true." She hooks a thumb underneath her necklace, pulls it back and forth.

Gid has a flash: His mother played with her necklace the first time she talked to his middle-school science teacher. And that man's now her husband!

This is incredible. Asking about other girls. Putting her bare feet on his chair. And now the necklace playing. He's taking his nail polish, and he's going to go tell Cullen that the bet is all about Pilar now, and he knows . . . she can sneak out of her room! He's going to have this tied up in no time.

At that moment, her tiny silver cell rings. She ducks behind a shelf of totally ignored foreign policy periodicals. Gid enjoys the view of her lower legs and the murmur of her voice. He pretends she is whispering to him. When she comes back, she tucks the phone into a tiny pocket in the front of her skirt and says, "That was a friend of mine who you know."

"Who?"

"A British friend," she says.

"I don't know anyone British," Gid says. "Oh, except those guys at the party. Dennis was nice to me."

"Dennis likes you," Pilar coos. "Because you protected me."

"Protected you? I don't have any idea what you're talking about."

He's still in the midst of saying the words as he gets it.

Dennis Tolland is dating Pilar. It all makes perfect sense.

Dennis encouraged him to go upstairs. To go and find Pilar, lie down with her. And Gid thought he was coaching him, well, not necessarily as an equal, but at least as a fellow guy. But really, Dennis was just thinking of him as a Boy Scout. Dennis was too drunk to go upstairs with Pilar, so he sent Gid, because he knew Gid would deter other suitors from trying to get into the room with Pilar. And that with Gid up there, Dennis could drink and strip-poker himself into oblivion and never wonder if anyone was macking on his lady. (Dennis's probable words of choice, not mine.)

Gid remembers Cullen telling him not to make the bed and feels a terrible chill.

The memory of every single fantasy he's had about Pilar since then blackens in his mind and fills his chest with ash. And that's why she moved rooms—to sneak out at night for her little Eurotrysts with Dennis Tolland.

"Are you okay?" Pilar touches his forehead. He wants to cry at how exquisite the feeling of her finger is and how heartbreaking it is that she always smells like roses. Dennis Tolland. That British asshole, whom he fantasized about being friends with. Repeatedly. Much more embarrassing, at this moment, than fantasizing about an unrequited love.

Pilar's phone rings again. Before she answers it, Gid glances at the display: DENNIS. Calling repeatedly. As lovers do.

"Bye," he says. He hopes Pilar hears the note of finality. Then he thinks, I could be like, Bye, you ruined my life, and she would just say, Good-bye, Gee-de-on.

totally
playing
the
dog

Pollard Theater is the newest building on campus. It was designed and built by someone famous and foreign. It's rectangular with a round porch, tiled in black and red. Large glass doors lead to its lobby, which is decorated sparsely and features randomly placed Plexiglas cubes that function as chairs. Molly, sitting on one of them, waves.

Gid notes that she looks pretty cute. She's wearing a skirt. Has she dressed up for their first night of rehearsal? He should probably say something about it. But what? He doesn't want to be too provocative. He could go for a sort of sly thing, like, "What's the occasion?" But that reminds him of his dad. Always trying to be so knowing, when he knows nothing.

"You're staring at me," Molly says.

Or he could just say nothing and make her really uncomfortable. "I'm sorry," he says. "I guess I am a little distracted." I love Pilar, he thinks. I like you but I love Pilar and every time I start enjoying talking to you I remember that I feel like an idiot because of her.

Molly tucks her skirt around her legs. "Why are you distracted?" she asks.

Her curiosity touches him. But not so much that he's going to actually say what's on his mind. He is amazed at how instantly he's ready with a good lie or half-truth. "It's my girlfriend," he says. "Well, I guess she's my ex-girlfriend. Though not officially. I came to school here, and I just basically . . ."

Molly smiles. "Never called her?"

Gid rolls his eyes. "I know it's not great behavior. It doesn't exactly make me look like a good guy to girls."

"What do you mean, to girls? Like, all girls? Are we on a team? Do we have uniforms?"

"Come on," Gid says. He shifts on the cube, which, as you can imagine, is not all that comfortable. "You know what I mean."

"If all girls are really on a team, I want to know what our team shirts look like. Are they baby tees? Are they pink? Do they say 'Princess' on them? Because I wouldn't wear that shirt. But a lot of girls would."

"You win," Gid says.

"I just feel like . . . guys think all girls have, like, one idea about how guys are supposed to act. I don't think I know how anyone is supposed to act. Do you know what I mean?"

Does he ever. But he doesn't want to admit that kind of vulnerability. Though the fact that she did is good.

It's quiet for a few seconds. Gid tries not to stare at her, or the floor, and ends up in a kind of spacey middle-distance thing which, if Molly were that alert, which she may well be, makes him look stoned. Which he is. But not as stoned as he looks. "Did you read this play?" she asks.

"It's pretty racy," Gideon says, reddening. "I'm not sure Ms. San Video will . . . uh, go for it."

"Oh, I wouldn't worry about that," Molly says. "She's essentially

European. They love it when kids talk about sex. She'll think it means we're smart."

Liam enters, walking fast, his hand held up in apology. "Sorry I'm late," he says. "I was sleeping."

This is an arrogant, annoying excuse, Gid thinks. Why doesn't Liam just say the prospect of being here with the two of you bored me? Then Gid remembers that he doesn't always have to go on the defensive with Liam. He's gained ground. Gideon stands up. "What's up, bro?" he says, slapping him on the arm.

"Nada, nada, nada," Liam replies, seemingly unmoved by Gid's bravado. And then he throws Molly one of his smiles. "Aren't you looking hot tonight, Ms. McGarry!"

Okay, Gid thinks, this has got to be considered overboard, right?

Or . . . not. Molly blushes, thrilled. "Wow, Liam, thanks. Do I really?" She's standing up now, and playing with her skirt. She tilts her head coquettishly, indicating that they should head to the practice space down the hall. She leads the way. Liam follows, staring the whole time at her butt and legs. Gideon, behind them, feels a sharp and sudden stab of ownership.

And Liam's not done. As they enter the practice space, just a dark plywood box down a stairwell between the theater office and the costume studio, he says, "You know, Molly, while I was napping, before I got here, I had a dream about you?"

This surely is not going to fly with Molly. She's going to make fun of him. She's got to. Gideon sits down in one of the metal folding chairs that are the only furnishings in the room, save a coatrack hung with a fur stole, and waits for this to happen.

It doesn't. Instead, Molly saunters over to the fur stole and, throwing it around Liam's neck, pulls her to him. "Did I do this in your dream?" she asks. Her head's tilted back and she looks right into Liam's eyes.

"No," Liam says, a little hoarse, "I would have remembered

that." Molly backs away from him, keeping eye contact. Gid knows that Liam is now fully aware of the fact that Molly is a little bit more than a stealth babe. This flirtation is throwing a wrench in his plans. And now Molly gets to choose between them. She's definitely going to pick Liam. If only because she'll be embarrassed to pick Gideon, because she knows him better. Unless that works the other way? Or is there no way that she would miss a chance to kiss Liam, just out of sheer respect for his handsomeness? So many stupid variables.

"I want to play the guy," Gid hears himself saying. He looks from Liam to Molly. Both wear neutral expressions. He keeps talking. "I am getting terrible grades, and Liam, your grades are fine. Ms. San Video already thinks I'm kind of lazy. This is probably my chance to change her opinion."

Liam's expression is still neutral, but he starts to step from side to side a little. He's nervous, Gid thinks. He's got to be thinking of a way to argue this without looking like he wants the part.

"You know," Liam says, "we all get the same grade for the project."

Just as Gid thought. This is about the only good point he has. If Liam keeps arguing, he's going to look like he cares. And there's nothing Liam likes less. This was his whole plan. Gid doesn't say a word. Let Liam keep talking if he dares.

"Well," Liam says, "what do you think, Molly?"

Gid feels the world go absolutely still. "Oh, no," Molly says. "This is between you two."

"I don't want to be a pain," Gid says. He looks at the ground humbly. "I just want to do well in school. I don't want to piss off my dad."

A masterful performance. Liam came in strong with the flirting, but he was no match for Gideon. "Sure," Liam says, "whatever."

Liam's playing the dog. Liam's totally playing the dog. He did it! And it wasn't even that bad.

Gid searches Molly's face for signs of disappointment or relief or excitement but she's not showing anything. Maybe she doesn't care.

Not possible, Gideon. When there's kissing involved, even if it's only make-believe, people always care. Especially girls.

They read through the play. Or, rather, Gid and Molly read and Liam alternately sulks and uses little corners of his script to clean things out of his teeth. "Do I have to bark in Spanish?" Liam asks at one point. "Because I don't understand how they spell out barking. I mean, ruff-ruff, that makes sense, but guau-guau? I can't say that. I'm going to look stupid."

"I'm going to go in the costume room and see if they have any plastic snouts," Gid says. He can't resist.

And really, why should he?

give
me
an a

"*Yo quiero el perro,*" Gideon reads, trying to make important eye contact and follow his lines at the same time.

"You're going to have to learn how to roll your damn *R*s," Molly says. "Let's take a break."

It's the following night. They've been rehearsing for about seven minutes.

Liam takes off his plastic dog snout. "Thank God. This is fucking melting my fucking nose," he says, lying down on his side. He rolls over to the other shoulder. Then he rolls over onto his back. "Lying on my side hurts," he says.

"No need to apologize," Molly says. "It's great. You're really acting like a dog."

She reaches down and rubs his stomach. Liam kicks out a leg.

Liam pushes himself off the floor. He frowns and brushes the dust off his perfectly faded Levi's. "Can I leave?" he asks Molly. "Seriously."

He pretends to beg. Molly pretends to throw a ball out the door and Liam chases after it and is gone for the night.

Right after Liam has left, the smile lingers on Molly's face just a few seconds longer than makes Gid totally comfortable.

"I don't know about you," Molly says, sitting in a metal chair, leaning back, and putting her feet up on the back of another metal chair, "but I think that the Spanish are a little too obsessed with death and love. I mean, would a rousing musical number kill them?"

Gid nods. He couldn't agree more. This play is even weirder than it sounds. Yesterday, Molly brought in a little information about the author that she'd gotten off the Internet. He wrote this play five years into his incarceration. He was married to a woman and a man, at the same time. The dog in their play, some people said, was supposed to represent Franco, who, Molly informed him, was once the dictator of Spain.

"Frank O.?" Gid asks. "You'd think if he was such an important guy, they'd use his whole last name."

Gid thinks this is a very erudite comment and is not at all prepared to see Molly fighting off a smile.

"It's one word. Like *Charo*. Or, if you don't know who that is, like *Sbarro*!"

Gid nods happily. He knows what *Sbarro* is. It's his dad's favorite place to eat on the highway.

"But back to Franco," Molly says. "It's not that I don't understand how a dog could represent a dictator. I just think it's kind of stupid. They're afraid of the dog, but they take care of it, they allow it to exist. Okay, I get it. They're afraid of the dictator, but they keep him around. Is that supposed to be profound or something?"

Molly is smart, Gid thinks. She is probably smarter than he is—though he imagines he himself is pretty smart. But the fact that he doesn't always get what Molly's saying can make it difficult to respond to her. He considers making a joke but can't think of anything particularly funny to say.

Gid taps his lips with his fingers. "I wish I smoked, sometimes," he says. "Wouldn't it be nice to be smoking right now?"

This is all he can come up with?

"You didn't even respond to what I just said," Molly says, annoyed.

This isn't good. He remembers his mother telling him that talking to his father was like talking to a banana. "Well," he ventures, "I guess I feel like, who am I to judge? I barely speak Spanish. How do I know what's good?" This is better. At least on subject.

Molly picks up the script. "Allow me to translate: I love the dog. You love the dog. We love the dog. We hate the dog. Who is the dog? The dog is the one who tells us who we are!" She flings the script back down. "I may be just a *campesina* from Buffalo, but I don't need anyone to tell me that is some of the most ridiculous shit ever written."

"Maybe we should do another play," Gideon says.

"No way." Molly shakes her head. "Ms. San Video is going to love this. She's so pretentious and annoying."

"Really?" Gideon says. "I think she's a good teacher."

Molly leans forward and puts her hands on his knees. Whoa. Not sure where to go with that. Boys have such a love-hate relationship to physical contact. "Why do you think that?"

"Uh . . ." Gid fights the urge to look down her shirt. She's at a prime angle for it.

"Because she's mean to you? Because she wears nice clothes?" Molly prods.

"I don't think she's mean to me. I think she's just trying to make me so ashamed of myself that I actually learn Spanish. It's working."

Molly laughs at this, as she should. She laughs hard enough, in fact, to drop her script. As she bends forward to retrieve it, he looks down the back of her pants. At first he is disappointed to see that she isn't wearing a skirt tonight, but then, when he sees that her pants were tighter than usual, he becomes elated.

He thinks her ass looks really good in those pants, and turns bright red.

"I think that's a pretty good observation of your psyche," Molly says.

"Really?" Gid is pleased. "I feel like you say things like that, like, five times a day." And he blushes more, because he knows that this is kind of like telling her that he likes her.

"Oh," Molly says wryly, and if she notices Gid's embarrassment, she doesn't let it show. "I'm sure one day you'll be as wise as me!" She pauses and looks at him. "Are you okay? You're all red!"

"I . . . I . . ." Gid decides to tell a very partial truth. "I was just thinking of something embarrassing."

He wants Molly to ask what it is. But she just nods and jumps up. "I do that all the time," she says. There's a tentative knock on the door. It opens, revealing Edie and her ubiquitous book bag.

"Hi," she says to Molly. "I need to show you my American history presentation." She gives Gideon a brief glance. "Hi," she says.

Gid stands up, to be polite. "You're in Cullen's class, aren't you? How did his thing with the little toy soldiers go?"

Edie waves her little hand from side to side, the international sign for so-so. "I laughed," she says.

"Were you supposed to laugh?" Molly asks.

Edie shrugs. "I was too busy laughing to decide."

Now they both laugh.

"What are you doing for your project?" Gid asks. You know, I don't know if it's obvious to Molly that he's only giving Edie the time of day to look better in Molly's eyes. Later in life, Gid's going to have to work on talking to all girls, not just the ones he wants to screw, so that when he talks to the ones he wants to screw, it won't be so incredibly obvious. Edie—whether she's on to him or not, I can't say—answers his question.

"I'm writing Betsy Ross's diary. Around the time that she's making the flag." Gid sees Edie redden, and the way Molly stands next to her at a solicitous, protective angle, he knows that Edie's not real big on sharing.

Gid nods.

Edie continues, "But it's not about, like, the war and stuff. It's just about the actual flag. Like, imagining the stores she has to go to and how she makes the cloth and how she has to get some guy to come to her house when her loom breaks. It might sound weird, but I'm learning a lot about the way the economy worked back then."

Okay, whatever. Someone needs to put the kibosh on all these hippie projects going on at this school. No wonder we are all nuts.

The next night is Friday. Cullen and Gid are sitting together at dinner, late, long after the other boys have evaporated. "You should blow off rehearsal," Cullen says. "Ask Molly if she wants to go for a walk."

"Go for a walk? That's so obvious."

Cullen leans forward, fixing his pretty eyes on Gideon's. They have yellowish flecks in them, and they've seemed to blossom over the last few weeks. Is it drug use? Has their friendship deepened to the point where Gid has more chances for close observation? "Girls like obvious," Cullen says.

Gid considers. "We have been getting out of study hall for the play," he says. "All the teachers think we're at rehearsal, and no one's checking up on us." But he frowns, looking out the window to the dark and cold. "But I think that . . . I mean, I think if I move too fast on her, she's going to think I'm weird."

Cullen lifts a giant glass of milk to his mouth and rolls his eyes.

He's laying off the chocolate for now, because Nicholas told him he was getting back fat.

"What?" Gid says. "All I'm saying is that I know you don't think she's, like, the most incredibly gorgeous thing on the planet . . ."

"Yeah," Cullen says. "Liam referred to her as stealth hot. Which I think is generous."

Cullen is getting back fat, by the way. I've seen it.

Gideon wasn't surprised that Liam told him he thought Molly was hot—excuse me, stealth hot. But he is surprised Liam admitted it to Cullen. This is not good news. His telling Gid was kind of like a tree falling in the forest. But Cullen matters. Telling Cullen means Liam might be prepared to do something.

Gideon says, "Great. Liam Wu. Great."

"Fuck Liam Wu."

"You don't really mean that," Gid says.

Yeah, he can't possibly really mean that. That's like saying, Fuck Pilar Benitez-Jones.

"Okay," Cullen says, wagging his head from side to side. "I don't really quite mean it."

"They flirt," Gid says miserably. "I mean, Molly really talks to me, but those two flirt."

"You're selling yourself short, buddy," Cullen says. "You're a lot more visible on campus now. I see a lot of girls look at you. I think she already . . . Oh God. Look . . ." His voice trails off. "Okay, shit, well, we're about to have a little moment of truth here. Molly's coming toward us," he says. "I am going to tell you whether she's ready for you or not. I'll kick you under the table. Okay?" His wink is so confident.

Molly is a little ramshackle in a shiny black slicker and oversize boots with a skirt. She has a knowing smile, and when she gets right up to the table, she opens her hands. In each of them is a plastic snout, identical to Liam's.

"Check it out," she says. "You know what we were talking

about yesterday, the dog represents the dictator, et cetera? Well, how about we wear the snouts too, not just Liam." She puts it on. "And it's like, we're all our own dictators. Whoa! Deep, right?" She laughs. Gid decides: She is excited to see me, just as Cullen kicks him, a little too hard. "She's going to love it. We can even be really bad, and she'll love it and give us A's, and we'll all go to Harvard, which is, let's face it, the only reason we all bother with this crap."

"Oh, come on," Cullen says, stretching his arms up on purpose—clearly forgetting about his love handles. "This place isn't that bad."

"For you," Molly says. "I mean, if I were a tall, handsome heir to a frozen diet cheesecake fortune and all I did was smoke pot and tell sophomores they were pretty, I'd like it here too."

The look on Cullen's face is exactly the same as the look Liam got on his face the night Gideon yelled at him about finding Molly. It is the look of extreme confidence shattered. He is pale, his features seem to curl in on themselves a little. He stands up. Gid stands up. The three of them walk out of the cafeteria in silence.

Passing through the alcove out of the cafeteria, Gid focuses on the notices pinned to the bulletin boards lining the walls: mini-fridges for sale, standardized test notices, offers of tutoring and summer programs and holiday rides to various locales on the eastern seaboard. Molly walks slightly ahead of them. She keeps turning around to look at Gid. Gid's torn between paying attention to her or to Cullen, who seems a little blindsided. "I thought your dad was a lawyer," Gid finally says.

"He is," Cullen says. "He opened up the cheesecake business when I was three."

So he hasn't actually been a lawyer for quite some time.

"You can ask him all about it over Parents' Weekend," Molly says to Gid.

Frozen diet cheesecake! He can see why Molly thought this would be an Achilles' heel. He had always imagined that Cullen's dad did something much more glamorous than that. He pictured a man in a dark suit, as handsome as Cullen, maybe with a little gray in his hair. Cullen's mother would be blonde and have tan legs from playing golf in short flowered skirts. Did Cullen's dad eat a lot of diet cheesecake? Was he fat? Was his mother fat? Gideon's mother had been fat when she was married to his father, but now she was thin. She and the science teacher were into power walking, which made them look like total assholes—part zombie, part windmill. But at least they weren't fat.

"Okay, well," Molly says brightly, "I'll see you at seven-thirty." She puts the dog snout into his open hand, then closes his fingers around it. "I entrust you with this."

"She's got a pretty nice ass," Cullen says as she walks away. There's something weird about the way he says it, though. It's a compliment, but I can tell that the frozen diet cheesecake thing got under his skin. There's a part of him, I would bet, that's trying to put her in her place. There's a little muscle under Cullen's neck that's pulsating in and out. Molly, Gid sees, got to him. She found a chink in his golden armor. A chink made of Splenda and fat-free cream cheese. He thinks about her ass. It's not just her ass. It's the way she walks. She walks like she's having a good time. Like no one's watching.

first
base

Rushing along the stretch of Route 215 that leads to the theater, buoyant from having turned in a paper on *Moby-Dick* that he actually thinks might not be that bad, Gid is struck with a revelation at once so brilliant and so obvious that he leaps into the air. And this is it: After five rehearsals, it's time to do the script for real. Which means making out. Ladies and gentlemen, my name is Gideon Rayburn, he says to himself, laughing appreciatively at his idea, and we are *off-book*.

Hey, I'm more than ready for sexual tension to become sexual. My feelings about Gideon aside, it's just how things are supposed to progress. And after all, pretentious Spanish playwrights don't just write sensual stage directions for their fucking *salud* (health).

When he arrives at the theater, Molly's sitting on one of the little Plexiglas cubes in the lobby, waiting, mouthing words over the script. Gideon's plan is so good that it even includes an opening line—not an especially inspired one but a start nonetheless— "Pollard Theater is a really ugly building."

But Molly holds off conversation with a raised finger. *"Qué nunca olvides este canción, la canción de la guerra, la canción de los muertos*" (That we never forget the song, the song of the war, the song of the dead), she murmurs. "God, what a load of crap." She closes the script and sets it down on her knee. Another skirt tonight, brown and soft against the whiteness of her skin. Her eyes soften to let Gid know she's ready to converse. "Pollard Theater," Molly says, "ugly indeed. Edie says it looks like an ice-cube tray fucked a roulette wheel."

Gid frowns. "That sounds a little dirty for Edie."

Molly fans herself with the script. "I think the 'fuck' part might be mine. But the sentiment, it's all her." She takes the script and taps him on the shoulder. (Molly's enjoying this whole actress thing. She might be wearing the skirt because she's into Gid, but mostly, I think she feels a little like a star and wants to dress the part.) "I suppose I should tell you that Liam is lying on the floor of the practice space, drunk."

Molly stands up. Gid notices she has cute ankles. Is he forcing himself to notice she has cute ankles? No, he decides, walking behind her, watching them as she walks. They're not quite as exciting as Pilar's breasts, but ankles have their charms. As a girl, I would pick ankles over breasts any day. I mean it. They last longer.

Liam rolls to one side and waves when they walk in. Even covered in dust from the floor and wearing a dog snout, he looks very handsome. Gid actually has a benevolent thought about his handsomeness. He sends out a silent wish for Liam Wu: Life is hard. May your totally unfair share of beauty make yours just a little easier. He's feeling generous, confident. He can do this.

"Hey, uh, Molly," he says, "I think that we need to start, you know, doing the play more as it's written. I think we need to get, uh, used to the . . ."

And here, he actually lifts one eyebrow, somewhat sexily.

"The physical parts," he finishes. He doesn't know if he's saying the right things, but he knows one thing: He's moving forward. Finally.

This moment isn't lost on Liam, who, alcohol-soaked as he is, begins to stir. His unfocused eyes sharpen ever so slightly with a sort of lascivious curiosity. He senses a plan, designs of sex and intrigue.

As far as Gideon goes, he could give a fuck. Here's what he sees. Molly likes his suggestion.

"Okay," Molly says, and Gid will be damned if he can't hear her trying to steady her voice, "let's get going, then."

Liam takes a giant swig from his flask, slips on his plastic snout, and, after walking a few feet across the room, slumps at their feet in a canine heap. Molly and Gideon put on their plastic snouts. *"El Perro que Compartimos,"* Liam slurs.

The first scene doesn't require any physical contact. At least not with each other. It does require that they stand over Liam taking turns patting him and exchanging observations about the quality of his coat.

"It is glossy."

"It harbors fleas."

"It is warm."

"When wet, it steams and festers."

"Hey," Gideon says when the scene ends, "I think I get what you said about the fascist stuff now."

"God," Molly says, "I thought you got it the other day."

Gid shakes his head. "You always think people know what you're talking about, and it makes it kind of hard to interrupt," he says. It's hard to talk with the plastic snout on. He takes it off and brushes plastic-smelling perspiration from his face. Shit. They're going to have to kiss with these things on. That's not going to be very sexy.

"Thanks," Molly says. "I mean . . . oh." She takes off her snout too.

They stand there, looking at their snouts. "Fuck," Liam moans. "I'm fucking bored. Come on, let's do the next scene."

Molly looks at the floor with more shyness than Gid has ever seen her display, and then quickly, like she's jumping into water, throws her arms around Gideon's waist. Strange, but with a girl's arms around him like this, he can really feel how his body has hardened. He feels happy, fulfilled, accomplished.

"Scene," says Molly.

Liam starts to giggle.

"Heel," Molly says.

Liam giggles some more.

If they do their little doggie-owner routine, Gid thinks, I will kill myself.

They don't.

It's a good thing that Gid doesn't really know what he's saying, because it's hard to concentrate on anything except the fact that he's got his arms wrapped around Molly McGarry. He always thought she was kind of small, but now he feels that she's surprisingly heavy, like a bullet. But not bad heavy, not like, "Hey, you should take up race-walking" heavy, just like, "She'd be sort of hard to pick up" heavy.

"*Tú eres el dueño del perro*," he says. (You are the owner of the dog.)

"*Sí tú me amas, el perro sea el tuyo también*," Molly says. (If you love me, the dog is yours too). She's actually not a bad actress. She's not seething with talent or anything, but at least you kind of believe what she's saying. Gid, by the way, is totally aware that he sucks, but he's smart enough not to add "lacks acting talent" to the list of personal shortcomings that are constantly piling up in his head.

"Now the dog is our friend, we are together, and the dog gives us something to talk about," Molly says.

And this is one of the places in the script where "*Oscar y Lucía se besan con pasión.*"

Molly and Gideon *se besan con pasión.*

This is a moment where being inside Gid's head is pretty weird. Because if I am Molly, of course, I know what to do. I know if he's not liking the kiss, and I can adjust. But what if I'm someone else, and Gid is kissing another girl, and liking it? I wouldn't like that. And he *is* liking it. Every aspect of it. The firm pressure of her hand on his back, the lighter pressure of her knee against the outside of his calf, the kiss itself—he doesn't know who started the tongue thing. Or if it's just part of acting. But it's definitely going on.

Over the kissing sounds, Gid hears Liam say, "Wow."

The *pasión* ends. Gid and Molly sort of pat themselves, arranging their clothes and hair.

Liam gets up and stumbles out of the room. He pauses for a second at the door. "I think that we might get in trouble for that. I'm definitely not needed here." They look at each other as they hear Liam make his way down the hall and groan as he opens the heavy glass door and disappears into the night.

"Let me be the first to tell you," Molly says, "we're going to get an A."

At first he thinks she means that they're going to get an A for kissing. And he's about to grab her, he's really about to, when he sees that she's getting ready to go. "Uh, I should really walk you home," he says. "It's probably best."

Molly pulls her hair free from under the collar of her sweater, which Gid notes is white and soft, and she shakes it out. "You don't need to walk me home," she says. "I mean, what, are you afraid the JV tennis team's going to pull a train on me?"

Gid reddens and looks at his feet.

"Oh, come on," Molly says. "Let's go."

They take the path that goes through the woods, site of Gideon's high-stakes crime night. He checks her for signs that the kiss has left her ruffled—he doesn't know whether to jump up in the air or puke—but she's totally smooth. She reminds Gideon of . . . a sailboat. That's stupid. Yes, it is, Gideon, you're right. Sailboat is stupid. At any rate, she seems utterly fine with the silence between them, but Gid, desperate to fill it, and vaguely hoping her answer will illuminate how she feels about him, asks, "So, what was it about the play that made you think we're going to get an A? I mean, you said yourself it's a dumb play."

"I know, because my parents are teachers. Anytime kids do something like this, without laughing, they're impressed. I mean, we're making out with plastic snouts on. How easy is that? Ms. San Video's going to think that we see some sort of symbolism in the whole thing. She's going to brag to all her friends at dinner parties how insightful we are. It's genius." Here, she stops and puts a mittened hand to her head. "I salute Liam Wu, in absentia, for picking this play."

"I don't know," Gid says. "I think that the kiss . . ." Molly puts her hands on his shoulders. He's pleased that she's touching him but knows it doesn't necessarily mean anything.

"Seriously," she says, "my sister's in college, and she just gave a presentation in her art history class comparing vaginas to hurricanes. Total bullshit. She got an A. The teacher told her she was, and I quote, 'one of the most brilliant students I ever had.'"

He was hoping that bringing up the kiss would lead to more talking about the kiss. Not this. Hurricanes and vaginas. These are two things he does not want to associate. Their walk back up Route 215, after this, is silent. And it's a girl silence, meaning she decides she wants it to be quiet. A boy silence is what happens all the time. Girl silences mean something. In this case, Gid hopes it means she's processing. Recovering.

Maybe she is. Maybe Gid's kiss just wrecked her.

Back at Molly's dorm, they settle themselves on a little cement step under the door to the basement. "Here we are again," she says. Molly wraps her arms around herself. Reflexively, Gid takes off his coat and tucks it around her shoulders. So now he's cold. He reminds himself sacrifice is part of the bet. "If you don't mind me asking," he says, going down another road altogether, "how did you end up coming to school here? I mean, if your parents are teachers?"

Okay, Gid, this is a good question. Direct, curious. Girls like this. Have you noticed that Gid really does just as well on his own as he does following the "expert" advice of his roommates?

"Thanks for the coat. That was nice and, once again, very Buffalo. I assume you were asking how I can go here because my parents don't make a lot of money, right?"

Gid wags his head from side to side, wishing to get around this, but Molly waves him off.

"When I was around four, my dad took me to a movie. We got popcorn, and lo and behold, we get to the bottom and a half-eaten bagel is lying there. Like with teeth marks. So we sued. And here I am with you fancy people!"

"Molly," Gid says, "I read that article the other day too." He actually reads the entire *Boston Globe* almost every day, at lunch. It's a good way of reminding himself that there are people in the world who have worse problems than being the new kid at Midvale Academy.

"You did? Damn. Anyway. I think the father's totally overreacting. The girl had all these shots and vaccinations. It's not like the bagel was soaked in human blood. Anyway, I thought it was a really good lie."

"It was only an okay lie," Gideon says. "Kind of adolescent."

Totally adolescent.

Now Molly reddens. "I . . . The truth is that my parents teach at the school I would go to, and they don't want me to go there, so they just use most of my mother's salary to send me here. Buffalo's not exactly expensive." She pokes at some gravel with her foot. "I feel a little stupid that I am always joking around," she confesses. "I sort of exhaust myself. But I just get nervous, and the only thing that makes me feel better is cracking jokes. Except then I get more nervous."

"Uh," he says, wanting to be helpful, "you could see a shrink."

Molly wrinkles up her face with distaste. "Nah. A shrink would be just one more person to be ashamed and embarrassed in front of. Who needs that?"

"Hey, Gee-de-on." No one mangles his name so beautifully. There she is. Pilar. Pilar in her new special fire-escape room. Now hanging out the window, waving, her hair hanging down like an Argentine Rapunzel.

Gid knows he should just wave. But instead he gets up and walks over to stand where Pilar hangs out. As if some force he had no control over were driving him there. Well, I guess you could argue there's a force he has no control over . . . he is a guy, after all.

But I don't know if I accept that. The whole no control–male libido thing is such bullshit. If Gideon were slightly more mature, slightly less selfish, he could have just waved to Pilar and continued to chat with Molly. But he's not. So he didn't.

"Hi, Gid," Pilar says. "What are you doing?"

"Nothing," he says. Whoops. Bad idea. He's torn between keeping an eye on Molly and looking up at Pilar. "We're just talking . . . we're doing a class project together."

"I was talking to Nicolito earlier," Pilar says. "He eats really weird food, no?"

"Uh, yes."

"Anyway, he told me he was going to be in New York for Thanksgiving. I'm going to be there too." She disappears for a minute, then comes back, pointing a tiny video camera at him. "Salute," she says. He salutes, self-consciously of course, looking over toward Molly. It's dark, but he can see the stiffness in her body, how she stares straight ahead. Gid, she's annoyed.

"I need to go," he says.

"Wait a minute," Pilar says. "I want to give you something. Wait! Wave one more time and say, 'Hi, Pilar!' "

He waves. And says, "Hi, Pilar."

Then she swings the camera over to the left. "Your new girl-friend got cold, I guess," Pilar says.

Gid's head snaps to the right. His jacket is in a neat pile folded on the fire escape's bottom stair. Molly's gone.

"You should maybe go after her," Pilar says. Not meaning it. Taunting, really.

"It's okay," he says. "She's not my girlfriend, by the way." Even though this is true, as soon as it's out of his mouth he recognizes it as disloyal. Lame. "We're just in a play. We'll probably rehearse to-morrow. It's going on in like, less than two weeks." Oh God, he thinks. A little more than a week until Halloween.

"Tomorrow? Aren't you going to be a little busy tomorrow."

"It's Saturday," Gid says. "I'm not doing anything." Holy Christ. Could she be asking him to get together? Could that fire escape in-deed have his name on it?

"Oh ho." Pilar laughs. "That's what you think." She waves a piece of paper out her window. "I have to go," she says. "But you might want to see this."

The piece of paper comes floating down from her window. It lands behind the Dumpster, and Gid scoots behind there and grabs it. It's some kind of brochure, printed on white paper. In embossed type, it reads: WELCOME PARENTS, over Midvale's seal—horse, rider, Latin—giving off beams of light. He opens it and reads: PARENTS' DAY OCTOBER 22.

Ten hours of Jim Rayburn. If he knows his dad, he's washing the Silverado right now. Rinsing out his coffee thermos. Getting ready for that predawn departure.

Gid sits down. He looks at the paper again, just to make sure it's right. There's something written on the other side. He turns it over. Beautifully, unexpectedly written there in a thick, glittery pinkish-brown lipstick is her cell number, again, and, PILAR!

Gid sits there behind the Dumpster for a while, absorbing the smell of garbage with the good and bad news. He looks up to Pilar's window. Her lights are on, she paces and talks on the phone. Molly's window, in the same position, on the opposite side of the dorm, is dark.

surprise
indeed

Early the next morning, there's a knock on the door. Gideon jumps up from his bed and looks out the window. The quad is empty, vapor coming off the grass, a marine layer hanging low over the brick vista of campus buildings. It is not a civilized time, Gid thinks, to knock on a door. The clock confirms this: 7:30.

He shuffles to the peephole. Sure enough, Jim Rayburn's standing there, thumbs through the belt loops of his black jeans. And also . . . Captain Cockweed? A most unfortunate pairing, Gid thinks, opening the door.

"I saw your father downstairs," Captain Cockweed says, "and I was kind enough to show him the way up."

"You're a real stand-up kind of guy," Cullen calls out, turning against the wall and hugging a pillow. His parents aren't coming. Colorado's a bit far to fly for a day. Cullen doesn't care.

Nicholas rubs his eyes and pushes himself up onto an elbow. "Yeah," he says, "when I wake up I want to be just like you." Nicholas's mother isn't coming either, because, as we know, she never leaves Manhattan.

Cockweed walks off, muttering.

Cullen gets out of bed, slips on a T-shirt, and comes over and shakes Jim Rayburn's hand.

"So nice to see you again, Mr. Rayburn," he says.

Golly, his father is practically blushing.

Jim leans in quickly before Gid can stop him and grabs him around the ribs. "You're a little fighter! Look at you! You didn't tell me you were working out!"

"I got Gid out on the track," Nicholas says. "And, you know, added some basic nutrition."

Jim Rayburn puts a manly hand on Nicholas's shoulder. "Fantastic," he says. "Fan-fucking-tastic. I thank you for that! Well, son, you had a surprise for me with that new bod of yours, but wait until you see what I have for you."

Gideon is terrified. Rightly so. Surprises can be great from the right person. But Jim Rayburn doesn't know him or understand him. So whatever it is Jim thinks Gid wants, he is probably way, way off base. Way.

But Gid plays along. "Great," Gid says. "What is it?"

"You're going to have to come out to the vehicle," Jim says.

He did not just say *vehicle*. No wonder Gid's mother left him for a guy who makes volcanoes out of baking soda and vinegar.

Gid runs into the bathroom and looks at his face in the mirror. He's so incredibly not up for this. What's the surprise? He goes through varying levels of horror, imagining it. Rubbers? A two-for-one coupon for Sbarro? A pony? He splashes water on his face.

In the hallway, Gid's father starts right in again. "Well, well, well, I can't say I've ever seen you looking this good before! Chip off the old block!" He snorts and—in his second aggressive and unwelcome physical act of the day—pokes Gid in the ribs.

Captain Cockweed is crouched at the far end of the hallway, feeding papers into an electric shredder. He grimaces.

Gid sees his father expanding, gearing up for his all-time favorite pastime—demanding attention from reluctant strangers.

"Killing two birds with one stone, eh?" Jim Rayburn bellows. "Keeping an eye on these hoodlums and watching out for that identity theft at the same time. You know, I had a buddy, two Spanish fellas got aholda his information . . . well, fourteen TVs, twelve velour living room sets . . ."

Captain Cockweed frowns.

"And God knows how many round-trip tickets to our Virgin of Guadalupe later . . ."

Captain Cockweed snaps off the paper shredder switch and regards both father and son.

"Anyway, seriously. On my way in, I saw a very attractive lady out here, your wife, I presume, with an electric can opener . . ."

On "very attractive lady," Captain Cockweed's eyes harden into gray stones.

"Come on, Dad," Gid whispers.

Unfazed, Jim Rayburn continues, "So I'm guessing you got an electrical situation going on in there. Am I wrong? I didn't think so. Well, why don't you let me take a look?"

"Dad," Gid says pleadingly, "my surprise, don't you want to show it to me?"

Jim smiles at him broadly. And poor Gid, for a second, he thinks he may have won. But then Jim says, "This is the kind of surprise you'd probably be happiest discovering on your own! So the Silverado is right out there in the, uh, lot behind that, uh, big building with the pillars out front . . ."

"That's our Humanities building." Captain Cockweed, company man, can't help but chime in.

Jim's fishing the keys out of his pants and handing them to Gid. Gid stuffs them in his pocket before Captain Cockweed can see the "Fish tremble at the sound of my voice" key chain. He looks at his watch. Eight o'clock. Ten hours and his father will be gone.

Captain Cockweed, defeated, opens his apartment door for Mr. Rayburn. "Won't you come in?" he asks, his mouth barely opening to say the words.

Outside, Gid breathes the cold, leaf-smoked smell of fall. This is my life now, he says to himself. He will leave prep school and then there will be college. Now, and for the rest of Gid's life, as unfortunate as conflict is with his father, at least it will have a beginning, middle, and end. This is the beginning, and that's hard, but he's going to be fine.

Speaking of fine, here comes Pilar Benitez-Jones, flanked on one side by a blonde woman in a short skirt, boots, and a sweater, and on the other by an older man with white hair and darkish skin. Pilar and the blonde woman seem to be moving slowly because of him. Gideon imagines they are her sister and father. But as they get closer, he realizes that, in fact, the blonde woman must be her mother; the dark man, an older grandfather or uncle. Pilar's mother wears a suit, a deep rose color, and boots with heels that taper down to thumbtack-size points. Aside from her slightly lined face, she looks like a girl. The man, in a dark suit and hat, is stooped over a cane and has the bearing of an extremely elegant turtle.

"Hello," Pilar says. "These are my parents."

Why, Gid asks himself, is it so incredibly sexy to him that Pilar's father looks like he's about to drop dead?

Pilar looks more beautiful and even more put together than usual. She's wearing low-heeled blue suede pumps with tight jeans, super low on her hips, and a white shirt, unbuttoned, Gid thinks, and frankly, so do I, to a level farther down than one imagines one's parents might normally approve. Her hair is pulled up on her head in a well-planned cascading mess. Her eye shadow matches her shoes.

Gid tries to give Pilar's parents the kind of smile he thinks might impress them, polite but enthusiastic. They smile back, but mostly, they seem to look right through him. Pilar's father, in particular, seems to be focused on something about one thousand miles in the distance. His clouded eyes don't move an inch as he takes Gid's hand and says what Gid imagines is "Nice to meet you," although it just sounds like "*Nun mah.*"

"So," Gideon says, "have you got anything planned for the day?"

"Maybe we will go into Boston, to a museum or two, maybe have some lunch, and maybe an early cocktail with some friends of ours now living here, who we knew from Barcelona." Mrs. Benitez-Jones, who has no accent and therefore must be the Jones part in this arrangement, gives a tiny shrug. She does say *Barcelona* the way you're supposed to, Bar-thay-lona. Gid doesn't notice, but I do. "And you? Do you and your family . . ."

"It's just his father," Pilar corrects her. "Gid's mother is not around."

If most people revealed this information about Gid, he might feel embarrassed. But he's so overjoyed that Pilar has any recollection of anything he's told her that he just accepts Pilar's quick sympathetic smile with a small, shy one of his one.

"Well," says Pilar's mother, frowning slightly at this information, "you and your father will do similarly, I suppose?"

Gid almost laughs out loud at the idea of his father having early cocktails with old friends from Bar-thay-lona. "I suppose," he says, thinking, somewhat randomly, Please let my dad not know there's a dog track near here.

Pilar's mother is checking her watch, a tiny diamond-studded thing with a pink face.

"We really should be going," she says. Gideon looks over at Pilar's father. His face is completely glazed over, he's smiling, but one of his eyes flutters a bit. He's paying absolutely no attention. His wife grabs his arm and shuffles him off a few feet. Pilar stays behind, looking at Gid.

"Wow," Gid says when they're out of earshot. "Your dad is

really old." Immediately, he thinks, I'm so stupid. I'm the stupidest person who ever lived. But Pilar bursts out laughing.

"Thank God, someone says the truth. Usually, people say, 'Your mother is so pretty,'" she says.

"To be honest," Gid says, continuing with this train since it seems to be a crowd-pleaser, "I didn't really notice, because I was so blown away by how old your father is. Wait a sec. He can't possibly be very cool about stuff like dudes. Like letting you date a rock star who is a lot older than you."

Pilar frowns. "Oh, they don't know about Dennis. They would kill me. After I finish college, I am supposed to get engaged to this Argentine guy. A *Porteño*."

"Is that a sports team?"

Pilar shakes her head. "No, it means a person from Buenos Aires. We are from Bahía Blanca. Anyway. He is thirty-six already. His father and my father own a company together."

"What kind of company?" Gid asks.

Pilar puts her hands on her hips. "Are you ready for this? They make industrial solvents out of beef fat."

"Holy shit." What else do you say to that?

"Anyway. That's not important. He will be around forty or forty-two then . . ." Gid blanches. That's how old his dad is. He imagines Pilar marrying his dad. Yuck.

"Pilar . . ."

"I have to go . . ." She reaches out and takes his hand. "Please don't tell anyone about what I told you," she says. She runs off, once again, inserting herself between her parents.

She confided in him! Wait a minute. Does she not want anyone to know about the industrial solvent made out of beef fat or the arranged marriage?

He decides he won't mention either.

It's only a three-minute or so walk to the parking lot, and Gid occupies himself daydreaming of interrupting Pilar's wedding six or so years from now. He's picturing the wedding taking place in a church in the middle of a big field. It must be the cow thing. Anyway, just as Pilar's father hands her off to the guy at the altar, Gid storms in. Pilar, resplendent but red-eyed in her white dress, faints into his arms. He revives her and they rush from the church. At the bottom of the church steps, a giant pile of cow shit obstructs them, and Gid lifts Pilar up and carries her over it. Pilar's mother watches from the church steps, glowering, resenting that her daughter will get to spend her life with someone so young, strong, and courageous.

Gid wishes he could just live inside that fantasy for the rest of his life, but he's arriving at the Silverado. And the surprise. He's approaching the pickup from the back. As Gid gets nearer, he swears he can see a bulge around the passenger seat neck rest. Is it a plant? It is a giant inflatable bottle? Oh Lord. It turns slightly to the right. It's a person.

Not just any person. A wronged person. Danielle. He sees her face in the passenger-side-view mirror. She sees him. She gets out of the car.

She's gained weight in the right places. Her hair is shorter, and those awful highlights that she did at home, with the help of a plastic pull-through cap and her friend Gillian Loh, have grown out. She looks pretty good for her. But she's not Midvale pretty. Her face has the hard look of a girl who has to share a room, beg for the car, and make and eat a fair share of frozen dinners when her parents are working late. Danielle just stands there, looking at Gid, for a good two minutes. A group of students in ripped jeans and ratty sweaters appear on the path behind her, smiling, pointing things out to their parents, who are identical versions of their kids but in neat pants and nice sweaters. They regard her quietly and quickly and move on. This girl standing there in the parking lot with a black corduroy purse from Old Navy is definitely no one they've ever seen before. They just keep walking, registering that this person probably isn't quite supposed to be here. But they're not all that concerned. Then Danielle starts screaming.

"You asshole! You chicken shit! What is your problem? Do you think I'm stupid? Do you think I couldn't handle it if you just broke up with me?" Now she's walking toward him. Before, the people passing by regarded her with mild curiosity and moved on. Now people are staring. She's a show. They're a show.

Gid backs away from her. But the parking lot's full of cars and there's really nowhere to go. He panics. She's still screaming. He needs to get her to be quieter. Midvale's a quiet place. She's at least four times as loud as anything I've heard here.

"Danielle, I understand that you're upset . . ."

"You don't understand shit. You think you could just fuck me, no, excuse me, you think I could just offer my virginity to you, and then you could just leave, and never talk to me, and that would be fine?"

It's amazing, Gid thinks, that she has such a specific story about what happened between them. When she said *offer,* does she also suspect it didn't quite happen? For him, it's haze and free-floating anxiety, but it's mostly just forgotten. He's never really—as she so clearly has—taken the time to put it all together. What a bad, unfair thing. He thinks—he can't help it—of Pilar, how awful it is to love her and not know if she loves him back.

Standing along the few concrete steps between the classroom buildings and the residential quad is what now could be referred to as an audience. Danielle, tired of screaming at Gideon, starts to scream at them. "Don't you have anything better to do? Don't you all want to go play polo or something? Organize your sweaters?" Their eyes stretch wide in their pale faces, their mouths are all thin, aghast.

Maybe they're thinking, What's so *wrong* with organizing our sweaters?

"Listen." Gid leans in and tries to put his hand on her shoulders. She bucks away from him. "Hey," he says. Gid stares at the black eyeliner seeping out of the corner of her eyes down her cheek. "Hey, stop. You should know you're still a virgin."

All the hard-edged tension seeps out of Danielle's body. She slouches. Gid tries not to look at the dark patches of faded acne around her mouth, beiged over with makeup.

"What are you talking about?"

"I mean," Gid says, "I don't think I actually, you know," and because he doesn't know what word to use next, he makes a fist, then taps his index finger against the crease. Danielle continues to stare at him. He finds there's something sexy about the patchy grayness of her skin. "So," Gid says, hopeful that he might have calmed her down, "do you get it?"

There's a long silence where they just look at each other. Gid is acutely aware of the pine smell in the air, and of Danielle's black clothing and roughness against the neat cheerfulness of the surroundings. He remembers what he liked about her. All kinds of girls, he thinks, are sexy. He likes the ones who glow and the ones who look sad and unhealthy. "You're still a virgin," he says again, thinking this is great news.

And then, suddenly, she is on him, fists pounding his chest and shoulders and, if not for the protection of his hands, his head. "You idiot. You idiot! I can't fucking believe what an idiot you are! This isn't about whether I still have a hymen or not."

Gid continues to protect his head. He can't really see. He wishes she hadn't said the word *hymen* out loud.

"It's about what a dick you are." Danielle's hands, arms, and wrists continue their rather ineffectual assault against him. He finds his mind starting to really float now, wondering how Danielle spent the ride up here. Did she plan out what she was going to say? Was she silent the whole time? What did Jim Rayburn know? What's all this shit about women being just as strong as men? Gid feels like a two-year-old is hitting him with a flyswatter. Of course, Danielle is pretty small in that teenage girl living off potato chips, Diet Dr Pepper, and frozen dinners kind of way. Then, miraculously, someone is pulling her off of him. He feels a few more swipes of the flyswatter. He uncovers his head slowly to see, of all people, Molly McGarry holding Danielle's wrists. Danielle strains against her, but Molly doesn't seem to be putting out too much effort. Okay, it's not just my imagination, Gid thinks. Danielle's kind of a weakling. Edie stands a few feet off to the side, clipping and unclipping the clasp on her book bag.

"Molly," Gid says.

"If I let you go," Molly says, "you can't hit Gid."

"I'm done," Danielle says in a defeated voice, and starts wiping up her eye makeup with the back of her hand.

Danielle turns to Gid. "I hate you. Do you understand that? So when I calmly explain this to you, don't think just because I'm being calm I don't hate you."

Then Jim Rayburn is coming up the hill, smiling victoriously. Gid can only imagine the massive victory he scored against Captain Cockweed's vulnerable electrical system.

"I guess your teacher's pretty grateful about what I did for him," he says. "And how do you like what I did for you? Is this a sight for sore eyes or what?" Jim puts an arm around Danielle's shoulder. Danielle, backing away from Jim, hides behind Edie.

Molly looks down at the pavement. "Yikes," she says.

Gideon talks to his father through gritted teeth. "Me and Danielle aren't really going out anymore."

"Ah," Jim Rayburn whispers. "She had me believe otherwise."

Gid nods. Danielle's smarter than he's ever given her credit for.

"Danielle, is it?" Molly says, clasping her hands together. "Look, I know you don't know us, but we're totally harmless. Our parents aren't coming until dinner. Why don't you come back to our dorm and just let Gid and his dad go? What do you think?"

Danielle crosses her arms and stares at Gid. "Sounds great," she says bitterly. Edie goes and stands with her.

Molly takes a step toward Gid.

"Thanks," Gid says, "you . . ."

Molly holds up a hand. "I'm not doing it for you. I'm doing it for humanity."

Gid won't let himself look at her ass when she walks away this time. He doesn't deserve to.

"Your friends don't want to come with us?" Jim asks. "Are you sure?"

"Yes," Gid says. "I'm sure."

They get into the Silverado and go a few blocks in silence. Strange to be here. Has it been only two months? He sees his father is thinking, trying to come up with the right question to ask about what's going on.

Which is too bad for him, because Gid has decided he's not going to tell him a fucking thing.

"Where we headed?" Gid asks, the Launch of Evasions and False Brightness already under way.

Jim—how Gid was praying this wouldn't happen—tugs on his mustache. "I thought we'd find a Sizzler or something."

Gid smiles to himself. What else can he do? Be optimistic, he coaches himself as they wait at the light down the road near the theater. Tell your dad what's going on. I mean, not really, but kind of. Maybe he can help.

The light turns green. His father guns it, and the torque presses Gideon against the seats.

"Fun, huh?" his dad says. "But if there're any cops around, they have another term for it: 'exhibition of speed.'"

The hostess at Sizzler appears to be around twelve. She's short and has a little Tweety Bird haircut. She has tattoos of birds on her forearms, and slouches, displaying a pink dragon on her lower back.

They follow her across the entire length of the restaurant, and she doesn't turn around once to see if they're keeping up. She seats them in a booth. When Jim declares, "Thanks, got a view of the whole place," she walks away without saying anything. Gid notices she has another tattoo on the back of her neck. She makes him sad. He stares at the salad bar, at the giant Plexiglas bowls of lettuce and pale tomatoes, and feels even sadder.

How can you not love a guy who gets depressed when he looks at a bad salad bar?

Jim, digging into a giant plate of various creepy hot foods and a salad drowning in blue cheese, curiously eyes Gid's plate of carrots, a scoop of cottage cheese, and plain tuna. "Gee, when Nicholas said 'basic nutrition,' he wasn't kidding!"

"When I got there, Nicholas said I was skinny fat and . . ." Gid trails off. The truth is, he doesn't have much of an appetite.

"So," his father says, "you and Danielle broke up?"

At the mention of her name Gid's stomach flips over. "'Broke up' is a strong term. I didn't exactly call her once I got here. She hates me." God, he wonders what she's doing right now. Was it a very bad idea to let her go off like that with Molly and Edie?

"Women always hate you no matter what you do," his father says. "And that's the honest truth."

This is sort of what Cullen and Nicholas have said to him. Though, of course, not in so many words. This is fantastic, if it's really true. It means that everything is okay, if in a backward kind of way.

"Did you and Danielle talk on the way up here?" Gid's curiosity about this isn't really personal. It's kind of a morbid fascination with what he considers a pretty weird pairing.

Jim wags his head from side to side. "I started out asking her about school. She gave the usual one-word answers. After that, we pretty much just kept to ourselves."

"Did she sleep?"

"No. In fact, she was awake the whole time."

Nine conscious hours in a car with Jim Rayburn. She must really have wanted to yell at me, Gid thinks, to have endured that. So she must really love me? Again, he thinks of Pilar. What a terrible world it is.

"So what did Mr. Cavanaugh have to say?" Gid asks, taking a sip of his Coke. It tastes good. Nicholas doesn't let him drink Coke.

"Funny you should ask. I told him that you seemed like you were doing very well here, and he told me that he thought Cullen and Nicholas might be a bad influence on you."

Gideon nods, feeling good again, realizing that he doesn't give a fuck what Cavanaugh thinks, aside from its being funny.

"Naturally, I was concerned. Then he starts telling me he doesn't have proof, but he thinks they do drugs. Drugs!" Jim laughs and takes a giant bite of something yellow, maybe an enchilada, maybe scalloped potatoes. "I about laughed out loud. I mean, I've seen people on drugs. Those boys, those two are nice-looking, nice boys in good shape. Drugs!" Jim shakes his head. Out in the parking lot, a wizened guy dressed in a filthy warm-up suit, squinting under his blue nylon baseball hat, limps by. He's missing teeth. Gid estimates his age as somewhere between thirty and ninety. "Now, that guy is on drugs," Jim says. "Like I wouldn't know if my own son was taking drugs."

really
okay

Charlie Otterman, Jim's former client, convicted drunk driver, and the man responsible for Gideon's attending Midvale, made Jim promise that on this visit, he would take a complete tour of the campus. "He told me Midvale was a special place," Jim says, setting a hand on Gid's shoulder. They're crossing the very same parking lot where Danielle made her previous assault. "He said to make sure I see everything." Gid leads him first to Thayer Hall, where Jim is suitably impressed by the vaulted ceilings and woodwork. Then to Pollard Theater, which Jim pronounces "very different." Then Gid finds himself leading his father toward the basement lounge of Proctor. It's a sentimental attachment to the night he talked to Mickey Eisenberg, and then met Pilar, that takes him there. Of course he tells none of this to his father, who surveys the ugly room, then simply nods and says, "Seems cozy."

For their final stop, Gid takes his father down the hill buttressing the south side of the campus to the track. A couple of football players, lumbering their way around, give them a cursory wave, and Jim yells out, "Keep up the good work, fellas!" They tip their giant heads to the ground, eager, Gid knows, to avoid further contact. Ordinarily, Gid would be mortified. Instead he considers the track's bright blue tone, smartly demarcated with white lines and numbers. This is the place, he reminds himself, where so much skinny fatness has been forged into strength.

Minute by minute, Gid manages to sustain that whole my-father-is-not-me feeling.

Jim kneels down, tugging at the grass as if to test its strength. "Okay," he says in a tone that lets Gid know he's satisfied. "Why don't we see if we can track down Little Miss Temper Tantrum?"

He's trying to bond with Gid, of course, but Gid feels a stab of defensive anger. Danielle, he thinks, hasn't been all that unreasonable.

Gid realizes now that he was so relieved to extricate himself—well, really to have Molly and Edie extricate him—from that initial situation with Danielle that he mistakenly thought that would be the end of it.

Walking back up the hill to Emerson, the girls' dorm, Jim Rayburn has the very good sense not to talk. Gid prepares himself for confrontation with more contriteness than imagination. *I will say sorry,* he tells himself, over and over and over again. *I will just keep repeating it and then Danielle will eventually just have to go away.*

There's a common space to the left as you walk in, but save for the poster of Sojourner Truth, it's empty. Gid leads his father back past the entrance down a short flight of stairs into another basement common room, as bleak as the one in Proctor.

A tenth-grader and a much younger kid, probably her brother, are watching television. Gid approaches the girl humbly. She's pretty, and Gid knows from having seen her around, from the imperious way she surveys the cafeteria before sitting down, that she's neither particularly secure or nice. "Have you seen Molly McGarry or Edie . . . uh . . . ?" He doesn't know her last name.

The girl narrows her eyes. She has straight blonde hair and is wearing green eyeliner. "Are they with some girl that doesn't go here?" she says.

"Yes, yes, exactly," Gid says, smiling, trying to let her know he's grateful.

"They're in the second-floor lounge." She looks back at the TV.

"Okay," Gid says. He stands there, waiting for the girl to say she'll go get them. Then the girl points to a sign on the wall, a simple sign printed on computer paper in a larger than usual, but by no means eye-catching, font: *Special allowances have been made for Parents' Weekend for men and boys to access the hallways and common areas in the girls' dorms.*

"Duh," she says.

Gid turns around. His father pretends to read an *American Heritage* magazine from 1986. His face has such a pathetic look. Like a dog searching for a place to go to the bathroom.

Gid bristles. "I didn't see it," he says. "I'm new."

"Duh," the girl says again.

"I always thought you looked like a bitch," Gid says. "I guess my instincts were dead on."

The girl seems to actually shrink. Her eyes widen and fill up her face, which has gone white.

Gid leads his father upstairs as if nothing has happened, but if he didn't have his hands in his pockets they would shake. Still, he feels good.

His father finally lets out a low whistle. "Jeez," he says, "you really let Miss Fancy Pants back there have it."

Gid doesn't turn around but just keeps trudging up the stairs. He can't look at his father when he uses phrases like *Miss Fancy Pants.*

"I just can't believe how friggin' confident you are."

Gid stops on the landing. No one has ever used this word to describe him. Ever. Even Danielle, who worshipped him, who wrote him notes covered with adjectives, *cute, sexxxy, hot, adorable, cud-*

dly, luscious . . . confident was never among them. Because he's with himself every day, Gid doesn't see himself change, but he tries to imagine telling that girl off when he first arrived here, and, well, there's just no way he would have. *Confident.* He'll take it. Even from his dad.

"Thanks," Gid says.

"I'm sorry I brought Danielle here," Jim says.

"It's all right," Gid replies. "I can handle it."

The second-floor lounge in the girls' dorm is a big room with a flowered sofa, a coffee table offering up a few magazines, and three round tables. It is decorated with oil paintings of dead headmasters' wives. Danielle, Edie, and Molly sit at one table, a nearly full Scrabble board in front of them, frowning over what's left of their tiles. He is amazed when he has an impulse to go to Danielle. The impulse confuses him.

Guys are always confused by how soft and sentimental they are. It's not like he wants her back. But he forgets . . . not long ago, he was pretty enmeshed.

Gid inches up behind her, stealing a glance at her letters—she has an *A,* a *C,* and a *V*—and the score sheet. Danielle leads with 187 points, Edie is second with 156, and Molly is last with 109. Molly and Edie are letting Danielle win! Molly gives him a quick glance over her shoulder, picks up her *C,* and puts it at the front of the word *reek* to make *creek.*

"Okay, eleven points," she says, writing it down. "Why don't you guys take a seat? We'll be done in a second."

Jim lets out a short, nervous laugh. "I was kind of hoping to get on the road before dark," he says.

No one responds.

Jim clears his throat, sits down, and begins to thumb through a three-year-old issue of *American Heritage.* Gid sits down too. He tries to smile at Danielle, but she seems to be concentrating on the game. She has reapplied her makeup and put on a clean shirt, which Gid is almost sure belongs to Molly. It's Edie's turn now. She twists her little face this way and that in concentration. Jim Rayburn taps his foot. Finally, she lays some tiles on the board. Gid sits up a little bit so he can see. Edie has made the word *mordant*. "What does that mean?" Gideon asks, relieved to have a genuine question.

"I don't know," Edie says. "But it's a word. And that's all my tiles."

Danielle wins anyway. Gid can see from the slight lift in her eyes that she is pleased with this. He knows he has to talk to her again. He knows about closure—his mother talks about it a lot, especially now that she lives in New Mexico and does yoga. Danielle excuses herself to go to the bathroom, and Gid, however grimly, accepts this as his cue to follow her for their closure chat.

But on her way out of the room, she passes close to him, puts her hand on his arm, leans in, and whispers, "It's okay. It's really okay."

Edie's busy putting away the game. Jim continues to read. Gid catches Molly's eye. He mouths, "She's not mad?"

But all Molly does is slightly raise one eyebrow. Okay. He's not getting anything out of her today. Fair enough.

Fair enough indeed.

She and Edie do accompany Gid, Jim, and Danielle back to the parking lot. Gid studies Danielle with some wariness as they walk, but she remains silent, guarded. She gives small, girlish hugs to Molly and Edie. She offers Gideon a hesitant smile, then climbs into the Silverado. Gid watches her for signs that she's about to blow, but she looks into the mirror on the visor, pretending, probably, to get something out of her eyes but just looking at herself in the way all girls who aren't totally ugly do whenever they get the chance.

He suddenly remembers his conversation this morning with Pilar, the secret arranged marriage, her turtlelike father, her blue suede shoes. He smiles fondly at all of it, then frowns, puzzled. He hasn't thought of her all day. It's almost certainly a record since he's met her. He usually doesn't go ten minutes, much less ten hours.

As he hugs his father, he looks at Molly over his shoulder. Gray afternoon light looks good on her sort of serious, librariany prettiness, particularly with her head turned the way it is, away from him.

tick
tock

The cold is starting to come in earnest now. As Gideon and Nicholas make their way back to the track on the Thursday following Parents' Day, the morning chill seeps from the hardened ground up into their toes. The light comes slowly, and a gray fog lifts a bit, then hovers stubbornly at the tops of the trees.

As Gid runs he thinks about Molly. She has spoken to him this week, but never unnecessarily, and never with any warmth. "Fuck," Gideon says, grabbing at a pain in his side.

"Run through it," Nicholas says, picking up the pace.

Gid grabs harder, twisting his body to one side. "You've got to be kidding," he says, but he manages to keep his legs moving. What's amazing about Molly is that she's also managed not to come across as cold, so there's so excuse to make an apology. Even in rehearsals, she said she had a cold sore and couldn't kiss. And she really did have one. He wonders if she made it out of stage makeup. He slows down. He doesn't want to run, he wants to think about how to . . . how to . . .

Now, how is he finishing this sentence? With "win the bet"? Or with "make her feel better that he stranded her on the stairs to go talk to Pilar"?

"Keep going," Nicholas says. "I promise, you'll feel better."

Eventually the pain subsides, then is gone altogether.

Just as they're easing into their cooldown walk, Gid looks out over the track to the access road that moves through the woods to the lower edge of the athletic fields. Coming through the fog is an early seventies muscle car, white, with blue-rimmed tires. Gid remembers the car from the driveway at the party. The car stops, the passenger-side door opens, and Pilar jumps out.

Dennis's car.

She's wearing a blue tracksuit trimmed with pink. Gid loves it when Pilar wears tracksuits. Her hair is in pigtails. Gid thinks she invented that look. I wish I could tell him that she didn't, because then he might be less enamored of her, less heartbreakingly impressed. But there are some things you just have to find out on your own.

"Pilar is like a cramp," Nicholas says. "Run through it."

Now, why couldn't I have made that point?

The car makes a hasty three-point turn and speeds off. Pilar trots up a wooded slope behind White, slips into the trees, and disappears.

Gid sends the message, I will always love you, into the morning mist. From near or far, always. He doesn't feel corny or embarrassed or totally sad. It's just . . . well, as Nicholas would say, the truth of the universe flowing through him.

So he can't say sorry to Molly. So what. He can still fuck her in time to win the bet. That's all that matters, right? He keeps seeing that empty stair in his mind. What if she really likes him? What if he hurts her? What if he already has?

Is it stupid to think he can pull it off?

When he walks into the mail room later, she's standing there. She is pale and dark-eyed and frowning. That's my disappointment, Gid thinks. I made that mouth look that way.

He thinks he only feels bad about that. But I know he feels good too. Powerful. He can't help it. It's not malicious. It's just that . . . well, growing up with such a sort of autistic father, he feels proud to be part of the world of feeling.

"I am so sorry," Gid says, before he even comprehends what he's saying. "I . . . shouldn't have gone over to talk to Pilar like that. It was mean." He moves toward her so quickly and with such a genuineness of feeling that he almost feels like he's floating.

Molly . . . I don't mean this to be mean, but she looks like she's thirty sometimes. Like, really mature. "I'm surprised you're apologizing," she says.

He wants to tread lightly here. Because it is not just a matter, he knows, of leaving one girl to talk to another. Because surely Molly must know that Pilar Benitez-Jones is no ordinary girl. And in apologizing, he doesn't want to make Molly feel, well, ordinary.

"I like that you said something to me," Molly says, and her voice is low and throaty and sends a little current through Gid.

The current is like alcohol and adrenaline.

"So . . . ," Gid says carefully. He doesn't want to ask, "You're not mad at me?" That implies that Molly is weak, that . . .

She's standing at eye level to his mailbox. She touches her finger against the glass window. "I bet you have a note from Danielle," she says. "That color is very her."

Gid opens the box. Inside is a light green envelope, with, ironically, a love stamp. Gideon walks outside the mail room and sits on a wooden bench. He opens the envelope and begins to read.

> *Dear Gideon,*
> *Hi. That was pretty weird, wasn't it? Well, at least I got to*
> *beat two prep school girls at Scrabble.*

Okay, that Scrabble line, for both me and Gid, is a heartbreaker.

> *I wish that things could have ended differently between us.*
> *But Molly explained to me that you were really upset and*
> *talked about me a lot and didn't know what to do. She ex-*
> *plained to me that you were really depressed and that you*
> *were just too down to deal with me.*

Oh my God, Gid thinks, Molly McGarry of the Buffalo McGarrys is a fucking genius.

> *And I just want to tell you that I understand, and that*
> *whenever you want to talk I am here for you. I just want to*
> *tell you also that I am not mad at you anymore.*

For a boy these are the most magical words in the world. Because all boys want to behave in a way that could get them in trouble, without actually getting into trouble. This is what being a boy is all about.

"I need a favor from you," Molly says, joining him on the bench.

"Anything," Gid says. He holds up the letter. "How did you do this?"

"May I read it?" Molly asks, not trying to hide the unmitigated delight in her eyes as Gid hands it to her. For a girl, reading things you're not supposed to, things meant for other people's eyes, is stunningly pleasurable. I guess that being inside Gid's head is sort of that same sensation. But it's been going on so long I don't even feel like I'm intruding anymore. I just feel like I'm with the person I love, but I don't ever have to wait for him to call.

Molly reads, almost immediately smiling in a mildly self-satisfied way.

"How did you do it?" Gid asks again.

"Wouldn't you like to know?"

Grateful as he is, Gid finds this a little exasperating. And who can blame him? Does she have to display her cleverness so constantly and with such aggression? Thank God, though, that he doesn't say this. "Just tell me," he says. "I'm dying to know."

Aware, perhaps, that curiosity, when it comes to the ladies, will get you everywhere.

"Just like it says here, I told her that you were really down." Molly shrugs with false modesty. "She actually believed you weren't calling her because of something that had nothing to do with her. You've heard of the whole 'I love you too much to be with you' thing, right?"

Gid has not. But he's intrigued. "Go on."

"Well," Molly says, "some guy tried it on my sister. . . . He said he really liked her, but he was so depressed that he didn't want to drag her into his hell."

"And she believed him?" He's enjoying himself. He's almost forgetting that this is business.

Molly snorts. "Please. My sister's not stupid."

Gid smiles. "Of course not. She discovered the unknown link between hurricanes and vaginas."

Molly laughs out loud. And she looks pretty. Not lit-from-within-by-a-thousand-candles pretty, but pretty.

"When I came to school here last year, I used it on my boyfriend in Buffalo. Greg Zhydoek. And he believed it. He believed it just like Danielle did. So," she rubs her hands together and holds them out flat, "they're happy, you're happy. People can survive anything as long as they think it's not their fault."

Gid thinks about this. "What's that supposed to mean, then? Are Danielle Rogal and Greg Zhydoek stupid?"

Molly purses her mouth. "Not stupid," she says. "Just romantic." Now she looks sallow again. Normal. God, this whole bet would be easier if she could just stay hot all the time. But then he probably wouldn't have a chance with her.

"Are you romantic?" he asks Molly.

Molly wags a finger at him. "No way," she says. "Not answering that."

Gid admires this. To keep things inside, well, that sounds to him like it takes a lot of courage. He is an unrepentant sharer of information.

"Anyway," Molly says, "let's talk about Halloween."

Gid's heart skips a beat.

"I think you'd agree that you owe me."

It skips two.

"Well, I want to go to the dumb Halloween dance as someone who came over on the *Mayflower*. And I want you to be my indentured servant."

"Let me guess," Gid says. "Your American history project." He groans. He hates dressing up. It's hard enough to act even marginally cool when he's being himself. "Can't you just use plastic soldiers?"

She puts her hands on his shoulders. "Why do I need plastic soldiers when you're life-size?" He can feel the pressure from her fingertips on his collarbone. He thinks there might actually be something going on in this touch. And she looks hot again. Hotter than before even. He wishes they could stay this way until Halloween.

the
yellow
ghost

I have never wondered what an artistic rendering of Gid's virginity would look like, but here we are, on the night of the Midvale Halloween Party, and I have to say I'm pleased to have been given an opportunity to find out. Cullen steps out of his closet in jeans, a T-shirt, and, over the jeans, an enormous yellow thong made especially for the occasion. "That tailor at the dry cleaner in town thinks I'm a giant pervert," he says. "But she is also under the assumption that I'm gay, which is good, because her daughter's hot, and in the spring, when I begin to pursue her in earnest, it will take that much longer for the mother to figure out what's going on." Nicholas has fashioned two giant red question marks out of cardboard, roped them together, and hung the whole apparatus over his shoulders, like a sandwich board. They practice. Cullen stands still in the middle of their room while Nicholas takes various poses around him. "What do you think, Gid?" Cullen asks. "You see, I am the thong itself, and Nicholas is, you know, the ambiguity around it. Does it look like that?"

Gideon, making his reluctant but dutiful way into a white lace-up shirt, a pair of old black knickers, and a worn pair of suede boots—all filched from the theater department costume vault—frowns. "I thought this was a private joke," he says.

"Look," Nicholas says, "you know me. Do I have any problem just ignoring people when they ask me questions?"

"No," Gid says, working out a knot on his shirt. "But Cullen does."

"Hey," Cullen says, "I just want to have fun. I just want to feel like your virginity." He snaps his enormous thong. "Hey! When people ask me a question, about what we are, I promise, I will just do that. Okay?"

"You guys are fucking douche bags," Gid says.

"But we're so clever," Cullen says.

"It was my idea," Nicholas says.

"Exactly," Cullen says, "and you would never, ever have had the guts to actually do it if not for me. Not the making-fun-of-you part, Gid. That's easy. The wearing-gay-shit part. You know?"

Gid knows.

He gives a resigned sigh. "What about me? Do I look like an indentured servant?"

Nicholas takes a break from looking at himself in the mirror—you have to at least respect someone who has the gall to consider himself hot even when dressed as a giant question mark—and checks him out. "You look like Peter Pan," he says.

Now Cullen gives him the once-over. "Gay Peter Pan," he amends. "Okay, truth? You look like a giant a-hole. But you are so winning this bet for Uncle Cullie tonight!" He puts his hand up, and he and Gid high-five.

Gid thinks too much, but he does have a boy's uncanny ability to ignore things that will only get him down. See, he's all but forgotten that if he doesn't score tonight, Cullen's whole position on him is going to change. But Cullen's boyish enthusiasm captivates him every time, so Gid sails out the door floating on top of that high five like a pink cloud. Good for him, right?

On the landing, he runs into Captain Cockweed, holding hands with his daughter, Erin, who seems to be dressed as either a ghost or a lollipop. Captain Cockweed clears his throat. "You know, Gid, I told your father I was very concerned for you," he says.

Gideon manages a fake grateful smile. "Yes, I know," he says. "He told me, but then he said I looked so great and obviously had such nice friends that while he appreciated your input, he himself wasn't concerned." Now an "eat shit" smile. He even pats Erin's head and says, "Oh, I hope that your electrical system is working better. Happy Halloween." He watches with extreme enjoyment as Captain Cockweed's whole body contracts with hatred.

The night air is cold and magical; the sky glitters with an almost impossible density of stars. Gid has that bursting-happy fall feeling. What's the unpleasant tug underneath it? he wonders. Fear. Sex with Molly.

Behind him he hears the clicking of heels. The heels are definitely a woman's but they aren't too dainty. They're gaining on him. Surprise. It's Pilar. Dressed in a cowgirl hat and cowboy boots and a one-piece white suit, a sort of glorified unitard, which, because my orthodontist gets *Vogue,* I know is called a Nudie. Nudies cost a lot of money. Pilar isn't the sort of girl to spare any expense with her Halloween costume, and what with the full financial power of the Argentine beef by-product market, she doesn't have to.

"Howdy," she says. "Are you supposed to be Davy Crockett?"

"I thought he wore a coonskin cap," Gid complains.

"Yes," Pilar says, "and one of these shirts too." She tugs on the laces, revealing a little of the left side of Gid's chest. He tries to breathe into that side a little harder, to puff it up. I would like to make fun of him for that, but when I walk around, I try to stick certain parts of my body out more than others too. It's an easy thing to fall into.

Gid shakes his head. "If I were him, I would make sure I had a coonskin cap, okay? So what are you?"

"I'm not a *what*, I am a *who*. On Halloween, everyone is a who."

"You're a cowgirl," he says. "And anyway, that's not true, some people are whats."

Pilar removes her hat. Her hair is pinned up into a sort of wavy bob. "I'm Patsy Cline. I know everyone is thinking I will be Carmen Miranda or something . . ."

Gid smiles inwardly at the idea that everyone on campus has formulated an idea of what Pilar might be for Halloween. And so do I. Even if I were Pilar, I would have to laugh at myself for assuming this.

Pilar continues, "So I thought I would throw them a curved ball."

"It's not *curved*, it's *curve*," Gid corrects her.

But Pilar shakes her head, her hair skimming her shoulders. "No, that's wrong," she says. "The ball is curved when it's thrown. Curved ball."

"Trust me. Curveball. The pitcher threw a curveball."

But she shakes her head again. "I don't believe you." The girl told the boy he was wrong.

"Fine. Suit yourself. I am American, you know."

"Oh, yes," Pilar says. "Your Americanness and its clean-cut charms has made itself evidenced to me many times. Anyway. What are you?"

A group of girls walk by, deferentially lowering their eyes. (Gid knows this is for Pilar's benefit, not his.) One of them, Gid is pleased to see, is the fading-green-eyeliner girl from the TV room. They're all in fishnets, short skirts, and ripped-up tank tops. A few feet away, another group of girls walk by wearing essentially the same thing. "They're all hookers," Pilar says, sensing Gid's confusion.

"American girls are always hookers on Halloween, so they can show off their tits. But anyway, please tell me what you are."

He tells her. Tells her why. Well, not entirely why. Just that he's a part of someone else's costume. She looks bored. Her violet-colored mouth goes a little slack. Or maybe she just looks a little sad? She's carrying a guitar case. She opens it up. It's filled with makeup, her cigarettes, and a bottle of water. "That's vodka," she says.

I should have known she was tipsy—the whole "Americans this, Americans that" routine.

She looks around, but they're in a protected area, a dark path between Thayer and the administration buildings. "Do you want some?"

It's going to be a long, emotionally challenging night, Gideon. Have some vodka.

He boldly stares into the shine in Pilar's eyes as he takes his drink.

"Boy, that burns," he says, handing back the bottle, keeping his gaze on (again, his words) the magic brown velvet of her eyes.

"But it burns clean. They won't smell it." She sets it back in the bag, kneels down—affording for Gid an exciting peek down her Nudie—and comes up with a photo.

She hands it to Gid and—wow, he was right—he sees that she is a little sad. It's them on the night of Fiona's party, sitting in the chair, pressed close together.

"I have to go," Pilar says.

"Hey," he says, "can I get another swig of that vodka before you take off?"

After a few chugs, Gid notices Pilar has rhinestones on her cowboy hat. She's a white flame, he thinks. Yet another ill-fated love metaphor for Gid.

Walking a few more steps to the party, he remembers casting his love of Pilar hopelessly into the morning mist. He laughs. He acknowledges that it may be the vodka that's making him laugh and that he will not always find this torturous connection between him and Pilar funny. But for now, he laughs.

He finds Molly sitting on the stone ledge outside the party, wearing a long ugly brown dress and a matching bonnet.

"Is that what people wore back in, what was it, 1620?"

Molly ties her bonnet string underneath her chin. "Yes. I got a book out of the lower-school library called *How Our Forefathers Dressed*. Which, clearly, I should have lent to you. You look like Robinson Crusoe."

"I've been getting various things," Gid says. "Robinson Crusoe is good."

Molly nods approvingly. "Well, Robinson Crusoe is more than fine. He's about a hundred years past the Pilgrims, but I don't think fashion moved very quickly back then. Anyway, here." She holds up some sort of leather strap. It's a leash. It *is* a leash.

Gideon's testicles contract.

"You want me to wear a leash?" Thank God for that nice vodka buzz he got from Pilar. Oh no! Pilar's going to see him on a leash. See? Already his love for her is no longer funny.

Molly's now slipped the collar over his head. She talks the entire time, in an informational tone of voice, as if this were no big deal.

"Amazingly enough, indentured servants were sometimes kept on a leash, especially when traveling. Too many opportunities to run off, you know, never to be, uh, indentured from again."

As they ascend the steps to the Student Center, walking carefully together so that Gideon doesn't get choked, he starts to relax. No one's looking at him. Everyone else is dressed up too. Most of the underclass boys are dressed as athletes in gold chains and jerseys, gold foil wrapped around their teeth. Liam Wu is Dracula.

Please God, Gideon pleads, don't let him bite Molly's neck.

With that, Liam swoops in, pulls a giggling Molly into the folds of his cape, dips her, and bites her neck. Molly bounces back up exuberant and flushed. They watch Liam swirl away through the crowd. "Do you need some Bactine for that?" Gid says.

"My, my, my," Molly says. "What a hostile tone you're taking. May I remind you that you're my servant? Is there something you'd like to take up with your master?"

Thank God for the sudden appearance of Devon Shine, bizarrely floozied out in a blonde ponytail wig, leopard-print mini-skirt, and high-heeled shoes. His face is powdered white, and his lipstick is bright red. "What the hell are these dumbass costumes?" Devon asks Gid and Molly. "Scooby-Doo and Velma?"

Gid thinks, Maybe Devon finally likes me.

It sounds like he's being mean, but Gid knows this is how Devon talks to people he respects.

"No," Molly says. "I'm a Pilgrim, and he's my indentured servant."

Devon nods. Gideon is pretty sure he doesn't know what an indentured servant is.

"Who are you?" Molly says. "Marilyn Monroe?"

Devon shakes his head. "Gwen Stefani," he says. "I'm hoping to have sex with myself later."

There's an awful blare of feedback, followed by a not especially apologetic "Sorry, folks." Mrs. Geller, the headmaster's secretary, seems to be playing DJ. This is the trouble with campus parties—there's a lot of buildup, then it's just the same people whom you see every day in the same space and an old lady who, thinking she's being cool, puts on Green Day's "Time of Your Life." Gid, Devon, and Molly, having exhausted the costume topic, can't find another. Gid looks around and sees that the whole room is littered with similar clusters, people just staring awkwardly at one another with no idea what to say or do. The awkwardness of his fellow Midvalians is soothing.

"I have some whiskey in here," Devon says, touching his

purse. "I think purses were invented so chicks could cart around booze. I wish I could always carry one. Anyway, why don't Gid and I go outside with the bottle, and then you and Gid can go outside?"

Molly nods and unhooks Gid's collar. "Now, don't jump overboard," she warns.

Gid bows.

Once they get outside, Devon ducks behind a bush. He guzzles whiskey from a silver flask, then passes it to Gid. As Gid drinks, Devon says, almost dully, "So I guess you'll be having sex with her tonight."

"What do you mean?" Gideon asks innocently.

Devon guzzles a little more, then cocks his head to indicate they should go back inside. His wig shifts. "Dude," he says, bounding up the stairs two at a time. "She wants your nut sack."

Now Devon's wig is also falling off toward the back of his head. A few red curls have sprung out. Gid reaches out tentatively, and Devon leans forward, letting Gid tuck everything back inside. "Thanks, man," Devon continues. "Okay, dude . . . she's got you on a chain. Man, I wish some hot girl would lead me around on a chain."

"Monster Mash" ends as they come back inside. One of the rappers pulls Mrs. Geller out of the DJ booth, doing a sort of modified twist, and one of his friends ducks in. Interpol comes on, and a riot of sophomore hookers fill up the dance floor.

"You think Molly's hot?" As much as he doesn't want to admit it matters, he wants to know.

Devon thinks about this. "If she led me around on a chain, she would be."

Gid finds this only slightly helpful. More alcohol would be very helpful.

Gid takes Molly out with the flask. Stands guard while she, careful with her skirts, ducks into the bushes. When she comes out her eyes are all glittery. "I'm drunk," she whispers as she resecures the collar around Gideon's neck. She gets in so close to him that the top of her lip actually bends the top of his ear.

"I'm surprised," Gid says. "I thought you were better behaved than that."

"This is itchy," Molly says, rubbing where the dress meets her neckline. "The booze makes me feel less sweaty and gross." Gid thinks of her sweating inside her dress and is aroused. He likes this night, the sneaking off, the itchy dress.

As if on cue, Cullen and Nicholas walk by, dressed as his virginity. "What are they?" Molly asks.

"You don't want to know," Gid says. But he smiles. He is drunk. Not too drunk. Not throw-up drunk.

Back inside, Cullen and Nicholas are the stars of the show, Cullen taking his few steps and Nicholas posing with his question mark nearby. They repeat this action several times. The dancing hookers cluster around them, giggling and pointing at the thong. Gid must be drunk, because as he surveys this spectacle, he's overcome with pride and flattery.

Molly tugs on his collar, uncomfortably flattening his Adam's apple. "Sorry," she says, "but I do want to know about Cullen's and Nicholas's costumes."

Nicholas stands perfectly still as Cullen pirouettes around him. Then they switch. Cullen's pirouettes are clownish and sloppy; Nicholas, even sandwiched between plywood, moves nimbly.

Suddenly, Gid's view is blocked by a giant black cape. Mrs. Geller frowns at him. Now that she's up close, Gid can see that she has a fake wart on her face so the frown's a little scarier. "What do you have around his neck?" she asks Molly. Gid tries to breathe out his nose so she won't smell the booze on him, and sends Molly desperate, silent signals to do the same.

"I don't know that I think it's appropriate for the two of you to be making fun of the slave trade," Mrs. Geller says. God, that wart's really grossing him out, even though it's fake. It seems to have been sculpted out of some kind of putty, and then painted.

"He's an indentured servant," Molly explains, using the same tone of voice she used earlier with Gid. "Indentured servants weren't slaves. They came over to America with—"

Mrs. Geller clears her throat. "I'm clear on indentured servants, Miss McGarry. Now, I have spoken to the other chaperones, and we feel your costume depicts a power dynamic we're really not comfortable endorsing. We'd like you to return to your dorms and change your costumes."

Molly stands up and faces Mrs. Geller. "There are, like, twenty white kids here dressed as rappers! And you're kicking us out? I am not endorsing indentured servitude, I'm depicting it. There's a difference. God, this school is retarded!"

Gid has a sense that this is going to be the thing that really gets them in trouble.

Sure enough, Mrs. Geller turns white.

"My son is retarded," she says.

A few minutes later, Molly and Gid stumble across the quad together. "We're wasted," Gid whispers, and slips a hand under Molly's elbow, hoping to steady them both.

"This school," Molly fumes, her face red, her eyes unfocused. "It's this weird combination of hippie stupid and totally uptight. I mean, can you believe Edie is writing Betsy Ross's diary for one of her classes? It's all in the same vein of this costume. It's not any different."

They are both stupid ideas in exactly the same way.

Molly continues, pausing at the John Midvale memorial. She starts to peel off her wool dress. She tries to pull it over her head and can't. She sits down on the marble edge of the memorial and starts pulling savagely at it with her arms.

"Uh, hey," Gid says, amazed and excited. But then, she's wearing another dress, a lighter cotton dress underneath it. "Wow," he says, "you're wearing two dresses."

Molly looks at him quizzically. "This isn't a dress, it's a slip."

This doesn't register at all.

"A slip? Your slip is showing?"

"Oh yeah, I've heard that before," Gid says. "I never knew what it meant."

Molly puts her hands on her seventeenth-century hips and shakes her head. "You really are incredibly clueless," she says. "I mean, like, it's logic-defying." There's something nice about the way she says this. It's as though she's saying she likes him because of this, not in spite of it. He opens his mouth and quickly shuts it.

Molly waves a hand in front of his face. "Hello?" she says. "What are you thinking about?"

Molly narrows her eyes, taking in his weirdness. Or so that's what he thinks. As a girl, I know that she's just really uncomfortable and that narrowing her eyes is the only thing she can think of to do.

"Okay," she finally says, "I guess me and my scratchy dress are going back to my dorm. This marble is cold under my butt anyway." She throws the dress around her shoulders, like an athlete would a towel. She starts to back away.

Gid has to think of a way to extend the evening. But without nightcaps, apartments, or walks along the promenade, he's got nothing.

Gideon decides to use the only idea he has. The only weapon in his arsenal.

"Molly," he says. "Do you want to know what Cullen and Nicholas's costume was about?"

"Of course I want to know," she says. "I didn't pull on your chain just for the hell of it."

Gideon hesitates. Confiding in girls, he knows, has helped him so far. That's how he got Pilar to like him, when he first met her and later, at Fiona's. It's how he got me to like him, though he doesn't know that. But Cullen and Nicholas, that's not how they get girls to like them. They're all cool and distant. Cool and distant is not going to work for Gid, because Gid's not gorgeous.

And he doesn't just want to confide because he feels good. There is also the guilt. Molly is the subject of speculation in a way that's probably not so nice. He owes it to her to tell her something damaging about himself.

It's funny that's how he thinks of it. Girls call this "sharing."

He stuffs his hands deep into his suede jodhpurs. "Okay," he says finally. "They're my virginity. Their costume is my virginity."

The Danielle story—the sounds of the brother making noise in the next room, his hand, working its way under the expanse of stretchy fabric, et cetera, all the way to the yellow thong and the question of is he or isn't he—comes out.

He's very detailed, open, and honest. Without, of course, breathing a word about the bet.

When he's done confiding—or more or less done, once the underwear is dirty, it's hard to think of what else you would say—they stand there in the middle of the quad under the bright hard stars. Molly's not quite smiling, but there's a peaceful sort of look on her face. "Shit, I'm drunk," she says quietly, then she lies down along the base of the memorial. It's circular, so naturally, she has to curve her body into a *C* shape. It's a process about which she is more matter-of-fact than sexy, and Gid smiles fondly, appreciating this. He lies down too, his feet near hers, so that their bodies take up almost half the diameter of the circle. The marble is freezing through his thin shirt, but he knows that lying down like this with a girl—even in a not very sensual position, even outside—is an opportunity he can't miss.

"Something similar happened to me," she says, "but I was on the other side of the thong thing. I mean, it happened to me with a boy. And I wasn't wearing a thong. They hurt my butt. But I always wonder if I am or if I am not. I mean, I probably don't wonder as much as you do . . ."

Gid is so stunned it takes him a second to feel insulted. "What do you mean, not 'as much as you do'?"

"Oh, you know," she says. "It's just not as big a deal for a girl."

"What are you talking about?" he says. "Virginity is, like, everything to girls! I think it's way less important to guys. I mean, you guys have, like, a cherry to pop."

"Okay," Molly says, "if I am so obsessed with my cherry, why did you stand there half in tears wondering whether to tell me your little story and I just up and told you about mine without even thinking about it?"

Gid doesn't know what to say. "Thongs hurt your butt?"

Molly makes a face. "Mostly. I mean, it depends on what kind of day your butt is having."

This is funny. They laugh. They laugh hard. They laugh so hard that they sit up, first just leaning against each other, but then they start clutching at each other.

They clutch at each other for long enough and are drunk enough that they start to make out. Being in Gid's mind was a lot easier before all this making out started. Gid making out drunk is different from Gid making out in rehearsal. I can feel his brain go totally slack, and where I usually hear him wondering what to do with his hands, now he's just kind of on sexual autopilot.

Molly pulls away from him. "You know what's good about this Halloween party thing?"

Gid shakes his head.

"No one's around. We can sneak back to my room."

Gid grabs her and kisses her again. A long, hard kiss, but with no tongue. It's a grateful kiss.

But he's not even thinking about the bet! He's just glad.

As they walk toward the door, Gid unconsciously reaches for Molly's hand. He takes it and kisses it. "I never kissed a girl's hand before," Gid says. See, now, he's just remembered the bet. He thought this was a good move. Suave.

The campus is totally, amazingly empty, a sea of quiet and cold green grass. They walk right in the front door of her dorm and upstairs without seeing a soul.

Over Molly's bed is a framed Picasso print from someplace called the Albright-Knox Museum. Gid looks closer. "Wow, Buffalo has a museum," he says. Edie's side of the room is papered with drawings of the American flag. He wonders, Is Edie, like, really patriotic or something? God, that would make her even weirder. But then he remembers her Betsy Ross diary. Okay.

Molly takes off her slip and hangs it over the desk. She's wearing a white T-shirt and white underwear. No thong, but they are cute underwear. Gid likes the way the curve of her butt and her breasts look in the dim light from outside. She's soft and girlish, she looks younger somehow. She gets into her bed. Gid takes off his jodhpurs and starts to unlace his shirt when Molly beckons to him and has him sit on the edge of her bed. She puts Gid's hands at his side, and then she starts to unlace his shirt. His heart starts to beat fast—and beats faster when he realizes she's looking right into his eyes as she's removing his clothes. He's actually in Molly McGarry's bed, on Halloween, and he's actually about to . . . win the bet. But better than that, a girl is undressing him. He has imagined losing his virginity, but this, this seems like a lot to ask for.

I don't think there's a person alive who doesn't like watching people have sex. Watching and hearing the narration, though, is a little weird. I almost feel like I'm directing them.

The door is shut. Precautions are on the nightstand. He puts his hands on the hem of her shirt and lifts it up, slowly. He wonders if she thinks he's being purposefully sensual, but the truth is, he's a little afraid to see her bare breasts up close. "Let me get the something," she says. Gid enjoys watching her cross the room dressed in just her undershirt and underwear. Molly opens up her dresser, producing a shoebox, from which she removes a fat yellow candle and a pack of matches. She lights the candle. She lies back down and smiles at him. Molly smiles at him! He kisses her cheek, her lips, her neck, then her lips again. Getting enough courage to look at her breasts. He puts his hand on one of them and thinks, I am touching Molly McGarry's breasts. He's here. He's really here. He's a can-do kind of guy.

Molly says, "You know what's good about this we-don't-know-whether-we're-virgins thing?"

Gid shakes his head.

"We can each take away, like, half of the other one's virginity. It's totally fair."

Okay, he's ready. But his neck is feeling a little stiff. That collar. It was worth it, but there's a little crick. If he hikes himself onto his elbows and just turns a little bit to the right, there. There. He's relaxing back onto the mattress, admiring the colors of the Picasso print reflected in the window, and . . . what is that underneath it? "No," he says, "it can't be," slowly turning, pointing at the door-knob. "Look," he says. "Look there." Hanging on the doorknob are a pair of yellow thong underwear. *The* yellow thong underwear. "Oh my God," he says. "Those are Danielle's. Danielle's underwear."

Molly sits up in her little twin bed, the sheet pulled over her chest. She rolls her eyes at Gideon. "Okay, why would I have Danielle's underwear in my room? They're probably Edie's."

"No, because, I remember . . . when you shut the door, I remember seeing your hand on the doorknob, because . . ." He blushes, because he really did, as boyishly idiotic as it sounds, pay attention to her hand on the doorknob, thinking about . . . oh, you know! "The point is," Gideon says, not sure, not caring whether Molly knows why he remembers her hand in this very place, "the point is, that was an empty doorknob. I know it like I know my own name." He seizes the underwear and holds them up. "Size six. Medium. You're a medium. Edie's a . . . I don't know, a super-small. These are Banana Republic. Shall I go on? I mean, these are the underwear!"

Molly is wide-eyed, shocked. And probably a little nervous.

"Oh, Jesus." Gideon starts to pace back and forth. "Okay, I didn't finish the thong story. I mean, the fallout from the thong story. I'm having sex with you, well, I was about to have sex with you—because of a bet. I mean, I like you, I'm attracted to you. But the whole reason this thing got started is because of a bet I made with Cullen and Nicholas, like, on the first few days of school."

"Why me?" She doesn't sound particularly mad. She just sounds curious. But Gid, so racked with guilt, doesn't hear.

"God." Gid sits down at the foot of the bed. Molly, he can't help but notice, inches away from him in various phases.

"So why are you telling me this?" Molly asks, now sounding a little more annoyed than curious.

"Why am I telling you this?" Gid shakes his head in disbelief. "What do you mean, why am I telling you this? Because it's mean. Because . . . I mean, you're the subject of a bet. Doesn't that make you feel, like, cheap?"

Molly takes a deep breath. As she exhales, her voice shakes a little, like she might start to cry. Her eyes are big and shiny.

"Please say something," Gid says.

Molly gets out of the bed. She looks smaller than usual. She pulls down her shirt so it is covering her again and pulls on a pair of sweatpants. She walks to the door, opens it, and looks both ways down the hall. "The coast is clear," she says. "I think you'd better go."

Gid's already dressed. He's about halfway down the hall when she calls after him. "You know what? I always thought it was sort of stupid that they didn't let boys up here. But now I can see why."

Gid would love to believe girls forgive boys for making dumb sex bets about them. He would love to believe that he and Molly can start over. But judging from what happens in Spanish the following Monday, when they perform the play, it seems like maybe he's going to have to adjust his expectations.

Molly makes out the way she's supposed to. It's weird how they're doing the same thing they did for real just a few days ago, but it feels totally different. Well. He opens one eye just a sliver while they're kissing and sees Liam, staring up at them, watching, interested. This is good, he tries to tell himself, now when I see actors kiss on TV, I will know how they feel. This is a good experience. Except it doesn't feel like one. When the class claps for them, they have to stand very close together, the three of them, on the classroom's tiny makeshift stage, and Molly digs the pointed heel of her shoe into Gid's foot. Hard. "I like very, very much," Ms. San Video says. "How you all wear the snout. Because in fascism, we are all pigs." She claps again.

They don't correct her and remind her they are dogs, because their dog snouts really do look like pig snouts. They get an A. It makes Gid strangely sad that Molly was right.

sour
november

On Sunday night, Cullen and Nicholas took the oversize question mark and the underwear outside and stacked them neatly beside the Dumpster behind Proctor.

Tuesday afternoon, Gid, Nicholas, and Cullen return from their afternoon classes to find both pieces of the Halloween costume and a note: THIS IS OVERSIZED TRASH. PLEASE HANDLE DISPOSAL BY TUESDAY AFTERNOON OR FACE FINE OR EXPULSION.—GENE CAVANAUGH.

Twenty minutes later, they're driving around the Boston suburbs in the seven-series, looking for a Dumpster without a lock on it.

Gid's in back, settling into his moroseness. He has a paperback today. They're still reading *Moby-Dick*. Mr. Barnes had one word for Gid's idea—that the whale represented man's drive, that the whale could have been a mountain, or a skyscraper, or a woman—and that word, written across the title page in dark red letters, was "Duh." On the part about the woman, Mr. Barnes scrawled, "Oh, Jesus!" He gave him a C. Gid thought, It sucks that I got such a bad grade, but I have to tell Molly what he wrote because she would laugh. But then he remembers: Dude, she hates you.

"Wait a minute," he says, suddenly energized. "You guys put the underwear on the door. You had motive, opportunity. The underwear."

"But you have the underwear in the room," Nicholas says with uncharacteristic gentleness, pulling out of a Target and crossing a state road to a Bed Bath & Beyond.

"I know you've been through a bit of an ordeal," Cullen says, pulling excitedly at his curls with one hand, smoking with the other. "I'm still not going to tell you in some split second while you were taking out and considering your tumultuous wiener . . ."

"Tumescent," Gid and Nicholas say in unison.

"Whatever." Cullen taps an ash out the window and continues, "You can't tell me while you were looking at your torpid wang in its last moments of virgin glory that one of us somehow soundlessly opened Molly's door and hung a pair of underwear—a common brand, a common color, a common size—on her door."

"Aha!" Gid seizes on this. "How did you know they were on her door?"

"You told us," Cullen and Nicholas say in unison.

Gid rolls down the window and inhales the comforting cool scent of ozone. "At least it's over."

Cullen puts his bare feet on the dashboard. He flexes his toes, smiles, unflexes. Still enjoying his feet, he says, "We love you. We love you a lot. You're so great." He holds his big toes in both hands, rocking back and forth. They are circling a mall parking lot about four miles from campus. It is teeming with public school girls in cheap fuzzy sweaters, big butts packed into tight jeans, small butts packed into tighter ones.

Gid is staring at one girl's eyes, marveling at how much makeup she has around them, when Cullen says, "The bet is still on. We're going to shift the dates, obviously, one month forward, but we're proceeding."

I can't believe it. I almost wish that I was inside Cullen's or

Nicholas's head just for the experience of being close to someone so insane that they would consider continuing a secret bet that is no longer secret.

"Uh, you guys, isn't part of the bet that she doesn't know . . . so . . . ?"

"Sure, sure, sure," Cullen says. "That was an important component of the bet."

"But now," Nicholas continues, "the fact that she does know . . ."

"Is an important component!" Cullen concludes.

Okay, so it wouldn't be that interesting to be in their heads. They're really just making it up as they go.

Finally, they find an open Dumpster—an employee had been filling it and he was wheeling his pallet truck back to the store when they pulled up.

"I'll get it," Gid says, wanting an excuse to get out of the car despite the rain. He takes the red question mark and the panties out of the backseat and heaves them on top of a pile of broken-down shoe boxes and packing peanuts. He tries to stuff them down but the Dumpster is too full. Finally, he stands on tiptoe to get some leverage and pushes with all his might, bending the panties and the question mark in half. He walks back to the car, rubbing his hands against his pants. He casts a look backward. The panties stay down, but the question mark snaps up again, like the bet, indestructible.

Back in the car, Gid is too stunned, too demoralized to speak for a few minutes. As they're pulling into school, he says, "You know, every time I talk to her she's going to think, You're trying to have sex with me."

"That might not be such a terrible thing," Cullen says.

What Cullen means is that girls like to be wanted. This is certainly true. But he's missing the point. No big surprise there.

They go directly to dinner, where Gid, hollow, empty, eats like he's forgotten about skinny fat. He sees Molly and tries to smile.

Nothing. He expected that, in keeping with her style, she would at least be cordial to him. But she looks right through him. Needing badly to disparage her, Gid thinks, That's so high school, then remembers, they're in high school.

Molly's actually the one thing about this high school that's not high school. And she hates him.

"You're not allowed to discuss the bet with anyone," Nicholas says, swiping a glass of chocolate milk out of Cullen's hand and replacing it with water.

"If anyone asks about it, deny it," Cullen says. "We could get in trouble."

"For what?" Gid whispers, because Devon and Liam are coming.

"Gambling," Nicholas whispers back, raising his eyebrows with subversive glee.

They can't be serious, Gid thinks. He wishes he could take a week off.

"Oh, and hey," Nicholas adds, "in all the excitement, I forgot. My mother wanted me to invite you home with me for Thanksgiving. Do you think you could come?"

Thanksgiving on Christmas Park Circle, since Gid's mom left, involves lots of college football, a badly cooked turkey, and lots of canned vegetables. And it's always just Gid and his dad. "I think so," Gid says, hiding his enthusiasm. Well, this is something to look forward to.

At this moment, Molly passes by their table. He knows that look. She's not looking at him, and she's trying not to look at him. She's aware of me, Gid thinks. She's aware of me, and I am not going home for Thanksgiving. Not an ideal life, but a livable one.

It doesn't stop raining. The boys do a lot of staying in, which results in a lot of pot smoking. But one night Gid is about to take a hit out of the Vaportech, and out of the corner of his eye he sees the *Moby-Dick* paper, with the *Duh* written across the front. "I don't think I want to smoke any pot," he says, passing it to Cullen. "I think pot's making me stupid."

"Dude," Cullen says a minute later, over a bulging mouthful of smoke, "don't blame your problems on pot."

"Okay," Gid says. "How about I blame them on you instead?"

Nicholas makes him go running every morning, despite the rain. "You seem down," he says. "You need to shake this off."

"Is that what you did with Erica?" Gid asks. "Shook it off?"

Nicholas, tugging his arm over his head, freezes and stares at Gid. "I wasn't upset about her; I was upset because she was upset. There's a difference."

Gideon writes Molly a letter, apologizing about the bet. How does he reconcile the fact that the bet's still on? He doesn't. Or if he does, in a tiny way, it's that he feels like he's a double agent. He used to tell Cullen and Nicholas everything he did with regard to Molly. But his remorse is a giant secret. He actually mails it, in town, with a stamp. He types the letter, even types the outside of the envelope, in case one of them sees her getting her mail.

> *Dear Molly,*
> *I feel bad that I made a bet about you. It wasn't a nice thing to do. I do really like you, and I hope you don't feel too bad.*
> > *Gid.*

After mailing the letter, he calls his father from the Student Center pay phone. As the phone rings, he prays with all his might for the answering machine, and he gets it. "Hi, Dad," he says. "I just called to tell you that I won't be making it home for Thanksgiving."

"Hello? Gid? What's this you're saying?"

"Uh . . ." That was all going so well, Gid thinks. "I'm . . . I'm going to Nicholas's, in New York City."

Jim laughs, but Gid can tell it's forced. "Well, I guess I can't compete with that, can I?"

Gid finds this question passive-aggressive. What's he supposed to say now?

Come on, Gideon. Remember you want your dad to think he's getting a good deal?

"You can compete with anything, Dad." Whoa, that was hard to get out. But he's glad he managed it.

"So the good news is," he says, "I'll see you at Christmas."

Good job, Gideon. You're getting it.

"Right, right." He can hear the relief in his father's voice. "The Big Apple."

"I knew you were going to say 'Big Apple,'" Gid mutters.

"What was that?" Jim Rayburn says. "That was just an ambulance going by."

Gid says he was just asking one of his friends to go buy him a Snapple. Jim laughs again and then tells Gid he quit drinking Snapple at lunch and lost three pounds in a week.

it's not
the
bet

On the Tuesday before Thanksgiving, an hour before leaving for New York with Nicholas, Gid pays a visit to the mail room, annoyed with himself as he goes. There hasn't been a response from Molly yet, so why should there be one today? The mail room has that bustling, pre-vacation feeling. Everyone is red-cheeked and happy and carrying a large duffel bag.

But there is an envelope. It's red, like Molly's coat. This makes Gid optimistic. He tears into it.

Gideon. It's not the bet. Molly.

Gideon winces. Couldn't it have been something just good or bad? Something he could hang a real mood on?

A few hours later, Gideon sits on the Amtrak in the window seat. Nicholas is next to him, asleep, still attracting a lot of attention. Prep school girls and college girls too—the hot ones in their heels and jeans and the shlumpy ones padding around in sweats and PJs—keep passing back and forth. They've clearly been sent by their friends to check him out, because they're all trying not to smile. The prep school girls tuck their embarrassed but excited faces into the placards of Fair Isle sweaters. The college girls just leer. The lucky asshole. He gets attention even when he's asleep. If I looked like that, all these girls wouldn't ignore me, Gid thinks. I would never have had the bet made about me. I would be going out with a girl like Pilar. And I wouldn't have been forced to be mean to Molly McGarry.

Come on, Gideon! Do you really believe you've been forced? He doesn't. He knows that the bet and he and the guys at some point all have become one. He just knows he didn't start it.

He presses the recline button and sinks back to think about whether starting something and not stopping it are the same thing.

"Excuse me." Gid turns to see a putty-faced man, dandruff dusting the shoulders of his shiny black suit. "This is a brand-new laptop. Watch it." Gideon hikes his seat back up, only halfway. The man fidgets and makes annoyed noises. Gid watches the cold, rocky shoreline of Connecticut, remembering a Discovery Channel special he watched in which some tribe in the deep forests of Brazil had to dedicate most of their waking hours to some ridiculously unpleasant, disgusting, and dangerous task—like the only food they ate was some venomous beetle that had to be picked out from the teeth of a charging animal, or they lived in huts that could only be held together with nails from some metal that could only be forged on the hottest day of the year. And after showing these miserable creatures and their hideous engagements with mere survival, the narrator said in a detached, matter-of-fact, and creepily drawn-out voice, "This is their wooooorld. They live under theeeese terms." And that just settled it. Well, in a weird way, it did.

I have my world, Gideon thinks, comforted by the tap-tap of laptop keys behind him. I have my terms.

Another Fair Isle–sweater girl walks by. She looks right through him, fixating on Nicholas instead. Gid feels no anger. She lives under her terms.

"You've been to New York before, right?" Nicholas asks as they pull into Penn Station. Gid feels important in the bustle of people arranging to get off the train.

"Yeah," he says. "I mean, I've been to, like, Radio City Music Hall and the Empire State Building."

"That's not New York, honey." A white-haired woman is popping out the wheels and handle on a black rollaway. She's carrying a canvas bag printed with the phrase WNYC: EXERCISE YOUR MIND. "New York is about jazz, art, cafés. You'll show him the real city. Some real nights on the town," she says, winking at Nicholas and then waddling off, duck-footed in rain boots.

"The real city," Nicholas says. "Those kind of people are so annoying. When they opened a Gap in the Village, she probably cried."

They take the subway, which is exciting and different. Gideon's heard a lot of weird things about the subway, how it's all homeless people just trying to rip diamonds off your neck and out of your ears, and is surprised to see mostly quiet, orderly people reading books or staring straight ahead. The ride takes just a few minutes.

They emerge to dusk and the pulse of Christmas lights, and Gid nods, contented, beginning to relax, feeling a buoyant anticipation he can't quite place.

I think I know what it is. I love staying with my friends' parents. Other people's parents are almost always great. They give you food. They have different stuff than your family, usually better. And otherwise, they basically ignore you. It's heaven. And Nicholas only has a mother. Single parents are always nicer than both parents. Single parents want to please you.

On the short walk to Nicholas's apartment Gid observes that this neighborhood seems to be almost entirely populated by doormen and old men and women, the women frowning in tweed, the men bleary-eyed in trench coats, walking small dogs. Most of the buildings are beautiful, with giant windows, draped with sumptuous amounts of pine boughs and red ribbons. A few, though, the newer ones, are white, ugly, and look like cruise ships, set upright from bow to stern. "Where are we?" Gid asks.

"This," Nicholas says ominously, "is Park Avenue. The heart of the Upper East Side."

A neatly dressed pretty girl about their age walks by wearing a red coat. Gideon thinks about Molly and her note. It's not the bet. It's sick-making and reassuring all at once. It's not the bet. What does this mean? That she hated him all along? No, she liked him. Her face when she talked to him, she always looked so happy.

I'm glad to see he's trying to work it out logically. Thinking. It's good for teenage boys to remember to think, because otherwise they just won't.

Okay, so when he told her about the bet, she didn't seem that upset. Right? Is he dreaming this? He heard about an artist once who tape-recorded all of his conversations. Maybe he should start doing that? It's not the bet. "Not the bet," he says out loud.

Nicholas groans. "Why are you thinking about the bet right now? Molly's not even here. Take a break."

Easy for him to say.

Then they're turning in to Nicholas's building, walking under a gated stone archway attended by a blue-suited doorman who calls out, "Nicholas!" He's white-haired and his uniform stretches tightly over his short, squat body. "Staying in trouble?"

Nicholas walks over to him and shakes his hand. "How's it going, Kenny?"

"I can't complain," Kenny says, patting his stomach. "At least not to the tenants!" He barks out a laugh that follows them into an enormous courtyard. Its expanse is dizzying. It's the size of a football field, with turrets in the corners and little stone outbuildings manned by more blue-suited doormen, some with clipboards, some talking on phones. It looks more like a medieval fortress than an apartment building. "You live here?" Gid asks. Nicholas's flat reply, "Yes, all my life," warns him that he should probably keep his amazement to himself.

Yet another blue-suited doorman greets them in the elevator, which is some gloriously rich wood, with brass fixtures polished to a mind-bending shine. He presses a button reading PHC. Penthouse C. Gid smiles to himself. Penthouse City!

"This is your real mom, right?" Gid says.

Nicholas nods. "If we were going to my stepmother's right now, I would be acting like a total asshole."

Gideon has always hoped Nicholas had some awareness of taking out his stress and anger on other people. This comment fills him with tenderness.

The elevator door opens. Advancing toward them, a white Pekingese beside her, is a slimly upright, strenuously youthful brunette. She takes Nicholas's face into her hands. "Darling," she says. She kisses one cheek, then the next. Then she stands back and regards Gideon.

"I'm Gideon," he says when he feels he has been stared at too long to not speak. "I live with Nicholas."

"Oh, Gideon!" She clasps Gideon's hand. The dog turns in excited circles. "You must be so thrilled to be in New York!" She bends down and ruffles the dog's head. "Who's Mommy's baby? Who is Mommy's baby bear!"

Dinner is order-in Chinese food. Gid stuffs himself. There are two different kinds of noodles, shrimp with broccoli, spare ribs, and, for Nicholas, some wet, unappetizing tofu thing. His mother's filled up the refrigerator with distilled water and jugs of green tea. She just sits there beaming and watching her son eat, now and then picking a few strings of vegetable from the crevice of an egg roll. Gid can't remember when he's seen someone look so happy.

And parental love is a powerful thing, because Nicholas seems happy too. The relaxed glow on his face is something new.

Afterward they go into a little paneled room dominated by a flat-screen TV. Nicholas lets him man the remote. "Where did your mother go?" Gid asks. He flips past the Powerpuff Girls, beefy-faced guys in suits, squirrels running up a tree.

Nicholas shrugs. "She takes the dog out. She wanders around."

So she's in training to become one of those old people that walks around the Upper East Side.

"She looks so young," Gid says. What he really means is, she looks weird.

Nicholas nods. "She works out for, like, three hours a day," he says. "She wants to get married again."

"Do you think she will?"

Nicholas walks to the door and shuts it carefully. "No," he says quietly, as if his mother could hear him in the streets. "No one wants to marry an old lady."

"She's not old," Gid says.

"She's not young either," Nicholas says. "I mean, she has wrinkles and she has to take calcium. And Metamucil."

Gid can't argue with this. They watch a show about tuna-fishing off of Japan. Some old British guy interviews Japanese fishermen, and one appears to get angry with him. There are subtitles. "We are not trying to do anything wrong. We are just doing what we know how to do. What we must do. What other option do we have?"

Gideon nods sagely. "This is their world," he says. "They live under these terms."

Nicholas smiles. He seems to understand.

"Hey," Gid says suddenly. "Show me a picture of your sister."

Nicholas's sister is at boarding school in Switzerland. She's not coming home for the holiday. Nicholas pulls out a couple of drawers, leafs through some albums, and hands Gideon a short stack of photographs. God. She is beautiful, a girl version of Nicholas. Electric blue eyes (scary husky!), dark hair, a ripe, naturally red mouth. She's prettier, actually, than he is good-looking.

"So level with me," Gid says. "Does she like Cullen?"

"I'm sorry to say that she does. I am the sole reason they haven't gotten together yet."

Gid smiles inside. If he wins the bet, he will become part of an important historical moment in their friendship.

Gideon gets his very own room. Mrs. Westerbeck shows it to him with much fluttering apology. "It's very small, but I think you'll be comfortable. At least I hope so!" The room isn't large, but Gid finds the Danish modern sofa bed, Japanese prints on the wall, and giant windows overlooking the median of Park Avenue completely luxurious.

"Now, shall we leave these drapes open?" She opens them. "Or closed?" She closes them. "What do we think?"

"It's okay," Gid says. "I can figure it out."

Mrs. Westerbeck's whole body deflates.

"Why don't you open them, then?"

Her body inflates again. "Fine," she says. With a flourish, she sends each drape sailing off to the edges of the window. Gid smiles at her, sharing in her small delight.

It's so cute how sweet he can be. And so sweet how cute he can be. I make myself sick. But seriously, he could tell that she wanted to fix the drapes for him, and he let her. Most guys wouldn't have picked up on that, and if they had, they would have thought she was just a lunatic. But Gid understands. She's in her element. And he knows how much he likes to be in his.

Gid notices a black-and-white photo sitting next to his bedside table of a man who looks like Nicholas. It must be Nicholas's dad. He looks away from it, but Mrs. Westerbeck grabs it up. "Tom," she says. "Nicholas's dad. Right after we got married. I met him on a blind date, my very last month at Vassar. I remember thinking, Oh, my, what a catch! What a wonderful man."

God, Gid thinks, maybe I should set her up with my dad. But he would be so uncomfortable here. He'd feel like he was going to break something.

No, Gid, he would just fix things.

"I guess he didn't turn out to be so much of a catch," Gideon says.

To his surprise Mrs. Westerbeck smiles fondly at the picture. "No," she says. "He was a catch. How do you think I got all this? Working?" She makes a wide gesture to include her large, well-appointed apartment. "The wonderful-man thing, well, I guess Lucy, that's Nicholas's stepmother, she might think so, but I . . ."

Gid wants to wrap this up. "It must have been very hard," he says.

Mrs. Westerbeck laughs a little—this time a little less kindly. "Don't believe everything Nicholas tells you," she says. "He thinks just because I miss him so much that I want a husband. I don't. I work out to fit into my clothes."

"I can relate to that," Gideon says. "I used to be skinny fat. In fact, I have your son to thank for getting me in shape."

Mrs. Westerbeck smiles with recognition. "Ah, yes. Skinny fat. Nicholas always says that about his stepmother. He thinks he needs to make me feel better. But I'm fine." She closes the door with a wistful half-smile on her face.

Gideon lies awake for a long time. He's never slept this far off the ground. What if there were an earthquake? Most people think there are only earthquakes in California, but Gid read once there could be a giant earthquake almost anywhere. What would he do if there were an earthquake? Would he call his mother first or his father? Would he appreciate life more after it, because he knew he could die at any time, or less, because he knew there might not be any point? He wonders if Molly could forgive him if she knew how much of a chicken he was.

I like it when Gid and I are both lying awake. It used to get a little exhausting listening to him, when everything was new, but now that I know him well, I can follow him a lot better. Now I almost don't notice the difference between our thoughts.

Gideon feels himself being gently shaken. He thinks he's back at school. "Cullen, leave me alone," he says reflexively.

"It's not Cullen, douche, it's Nicholas. Hello, you're in my apartment." Gid opens his eyes, his heart beats fast, and for the split second when he still doesn't know what's going on, he thinks he's a scared little kid. Then he acclimates himself to the room, the giant windows, the towering bookshelf. When his eyes fall on the black-and-white photo of Nicholas's father, he finally knows what's happening.

"We're going out," Nicholas says.

"But I don't want to go out," Gid mumbles. This is a really comfortable bed. Mrs. Westerbeck explained to him it was some special mattress from Sweden. Gid thinks it feels like he's lying on a giant piece of bread. When he finally fell asleep, it was with the image of an entire special Swedish mattress full of Swedish girls. It was a little unpleasant, but I got used to it. It was kind of like watching a spring-break movie where all the actresses have blonde braids piled on top of their heads.

"Whatever," Nicholas says. "I just can't sleep, and Liam and Devon called me."

No reason to leave this Scandinavian heaven. None at all. Gid can most certainly make it until Sunday without seeing those guys.

"And they're with some girls, at a bar that's not far from here. Madison, Mija, Pilar, some friends of theirs."

Pilar in New York. In her natural habitat. In a bar. How exciting was that!

To you, Gid, extremely. Me, I just wish we were still asleep.

Pilar did say she wanted to hang out with him here. Her number is floating around somewhere in his duffel. He hadn't dared think he'd have the courage to use it.

Gid says, "I have Pilar's number written in lipstick in my bag, and I was thinking that's the only way I will ever get her lipstick to touch my underwear." He laughs again. "Oh, Jesus," he says, "is life ridiculous or what?"

Then he sits bolt upright. The amazing Swedish bed barely moves underneath him. "Wow," he says.

"Look," Nicholas says, "are you coming or not?"

"Just be quiet for a second. I have to tell you something. Something weird just happened to me. I . . . did you notice that? When I just said, 'Is life ridiculous or what?' "

Nicholas nods slowly, with mock patience.

"Well, I really did think it was funny. The idea of Pilar not liking me, because I'm lame, or too short, or not cool enough, well, usually when I think that, I get sad. But this time, I actually laughed about it." He pauses, thinks. "Okay," he says, "it went away. I just thought about how I was a dork and she would never really like me, and as usual I felt bad about myself. But for a second there, it didn't matter. None of it mattered. I felt good. Isn't that incredible?"

Nicholas stares at him. "I think that maybe what you're saying is beautiful. Can we go now?"

A few minutes later, they're stealing down the service entrance stairway of Nicholas's building. "The doorman and my mom are tight," Nicholas explains. "At least when it comes to my behavior." At the bottom of the stairs, they pass through a grim hallway crowded with garbage cans and pause at a heavy steel door with a sign that reads: BUILDING PERSONNEL ONLY.

"Just wait." Nicholas whips out his cell phone. "Cullen? Hey. Yeah." He laughs and covers up the phone for a second. "He's in a bar in Denver, trying to pick up some woman who has three kids." He talks into the phone again. "I'm sure she is. I have a proposition for you. Okay, full disclosure: Pilar wrote her phone number for Gideon in lipstick. Did you know that? Yeah, neither did I. It's not, like, the biggest deal in the world. It's not like automatic sex. But it's good. Okay. Here it is. I say, Gid and Pilar, tonight. No, I haven't changed my mind about Gideon. I still think he's a giant loser." He smiles at Gideon. Gideon likes Nicholas's calling him a loser—likes it the same way he liked it when Molly told him he was clueless. "I just have a hunch. I like the way Gid's representing himself tonight. I think he's really tapping into something."

After he hangs up, Gid says, "The bet's not really real, is it?"

They've changed the rules enough times that Gideon's finally figured out: There are no rules.

Nicholas mashes his lips together and puts the phone into the pocket of his blue fleece jacket.

"I mean, it's as real as it is not real. We are all kind of watching me try and get something because, you know, what else is there to do? But the car . . . you're going to give me the car at the end of the year regardless, because you drive it whenever you want to anyway, and it's not worth a lot even though it's a Beemer—I looked it up: Blue book's only, like, three grand."

"I don't know what a blue book is," Nicholas says haughtily, "but the car's worth four grand."

They step onto Ninety-third and start to walk east. Again they're sharing the sidewalks with old people and little dogs—there are just fewer of them. "It's not that the bet's totally bullshit," Nicholas says carefully. "It's just that we don't really care how it turns out. Let's say Cullen wins. He may sleep with my sister, he may not. If I still don't want him to—and I would never tell him, he would just know—he wouldn't. And if I won, well, would I really make Cullen go out with some girl for a whole year? I don't know. We might do that anyway next year, whether Cullen sleeps with my sister or not. That's going to be fun, by the way. Thank God we didn't get kicked out."

Gid's hovering somewhere between anger and relief. The relief is pretty strong. That bet is, was, such a ball and chain, a constant reminder that he didn't quite own his own time. But he put so much into something that wasn't even there. "I fucking . . . I kind of hate you," he says. Nicholas whitens. Gideon immediately regrets this, but he doesn't stop. He deserves to say this. "I tortured myself over that bet."

"Oh, come on," Nicholas says. "Are you really that miserable?" A fair question.

Gid hugs himself and looks up, feeling cradled by tall buildings on both sides of the street. The air is cool but not uncomfortable, and he's wearing a jacket of Nicholas's that smells like a fireplace and, if you get close, a little like Nicholas's mother. He's still full of Chinese food, and he's going to have a drink in Manhattan. No, he's not miserable. "I'm not," he says. "My life is not bad at all."

Nicholas appears relieved. "The bet wasn't . . . isn't . . . nothing," he says. "We are serious about it in a way."

"It's just in another way, you're not serious about it," Gid says. "Right?"

"Well," Nicholas says, "we were kind of trying to distract you from your virginity."

God, that hadn't occurred to me. But the bet did have that effect.

"No way," Gideon says. "It worked."

"Please," Nicholas says. "Don't tell me what I already know."

Gid and Nicholas smile at each other, though Gid shakes his head to let Nicholas know he's never going to be as innocent as he once was. Then, suddenly, he says, "Shit. Molly. I knew there was a reason this wasn't all okay."

Nicholas stops, letting Gid talk. It's the least he can do.

"I think I really hurt her."

"Well," Nicholas says, "I don't want to be flip, but she did say it wasn't the bet."

Gideon scowls. "Of course she's going to say that." He starts walking again. "What else is she going to say?"

"From what I know of Molly McGarry," Nicholas says, "she usually says what she means."

"So if it's not the bet, then it's me, of course. That's worse," Gid says helplessly.

"I don't know what you're so upset about," Nicholas says.

I have some ideas. But I'm not entirely sure.

"Molly McGarry's in Buffalo, and she's fine. And Pilar Benitez-Jones, she's fine too. And she's here. In New York. Waiting for you."

please
don't
talk about
love
tonight

Gid always imagined any bar in Manhattan would be really stylish. He imagined walls made out of fish tanks. The men would be wearing suits, and the women would all be in tiny dresses holding martini glasses carefully as they navigated light-pulsating walkways in spike heels. But this is just a bar, with Formica tables, ugly, low-hanging lights with faux stained-glass shades, and a neon beer sign.

New York isn't all that, he thinks, but he's not disappointed, he's comforted. He can totally deal with this.

Gid has planned that he's just going to hang back and wait to make his move. He steps up to one end of the bar, edging himself between a blonde in a scarf, drinking white wine, and a freckly black-haired girl drinking beer out of a bottle. "We were having a chat," the black-haired girl says. She's Irish.

"God, I'm sorry," Gid says, backing away. They both burst out laughing. Gid smiles nervously, not sure if they're laughing at him or laughing because they just want to look happy in front of him. He thinks girls are capable of this. Even older girls.

He's right. And that is what they're doing.

Nicholas studies the jukebox with sober focus.

The blonde pats her chest and pulls the clasp of her pearls around to the back. "Go ahead, go ahead," she says. "We were just laughing because you're so polite." His brown eyes narrow, and she leans in, whispering, "That girl at the end of the bar is looking at you."

Gid leans past her to see Pilar, seated four or five stools away. She's holding a martini glass containing something pink and festive, and a group of older guys, uniformly handsome, surround her in almost perfect symmetry. She softens her eyes and moves them a little to the left. At Gideon. She smiles now, slowly, her expression sexily suspicious but playful. Like, "Well, well, well, what are you doing here?" Although of course Madison, her friend, called them to come. She touches the glass to her lips.

So cheap! Effective. But so cheap.

"Damn," says the Irish girl. "I wish I looked like that."

"Not me," the blonde girl says, lifting and dropping her pearls. "What a giant pain in the ass. Seriously, though." This to Gideon: "Let her come over here. A girl like that has to come to you. Trust me."

The Irish girl laughs out loud.

I like these girls. They could be my friends. I think Gid likes them too. Why, he thinks, can't Cullen and Nicholas be more like them? Friendlier in their harshness?

Gideon's radically insufficient age is no impediment in procuring a beer from the thin-lipped, unsmiling bartender. He gets a Guinness for Nicholas, who is feeding dollar bills into the jukebox. Madison appears, raking through her hair with her fingers. "Hey, doofus," she says to Nicholas and bumps him with her hip.

I wonder what Madison's going to be like as a grown-up. I think she'll just marry a rich guy and do Pilates all day.

Nicholas ignores her. He presses B16, "Get Off of My Cloud."

"So cool with the classic rock," Madison says. "You know, Erica was going to come, but she didn't, because of you."

Nicholas continues to punch in selections: R12, "Teenage Wasteland."

Gid speaks up. "I feel bad for Erica. I think she's a nice girl, and," he adds, because he knows that this will increase his credibility of the controversial viewpoint he's about to offer, "an excellent soccer player. However . . ."

"Oh, God," Madison says, "I am going to need more alcohol for this one." She sips. "Okay, go ahead."

"How long has Erica known Nicholas?" he asks.

"Forever," Madison says, thrilled to be in the know. "They've known each other for years. Nicholas went to Dixon's, and she went, with me, to the sister school, Saint K's, which is, like, the best girls' school . . ."

Gid and I wonder simultaneously what it might be like to parade around with Madison's severed head on the end of a stick.

The music's loud, so Nicholas either can't hear them or can get away with pretending he can't.

"My point is," Gid says, "Nicholas's mother stares at him when he eats. She sits there and pets him. Now, I love Nicholas." He pats him warmly on the back. "And Mrs. Westerbeck is a nice woman. But my point is, simply, if you know that a guy's mother pets him when he eats, all I'm saying is his behavior is totally predictable."

Nicholas is staring at the tops of his shoes and smiling. Gid is loving himself.

Gid notices Pilar working her way toward him. This is what it's all about, Gid thinks. Don't lose your nerve. If only his stare wasn't so blatant. Why does Pilar have to wear white all the time? As if she knows that it just makes Gid lose his mind. She smiles her deeply shiny lip-glossed smile.

Gid, don't stop staring at girls. Some of them might not like it, but the ones who do, well, they'll make up for your trouble.

"He's telling us why Erica was stupid to have sex with Nicholas," Madison says.

"I didn't say stupid," Gid says. "I never said stupid. I am only saying that she shouldn't have been surprised by the outcome."

"I agree. I agree, and I'm impressed," Pilar says. Pilar presses into him. What is with her, this way of making it seem like she's in a tight space, like she just can't help but sidle up to you, when in fact there's plenty of room? Not that he minds. She smells like slightly sweet cucumbers. "Do you want another beer? I'm empty." She wags her glass in front of his face.

"Sure," Gideon says, pouring the rest of his beer down the back of his throat. She takes the bottle from him.

"Let me get it for you," she says, with that slow-eye flutter Gid really likes.

He watches her walk away. Nicholas just sits back and watches it happen, a wondrous smile on his face. I watch too, a little more subdued.

Gid, though, of all the people watching this seduction unfold, has the best view and is the most amazed. He feels like someone programmed his body to know exactly what to do. He slips easily off his stool and guides her off of hers when she goes outside to smoke. When he lights her cigarette, even though the wind is blowing hard up the avenue, he cups the matches perfectly, and they never blow out. Inside, he raises his hand to the bartender, keeps his eyes on her even as he reaches into his pocket for money to pay for her drinks. She tells him a story about her uncle running for district president of some small district in the southern part of Argentina—Patagonia, the place that he had no idea was really a place. Gid doesn't really understand what's funny about the story—something to do with a blind dog, a roasted chicken, and a farmer—but he manages to laugh in all the right places. He feels—a feeling that increases with each drink—like there's a beam of light connecting their faces, even their bodies, a beam of light that lifts him up a bit, makes him feel weightless.

He tells her the story of Mrs. Frye and the ranunculus and how he was mean to Liam Wu and watching the bloodhound show on the Discovery Channel. He's careful with the parts about Molly Mc-Garry. He says enough so that she knows other chicks dig him but not so much that she doubts his interest. She's leaning in closer and closer, hanging on his every word. She smells like warm flowers and cucumbers and sugar. He puts a tentative hand on her leg. She lets it sit there. She puts her hand on her neck, arranging and rearranging her fragrant dark hair.

When girls start playing with their hair, Cullen says it is fucking *done,* and I can't say I disagree.

Madison saunters over. She takes note of Gid's hand on Pilar's leg.

"Awfully cheeky for a new guy," she says.

"Madison," Gid says, reaching out with his free hand and chucking her under the chin. "I'm not the new guy anymore. I'm just . . . the guy you'll never have and dream of forever."

Madison actually laughs at this, genuine, friendly laughter. Most important, she turns on the heel of her Marc Jacobs wedges and leaves them alone. Gideon slides his hand farther up Pilar's leg until he's got underwear. Pilar pulls away. Gid is on the verge of saying sorry when he instead meets Pilar's eye and just stares at her. It's a good move. Girls hate sorry. Like, unless you do something really bad that you didn't mean to do. But shit, thinks Gid, I can't apologize for trying to do the very thing in this world that I live for.

"I don't take my underwear off in bars," Pilar says. "But my parents are in Rome."

"Okay," says Gideon slowly, having no point of reference for such a thing, wondering, drunkenly, if Rome is a restaurant.

Then they're making out. He inches his hand down toward her breasts, which, in particular, is something he's been dreaming of doing for so long that it almost plays like déjà vu.

She stops him, but only to say, "Seriously, my parents aren't flying in from Rome until tomorrow morning. Let's go back to my place."

Everything is arranged so quickly. Nicholas is going to tell his mother Gideon went out for a run before they got up, and he's going to leave jogging clothes for him at the tenth-floor landing on the service stairs. Pilar stands there smiling and almost blushing. When did she become so girlish?

Nicholas slips him a single apartment key. "You realize now," he says, "that my mother is going to be petting me all alone tomorrow. She pets harder without an audience. Get back by nine. She won't suspect a thing." He stands back and regards Gideon with much respect. "You have become the creature I believed you could become."

Gid breathes in the moment like it's mountain air.

And then he's outside, walking the streets of Manhattan at three o'clock in the morning, with not just a girl but literally the girl of his dreams. She's holding his hand. She's glassy-eyed. She's wearing high-heeled boots and a short skirt. Oh my God, Gid thinks. I've never had sex before. This is a terrible idea. But he can't think that. This is the opportunity of a lifetime. Try not to think so much like you usually think, he instructs himself.

They're in her apartment now. Her parents' apartment, which is a vast expanse of glass, leather, and right angles. They make out against giant walls of mirrors. His natural abilities return, his sense that he knows how to behave, what to do. They make out all the way down a hallway, first her up against the wall, with one of Gid's hands under her shirt and the other one on the inside of her thigh. She pushes him away, and he thinks he's gone too far, but no, now he's against the wall, and Pilar's unbuttoning his shirt and pushing it off of him. He touches the top of her warm head as she kisses his chest, and she looks up and stares at him.

"Are you okay?" she says.

He nods.

She leads him into a room with a giant white bed, which she falls onto, giggling, her legs, bare above the boots, bouncing provocatively up in the air. Jesus, Gid thinks. This is it. This isn't just *it*, this is the end and the beginning of everything. He feels like he should say something before it starts, and after some thought he settles on "You look so good in white."

"Thanks," she says. "I got the idea from J. Lo."

"You got the idea from J. Lo? I don't understand. Did J. Lo invent white?"

Pilar smacks the bed, instructing him to get on it. "She didn't invent white, but she kind of made it popular," she says as she runs her fingers down the front of his chest. She has nails! Adult nails. It's almost . . . well, it's sexy, but it's also scary. Like anything could happen. "Anyway, don't tell anyone."

Gid frowns. "I think a lot of people know who J. Lo is," he says.

"No," Pilar says, now straddling him. "Don't tell anyone I got my idea about always wearing white from J. Lo. Or if you do, make sure they don't tell anyone."

He doesn't know whether to be happy that she's straddling him or to burst out laughing at the idea of himself actually saying the following sentence to a fellow human being: "Pilar wears white because of J. Lo. But don't tell anyone." God, Molly would think that was funny. Molly. But there's no time for that. Pilar is bearing down on him, kissing him, her movie-star hands undoing his pants, taking off his shirt. Gid's mind feels like it's going to fall out of his head. It feels like it might fall out of my head too.

Then Madison Sprague comes tumbling out of the closet. Holding a video camera.

"Oh, shit," Madison says.

Gideon's first impulse is to feel incredibly, overwhelmingly grateful that he's still wearing his underwear. Once he's processed that, all he can think of to say is "I didn't even know you two liked each other."

Pilar sits up in bed. Gideon looks at her breasts and thinks, with a surprising sense of removal, Those were just in my hands. "I thought we called this off!" Pilar shouts.

Called this off? Pilar's stepping back into her pants, turning to the wall, suddenly modest, to slip back into bra and shirt, a sexy film in reverse. That means that Pilar has talked about Gid when he's not around. That . . . God, that was all he wanted. He has been imagining her thinking of him since she met him.

"Gideon," she pleads. "I really do like you. We planned this, like, a little while ago, and I thought I told her not to come over. I really don't want you to be mad at me. I really like you."

Gid thinks. He wasn't mad when he saw the video camera. He wasn't mad when he saw Madison. You could do worse than lose your virginity to a really hot girl while another hot girl taped it. Even if the girl taping it isn't as hot as you used to think she was. Does that make it even hotter?

"I really like you," Pilar repeats. "I don't want you to think that I don't like you."

Yes, this is definitely the part of this whole experience that's annoying. Because she was just all over him, and she didn't seem to be acting, so it's like she's apologizing because she thinks he could never believe she would actually be hot for him. That he would be worthy of it. But in fact, he totally believes it.

It's not the bet, Molly wrote him.

He didn't understand, but now it is so incredibly obvious. Both what she meant and what he has to do.

He starts to dress himself, checking his wallet for his emergency credit card.

"What's going on?" Pilar asks, chasing him to the door wearing a white comforter like a toga. Gid tells himself not to look back, but he can't help it. "Damn, you're hot," he says, shaking his head.

"Why are you leaving? Where are you going?" Pilar supports herself against the mirror with one hand.

"Buffalo," he says, putting on his coat. He takes a final look at Pilar. He can't tell if she's angry, desperate, or just wasted. He decides he'll never know and steps out the door into the foyer. It's one of those apartments where the elevator comes right to your entrance. He can hear what's going on inside.

"Buffalo?" Madison says. "Who lives in Buffalo?"

"I don't know," Pilar says. "That girl Molly McGarry lives there, I think."

"I don't know if I know her," Madison says.

"You might not," Pilar says. "She's not really all that pretty."

This would have stung Gid before. He would have thought better of his judgment, but all he thinks now, and what I think too, is Don't hate Pilar and Madison. They just live in their world, under its terms.

the
queen
city

At five-thirty in the morning on the Sunday before Thanksgiving, Gideon's one of eight people in line to buy an Amtrak ticket at Penn Station. There's only one window open, and the man behind it has the longest face Gid's ever seen. Even on the happiest day of his life, the man must look about ready to pack it in. The alcohol's slowly leaving Gid's system, and his skin feels prickly, his brain jumpy. If he weren't so nervous, he would be happier than he's ever been in his life.

Seven people come and go from the window pretty quickly. The last, an old lady, has a problem. She smacks the counter repeatedly with her wallet. The man with the long face doesn't look like he's having a good time, but he doesn't appear to be getting riled up. Finally, Gid sees her credit card come out. She signs her ticket, still glaring. "Have a safe trip," says the man. "Next."

Gid steps up. "I want to go to Buffalo," he says.

The man's face lights up. Gid's startled by the transformation. He looks like a different person. He says, "I'm from Buffalo."

"No shit," says Gideon. He hands the guy the credit card. He's hoping the fact that he hasn't used it at all yet will make up for any debates about what constitutes an emergency.

The man is shaking his head, all smiles and reverie. "I like New York," he says, "but Buffalo's my town. Why are you going there?"

Gid doesn't want to say "To lose my virginity," so, inexplicably, he says, "I'm going ice fishing."

The man's delight collapses and disappears. "Have a safe trip," he says.

As Gid walks away, he realizes that it's barely winter and that the lakes aren't frozen yet. The guy probably thought he was making fun of him. He'd like to go back and tell him the real reason. Man to man. But his train leaves at six A.M., in five minutes.

He settles himself in for the ride, taking from his bag a bottle of water and a newspaper, because he's always thought it looked fun to read a newspaper on a train and he never has. His train won't get in until early afternoon. He has a long time on the train to think about what he's going to say to Molly. He even starts to write it out, but almost three hours later, he finds himself in Albany staring at fourteen Amtrak napkins covered in adolescent meanderings. He realizes he can't think of how to explain his presence in Buffalo to Molly when he himself doesn't exactly understand it.

Start at the beginning. Start with Cullen and Nicholas.

Okay. Gid draws their pictures on a napkin, representing Nicholas mostly by his keen eyes and pretty mouth and Cullen with a big head and perfectly messy hair. He smiles fondly at his flawed but evocative representations. Before he met them, he thought he was forever fated to that present level of confidence, that he was going to have to go through life like Jim Rayburn. He no longer believes this.

Clearly, these guys know a lot about girls that's worth knowing. And Gid is grateful for having been taught most of it. But it's not like he actually wants to be like them. Cullen, well, he's happy the way he is; girls are like prizes to him, and he likes that. And maybe,

Gid thinks, if I were as handsome as he is, I would be like that too. But I'm not. And when you don't have that handsomeness to protect you, don't you need a girl to be your friend?

As for Nicholas, well, half the reason he's even going to see Molly McGarry—well, he thinks, a third of the reason, maybe—is to tell her what he's figured out. Nicholas punishes Erica, delights in it, because he can't yell at his own mother. And the sad thing is that if he did yell at his mother, she'd certainly recover.

Will Erica? Probably, and probably all of Cullen's girls along with her. And Pilar Benitez-Jones is probably the damn finest piece of ass he'll ever see in his life. But at the end of the day, Gid knows that he's too much like Erica, really, to let Pilar have sex with him. He would hate waiting for Pilar to call. He would hate himself for hating to wait.

They say girls are the only ones who care about virginity. That we're the only ones who care about anything. It's not true.

He throws the napkins out in the Buffalo train station men's room, still unsure of what to say. It's six in the evening, grimy, wintry, and dark. The train station is just a hideous shack, like a beach snack bar, beneath an underpass. Snow is coming.

He gives Molly's address to a cabbie outside. "I thought Buffalo had a nice train station," he says, trying to strike up a conversation. He actually knows the truth, that they used to, and he's hoping the cabbie will discuss this with him.

But the cabbie just runs his finger along the inside of his gums and, depositing something in his ashtray, says, "Nope."

Molly's house is a modest two-story brick thing on Highland Avenue, built sixty or so years ago by someone careful but without passion. He knocks on the plain wooden door, set to the left side of a painted white porch. A little boy answers, clearly Molly's brother. This is good. He's small and dark-haired, and looks annoyed.

"My parents aren't here," he says.

"I'm looking for your sister," Gid says.

"Molly or Jasmine?"

Jasmine? She has a sister named Jasmine? Gid smiles. No wonder she wrote about hurricanes and vaginas.

"Molly," he says.

The kid runs off without saying anything.

In a minute or so, Molly pads down the hall, dressed in jeans, mismatching socks, and a T-shirt with no bra. "Gideon?" she says, with the surprise of someone waking up in a different room than the one where they fell asleep. "What are you doing here?"

"What do you mean, what am I doing here?" he asks. "What reason would I possibly have for coming to Buffalo, other than to see the famous antifreeze pond?"

He thinks maybe she's smiling? Or about to smile?

"If you are happy to see me, I'll tell you the real reason."

Now she's smiling.

"I came here to lose the other half of my virginity," he says.

No one would ever recommend that you say this to a girl, but somehow, it's exactly the right thing.

Molly doesn't smile, but she doesn't not smile. "How did you get here?" she asks.

He tells her about Amtrak, and the old lady, and the man with the long face. "I feel bad about the ice-fishing comment," he says.

"Don't feel bad," she says. She pulls him into the hallway. The little kid lurks in the background, behind a metal radiator. "Get out of here," she barks at him. He takes off. "I think he's gay," she whispers. "All he does is read biographies of ballet dancers. He's either gay or an aesthete, I guess, both of which are not good matches for this town." She takes Gideon's coat and hangs it on a tree, on top of a lot of other coats. It falls to the ground. "Do you mind?" she asks, leaving it.

"Not at all," Gid says.

"My parents aren't home," she says. She indicates he should follow her upstairs. She takes his hand, as she did walking across the quad a few weeks ago. He kisses it. Molly winces.

"That was kind of gay. Not gay like my brother gay. I didn't say anything last time, but I'm feeling a little more confident this time."

"I get it," Gid says. They've paused on the landing. The stairs are lined with family photographs. Molly has looked the same since she was about four. He touches the silver frame on one of them, showing Molly at nine or ten, standing on her ice skates on a pond, in the middle of a park. "Is this the pond?"

"The very same." There's some movement downstairs, footsteps, kitchen cabinets being opened and closed. "My sister," she says, jerking her head, indicating he should move faster.

Her room isn't like Danielle's, but it reminds him of that. It's carpeted, and not with interesting carpet, just carpet. There are dumb posters on the wall left over from childhood—Christina Aguilera and a photo of the mayor, Anthony Masiello, shaking hands with Hillary Rodham Clinton. Downstairs, he hears the patter of feet and a toilet flush. This is a nice place to lose your virginity, he thinks. The TV hums up through the floorboards. Molly's bed is warm, with flannel sheets printed with daisies.

Gid lies down looking up at Molly. "You can get into bed with your clothes on if you want," Gideon says. "I could take them off for you."

She grins down at him. "Do you think you can handle that?" she says. She takes off her mismatched socks and lays them on a pile of old *Seventeen* magazines on a plain wooden desk. She snuggles in next to Gideon, her head rests on his shoulder. "You can take off my clothes if you tell me what you're doing here," Molly says. "And remember, you're not trying to convince me of anything. I just need to believe you."

Gid closes his eyes. "About twelve hours ago," he says, "I was going to have sex with Pilar. And I realized I didn't want to lose my virginity to her. I mean, I want to maybe have sex with her, or a girl like her, someday. I mean, who wouldn't? Not that you're not a girl like her. I mean, you're . . ."

Molly laughs and readjusts her head on his shoulder. Gid panics that his shoulders are small. But her head is pretty small. He relaxes. "I know that I was supposed to have sex with you because of the bet, and I probably wouldn't have thought of it on my own. I probably wouldn't have. But once I knew you, I liked you."

Molly looks down, the compliment making her shy.

"And I know why you were mad at me. You weren't mad because I had a bet about you. You were mad because I thought you would have a nervous breakdown if I had sex with you for any reason other than that I was madly in love with you."

Molly is shocked. She props herself up on one elbow. "How did you figure that out? I mean, that's pretty involved."

Gid shrugs. "Partly a conversation I had with Nicholas Westerbeck's incredibly insane mother. Partly because Madison Sprague nearly captured on videotape, from the vantage point of a forty-square-foot custom closet, me losing my virginity."

There's a knock on Molly's door. "What?" she says.

"What are you doing?" It's the little brother.

"If you go away, we'll watch *Flashdance* in, like, an hour."

There's the sound of feet disappearing down the hall.

"Go on," she says.

He shrugs. "If Madison weren't so clumsy, and such a drunk, I probably wouldn't be here right now. I can't lie to you. Pilar is incredibly hot. But that's all she is, or most of what she is. Which is probably why she's so hot. These are issues I will have to work out. But seriously. Do you really think we're going to have sex for a whole hour?"

Molly considers this. "Only if we do it more than once," she says, kissing both his cheeks.

All of Gideon's nervousness melts away.

"Why didn't you just wait until we got back to school?" Molly whispers as he's taking off her clothes. "And don't tell me it's because you couldn't wait another day."

Gideon laughs. "If I'd stayed in New York, I probably would have hooked up with Pilar eventually. She's very persuasive. But seriously. I . . . just thought this might be . . . a lot more fun."

They kiss for a long, long time. Gideon obviously has been kissed before but never this extensively or, it seems, this well. Molly McGarry's face and lips and hands are all a couple of degrees warmer than any skin he has ever felt, and thinking this, he lays a finger along her cheek and opens his eyes. "To me," he says, "there is no one more beautiful than you. I somehow know that you need to hear this. And, well, plus, it's really true."

The small but ever-present shadow of suspicion that resides just above Molly's left lip vanishes. When it is gone, Gideon realizes he noticed it for the first time right before it disappeared. The planes of her cheeks and forehead soften. I want to say that she looks luminous, but I think I might hate myself. Oh well, I will take that chance. She looks luminous. Oh, wow. I don't hate myself at all.

Molly smiles back at Gideon. "There is no one more beautiful to me than you either," she says. They press themselves tightly together.

So tightly, in fact, that I am not sure where to go.

happily
ever
after

He's been with Molly for about two months now, and Gid hasn't looked at another girl once. Pilar gave him ample opportunities to look down her shirt, but he didn't even notice. He's so enraptured with Molly—with her broad cheekbones and wide, sarcastic Irish mouth, her humor, her wit, the way she makes him feel so stupid and smart all at once—that no other girls seem to exist. At some point in the not too distant future, his attention will wander. Maybe not forever. But it will. But right now, if you told him that, he wouldn't believe you. Molly really gets him, he thinks. It's amazing. Almost miraculous. That league stuff. Well. It's not like it doesn't make any sense, but in a way, it doesn't make any sense.

He's thinking this one day as he hustles down the fire escape after one of his many illegal visits to her room. *Moby-Dick* is long over, now they're reading *For Whom the Bell Tolls*, which is so easy he finished it in one night, sitting on that ratty basement couch, with, of all people, Mickey Eisenberg. In Art History the other day, he said Renoir idealized girls so much it seemed like he may have hated them, and the teacher told him this was a very interesting and original point. Cullen and Nicholas are his friends, but they're not his everything. They can still be mean, but it's easier to ignore, also, much easier to retaliate.

Most important, his girlfriend is pretty and funny.

One cold January afternoon, he and Molly cross the quad together: She's headed to a yearbook meeting, he's off to play some foosball with Devon Shine. They're not overtly groping per the standards of behavior both adhere to but still pleasantly knocking hip joint, elbow, knees, and he's filled up with a sensation of happiness and perfection. He's not so in his head anymore. He feels good. Could it be that the bad part is just over, and now, it's all going to be fun from now on?

"Don't bet on it," Molly says.

"Excuse me?" Gid says.

"I said, don't bet on it," I say, and parting from him, walk quickly up the stone steps to my yearbook meeting.

I never did figure out how Gid got into my head. If I had to venture a guess, I'd go with those wacky *Journal of the Zen Hut* mind games Gid was playing when he and Jim Rayburn first drove onto campus. No one hates to admit this more than me, but some of that stupid hippie shit is surprisingly powerful.

The question now, of course, is how am I going to get him out?

Naturally, I was pleased to know that the first time we did it Gid thought I looked luminous. Because I totally did. Still, it was one thing when I was yearning for him, and needing to know his every move. Now that we're in love and everything is so perfect between us, well, I wouldn't mind being a little less well informed.